THE OTHER HALF

By

Kimberly Atwood Balser

Dedications

To my mom, Kathleen O'Brien- Thank you so much for encouraging me to keep working on this novel! It's been a long journey, but an exciting one and as well as a great learning experience! Your help with editing was invaluable. Love you, mom!

To Myrna D'Ambrosio-Your positive feedback and kind words helped me to keep going when I felt like giving up on publishing my novel. Thank you for all your editing help, as well reading a finished draft.

To Wendy Allmendinger-I'm so grateful to you for offering to read, edit and give feedback on my final draft! Thank you!

Table of Contents

Prologue

The wind and rain whipped her blonde hair in wet strings around her face as Krista ran, glancing back to make sure she'd put a safe distance between her and whoever was chasing her. She couldn't see anyone, but she heard footsteps above the downpour of heavy rain. Adrenaline and instinct kicked in and she ran faster than she thought possible. Suddenly her foot caught on a mossy log and she was thrown several feet, landing in a pile of wet bushes.

'Get up!' Krista screamed out loud, managing to get to her feet. She was slipping in the mud as she ran, not sure which direction to go. She looked back again, and this time she could see a shadow of the figure chasing her. She struggled through the thick brush just as she felt someone upon her. She could feel fingernails on her ankle as if it was being grabbed. Running through the branches, she was fighting for breath. She didn't know who was chasing her or why, but knew if she was caught she would be at their mercy. She fell again, only to see that she had run to a cliff with a drop to the ocean with nowhere to go but down. Krista froze, crouched in a squat position, frantically looking around for another route. Suddenly the footsteps stopped. Her stalker was right in front of her.

Krista tried to scream, but no sound came out. The whitecaps from the huge waves were frighteningly close, threatening to sweep her off the cliff. She caught a glimpse of whoever was chasing her. It was if she was looking in a mirror, except that she wasn't rain-soaked like Krista. She was in fact identical, down to Krista's blue pajama pants and white tank top. She was even wearing a gold half-heart pendant necklace like Krista. She saw her moving her arms and saying words, but she couldn't hear her over the sound of the waves. A sudden huge wave came toward her and reached the cliff, sweeping her away in a wall of water. She was drowning. She tried to cry out, but the water was filling up her lungs. She struggled, feeling smothered with the weight of the water.

Krista felt someone shaking her shoulder. It took her more than a few seconds to realize that she was in her own bed and the person shaking her was her husband, Chad. "Honey, c'mon, wake up. You're having a nightmare!" Krista opened her eyes, feeling very disoriented. She was shaking, hyperventilating, and clinging to Chad as if he was keeping her from drowning. "Shhhh…it's okay. I'm here. It was just a dream," Chad whispered into her ear. The sound of her husband's voice was somewhat calming, but the terror of the dream was still overwhelming. She lay in bed for a few minutes to let the memory of the nightmare subside. She was angry with herself that she continued to let these dreams bother her in her waking hours; this wasn't the first time she'd had this same nightmare. She looked down at her tank top, soaked with sweat. She took off her clothes and went to shower. As the water poured down, she was finally able to regroup and relax. She stood under the warm water for what seemed like an eternity before finally getting out and putting on fresh clothes.

"Kris, what are you doing? It's 3:00 in the morning," Chad said, his voice was slurred with sleepiness.

"I just needed to take a shower. I'm okay." Krista replied. "Go back to sleep. I'm fine." Which was far from the truth, but it was nothing new for her to keep the truth from her husband. She'd stopped telling him anything important a few months ago.

"Are you okay now, babe?" Chad asked sleepily.

"I'm okay. It was just so real. I can't even explain it." Krista was hoping she would feel comforted by her husband's concern. However, she was still upset by the dream. She knew it would fade and she'd be right back to what she was feeling most of the time. Alone. In the past 6 months, Chad had been coming home late, watching TV while eating dinner, and going to bed at 9:30. She couldn't remember the last time they did anything together, with the exception of their random work related events.

Chad gave her a half-hearted, sleepy hug. "Kris, it's a dream! Go back to sleep!"

Krista only nodded and closed her eyes, but she couldn't sleep. The nightmares were becoming more intense and upset her. What was worse was that she could sense that Chad was pulling away from her and she wasn't sure what to do.

When the alarm went off at 5:30, Chad didn't hear it and Krista reached over and shook him gently. "Time to get up, sweetie. It's

5:30." She kissed him on his cheek as he mumbled and opened his eyes. "I'm up." Chad rolled over and got out of bed, moving slowly, as he usually did in the morning. "So tired. Got a late day today too." He grumbled as he headed toward the shower in the master bathroom. Krista sighed, and didn't bother to answer. She was tired, too. She'd started having a nightmare about someone chasing her about two months ago. This one was different. This time she'd seen who was chasing her; someone identical to herself including the necklace she was wearing. She touched the half- heart pendant on her neck to make sure it was still there. It was a gift from her father given to her as a young child and always made her feel more secure.

She started the coffee, making it strong not just because he liked it that way, but she needed the extra dose of caffeine this morning. Chad was the definition of "strong" as far as she was concerned; strong face, strong body, strong personality, and strong bread-winner. He'd been the top-selling realtor for her father's real estate business for the past year. Having only worked for Carson Realty for two years, he was bringing in more sales and commission than the eight other associates. They'd only been married a year, and she knew the neighbors whispered behind their backs. Although Chad was handsome and in good shape, it didn't change the fact that he was thirty-nine years old, and since she had just turned twenty-eight, there was a lot of speculation about the relationship, even within her family.

When they'd met two years ago, her father, William Carson, had problems with the age difference.

Krista had to initially tiptoe about her relationship, because of Chad's age, and the fact that he was her father's employee. Once he had gotten to know Chad, he admired the business-like attitude and his way of protecting those around him, and he wanted that for his only daughter. Krista's mother left when she was only three years old, and William did his best to be both mother and father to her.

"What's going on here? Breakfast?" Chad startled her for a second as he came into the kitchen freshly showered, and dressed in his usual suit and tie. Krista had just finished a pan of scrambled eggs, and glanced at her husband. His dark wavy hair with just a hint of gray set off his green eyes; along with some slight facial scruff making him overwhelmingly handsome. Krista could tell that other women thought so too. Whenever they went somewhere together, there were multiple double takes in his direction.

"It's my way of apologizing for waking you up." Krista gave him a kiss as she buttered the toasted English muffins. Despite being overtired, she was trying to evoke a closeness she felt was lacking in their relationship.

"Keep having these dreams, Kris, I like this five-star treatment!" Chad kidded and patted her on the butt as she walked away to grab the orange juice.

"You wish! I hope I never dream again!" Krista tried to joke, but the lingering remnant of the nightmare was still bothering her.

Chad dug into his breakfast while opening the paper. "They're just dreams, Kris. Everyone has bad dreams once in a while. Besides, the nice thing about bad dreams is that they aren't real." He turned his attention back to his newspaper, signaling that he was only half-listening.

"I wish they didn't seem so real." Krista said in a low voice, more to herself than to Chad.

"What's that, babe?" Chad asked, still reading the paper.

"Nothing. I have to go get ready for work. Have a great day, honey." Krista gave him a kiss on his cheek, and headed up the stairs to shower.

"Have a good day, babe! Love you." Chad replied, his nose still buried in the paper.

"Love you too." Krista said and headed up the stairs. As a real estate executive, Chad started his day earlier than she did. Her job as a school counselor started at 8:30, which was nice, as it gave her some alone time in the morning.

She tried to forget about the haunting dream as she showered and got ready for work. She knew she was lucky to find someone like Chad. He was older, handsome, successful, and had never been previously married. They'd met at one of her father's corporate Christmas parties. Despite their eleven- year age difference, from the time they'd met, there was a bond between them that was rare. Both had grown up with an absent parent, and they confided in each other early on in their relationship about their childhood years, which enhanced their instant attraction. They'd also found common interests in music, sports and comedy shows. Their age difference, plus their personalities brought out the best in each other. Krista had always been somewhat of an introvert and struggled with depression since she was a teenager. In contrast, Chad was outgoing, social, and always wanting to try new experiences. They'd only been seeing each other a year, when Chad surprised her with a proposal during a weekend trip to Cape Cod; complete with a beautiful 2 carat ring that he'd selected. They'd had a destination wedding in beautiful St. Thomas.

It had been an intimate ceremony, and the only person that was missing was her mom. Krista sighed as she thought about her mother. She often wondered what her mother would think if she were here now. Would she be proud of her? She had a few fragmented memories of her, mostly from the photo album that her father had given her when she was six. She would like to believe that the mother in those pictures still cared, that she would miss her and come back. She also had the feeling that someone besides her mother was missing, but never could put a name to the feeling. When she told her father about seeing and playing with her sister, he took her to a number of different therapists. The therapists concluded that it was an "only child" syndrome and not to worry about it. "She'll get over it, it's just the age."

Krista finished getting ready for work, dressed in a simple black dress with a blue cardigan that brought out her bright blue eyes. She straightened her long blonde hair so that it cascaded over her shoulders. She stepped into some sling-back black sandals and grabbed the keys to her black Lexus that Chad had bought for her for her 28th birthday last month. She turned the key and cranked up the radio to her favorite hard rock station in an attempt to forget about the nightmare and to focus on the day ahead of her.

Chad

Chad Burton arrived at work early as usual. His secretary Nancy, handed him a cup of coffee, black with two sugars. "Thanks, Nancy!" He gave her a wink and smiled at her as he made his way to his office. "Let me know if you need anything, Mr. Burton!" Nancy smiled back, purposefully running her hand through her long, dark, wavy hair. She was anxious to please. Between his 6 foot 3 inch frame and dark-haired good looks, he commanded attention. He'd obviously captured hers. Chad opened the door to his corner office at Carson Realty, relieved to be away from the drama at home. Krista had been so disruptive with her nightmares, waking him up and needing attention when he needed to sleep. It was getting to be too much. He feared she was becoming too needy, which was not like her. This nightmare shit needed to go, and if it didn't, he wasn't sure how much more he could take.

He'd started working for William Carson a few years ago, after working countless low-paying sales jobs that barely paid the rent. With only a few college courses under his belt, it was hard to find a job that actually had any challenge, let alone pay the bills. He met William at one of the corporate parties that he always hosted at the holidays. He became the plus-one for his friend Paul because his date had backed out at the last minute. No one what have guessed how much his life would change. That night he'd met his future wife and was offered a great job opportunity. Now he was living the life he'd always wanted. No doubt his brothers would be jealous now if they knew. His older brothers, Joe and Evan, had always given him shit for as long as he could remember. "Chad, why don't you finish school? You're always going to have crappy jobs if you don't!" His brother, Joe was the one that was always on his back. "Good old Joe, the golden boy," Chad thought to himself, especially when he was always reminded of how he never lived up to his older brother's standards. Joe lived in a multi-million-dollar house in LA, after becoming a plastic surgeon. Evan was equally successful, as a partner in a high profile law firm in LA. Neither one of them had a clue what it was like to feel unwanted, like an outcast. Chad knew he was on his own and hadn't spoken to them in years. After he dropped out of college because he was sick of school, they gave their advice and he avoided them like the plague. The fact that he had a reputation as a player with the random one-night stands, and no relationships lasting longer than three months, didn't improve his image with his brothers. They'd settled down, gotten married and had children.

Chad viewed William Carson as the father figure he'd never had. His own father, Martin Burton, had been a worthless, alcoholic piece of crap and he stopped talking to him as soon as he finished high school and moved out on his own. Chad winced as he thought about him. He had no more time to waste on thinking about the past, the people that he never wanted to see again, or the pain they'd caused him.

The phone rang and Chad answered, glad to be distracted from the past, which he tried to forget on a regular basis. Nancy informed him that Krista was on the line and Chad rolled his eyes and took a deep breath. She knew he didn't like calls at work. He had work to do! "Thank you, Nancy," Chad managed through gritted teeth. He had to get himself together before answering the phone.

"Hey, Kris, what's up? I'm really busy." Chad tried to be sympathetic to his wife's anxiety, but she was becoming obsessive. She was calling on a daily basis, and it was getting on his nerves. It made him feel like a teenager, having someone constantly checking on him.

"Are you busy? I was just thinking about dinner. Is there anything special that I can make for you? What's your pleasure?" Chad could tell his wife was trying to please him by being thoughtful, and he suddenly felt guilty.

Chad smiled, "Whatever you want to make is fine with me, Kris. Is that the only reason you're calling?" She didn't answer immediately.

"Kris? Is something wrong? Chad inwardly groaned because he knew what was coming.

"I don't know. I'm still feeling confused by these constant dreams. They really bother me." She sounded upset, despite the fact that the dreams had happened at least seven hours ago.

"Kris. Seriously, they are just dreams. Nothing is going to happen, okay? I promise. I'm here for you." Chad tried not to sound as irritated as he felt. This had been the theme over the past few months and he still loved his wife, but this was getting old. She was so distracted by these dreams it was starting to make him wonder if she needed psychiatric help. He found himself avoiding her and staying late at work. He was beginning to wonder if their marriage was going to survive this.

"I know. I'm okay. I'm just tired of the dreams. I'll be fine, don't worry. I'll start counting sheep before bed," she teased him, laughing. "Okay, then. I'll see you later. Love you." Chad was glad that she seemed to be coming to her senses. It was rare that when he hung up the phone, after talking to his wife, that he'd actually smiled. There was a knock at the door. "Come in" Chad said. Nancy poked her head in.

"Is everything okay, Mr. Burton?" Nancy asked. She knew she was being nosy, but she couldn't help herself. Every time his wife called, she always pondered the outcome.

Chad smiled. "Everything is fine, Nancy. Thank you for asking," he replied in his best professional tone and looked back at the paperwork on his desk in an effort to dismiss her. Nancy frowned and slammed the door behind her. Chad immediately felt remorseful, but she knew he was married. He couldn't treat her differently from the other staff. It would only instigate rumors, which could ruin his career and his marriage.

Chad~ Two years earlier

Chad was pissed. He'd spent two months on a difficult math course and almost flunked it! He was furious, tired, and basically felt he was wasting his time with these community college courses. He knew he'd never live this down if his brothers found out, which made him more frustrated. The phone was ringing and he debated answering, but picked up anyway. "Hey Paul, what's going on?" Chad tried to sound cheerful. Paul was the only friend that he trusted. The rest of them continued to mooch off their parents, even in their thirties, taking advantage of the fact that they could. He didn't have that luxury, and he despised their lack of motivation. He'd practically grown up at Paul's house, because of his alcoholic father and a mother who was busy working and taking care of the family. His father died three years ago. He barely kept in touch with his mother, who now lived in Pennsylvania and married a man with a teenage daughter. He didn't have anything in common with his brothers who were too wrapped up in their own lives, and he often wondered if that was because they weren't close in age. It would've made life growing up a little easier.

"Oh, man, what's up? You sound pissed or something." Paul knew Chad's voice and decided to go ahead with his message anyway. "So, you need to go to this party tonight! I'm serious and I'm not taking no for an answer."

"Who's hosting this party?" Chad was realistic. Although Paul was a good friend he didn't always give great advice. But at the same time, his sales job at Hugh's, a local furniture store, wasn't really doing much for his career.

"It's a corporate party. Have you heard of William Carson?" Paul was teasing.

"Are you talking about William, as in 'Carson Realty'? Seriously? You have an invitation?" Chad thought he was bluffing. Although Paul had good connections in the real estate world, he was nowhere near the level of Carson Realty. Carson Realty was the Elvis of the real estate world, at least in Rhode Island.

"Yup. Don't ask me how, but I'll just say that my latest girlfriend has connections and managed an invite with a plus one."

"So I'm the second choice? Aw, thanks, that makes me feel cheap!" Chad joked. Then again, Chad knew his friend's 'player mentality. Paul's idea of a 'girlfriend' was a one- night stand that he actually called for another date. "Aw, dude, you know me. Never found one to keep my interest for very long." Paul laughed. He knew he was a player and he didn't give a shit.

"I'm there. What time?" Chad began looking through his closet, and groaned at what was available. Knowing it was a corporate party, it was probably a black tie event. Not a tux in sight, just a few casual business suits. Shit!

"Around eight. Get dressed. Black tie." Paul advised.

"It's six now. I've got no tux. How is this going to happen?" Chad was stressed. He didn't want to blow this opportunity off because of a wardrobe issue.

"I've got you covered. Pick up a tux at Men's Wear House on Blanden Street and I'll meet you there." Paul confirmed.

"Got it." Chad hung up, took a quick shower and took off to meet Paul. He grabbed his tux and they were off. When they arrived at the Crown Plaza hotel in downtown Providence, they were greeted by the valet. Chad still couldn't believe his good luck as he walked into the elegant lobby. He gazed around at the crystal chandeliers, the regal red carpet and marble flooring everywhere. Even if this didn't get his career going, he was going to enjoy the experience of first class. He got a drink from the open bar and then sat down with Paul, just as the gala began with opening speeches. William Carson came to the podium to discuss the expansion of his real estate business. Chad found himself getting distracted until Mr. Carson brought up his daughter. She caught his attention and he sat up in his seat. Krista was beautiful, that was obvious, but it was her energy that drew him to her. He nudged Paul. "Hey, what do you know about her?" Chad wanted to know.

"She's the daughter of William Carson. Need I say more? Pretty hot, huh?" Paul smiled.

"Do you know her?" Chad knew Paul probably didn't but hoped for the best.

"I've met her. That's my connection. Phoebe is friends with her. Why? You interested?" Paul gave his smile again. "This isn't a girl that you can do the player act with, just warning you. Her father and his army would hunt you down!"

"Just wondering." Chad tried to play it cool, but Paul knew better. "I'll get you an introduction."

After the speeches and people began circulating, Paul kept his word and introduced Chad to Krista. The minute he touched her hand to shake it, there was an instant attraction between them. She was even more beautiful up close without all the harsh lighting. Her blonde hair was in a bun with small pieces coming down, eyes that matched her sky-blue dress which showed off her petite figure. She was much younger than him, yet he was drawn to her, and she seemed interested as well. As the evening progressed, Chad was smitten and knew that he wanted to get to know Krista better.

As they danced to Ella James' "At Last," the final dance, Chad asked to see her again soon. Krista smiled and nodded. "Can I get your number?" Chad was a man of details. When he wanted to do something, he needed to make sure it would happen.

Krista gave a precocious laugh. "I'll give you my number if you tell me something you've never told anyone else."

Chad grinned. She was beautiful, and had a sense of humor. He thought quickly and knew the only thing he'd never told anyone else. "I once had to lie for my dad." Simple words, no explanation needed, and he wouldn't give one if she asked. Having a deadbeat alcoholic father was not something he had ever shared with anyone, with the exception of Paul.

Krista smiled and looked at him. His face was suddenly serious and she knew he wasn't playing a game with her. "Thank you. I'll give you my cell number when we finish this dance." Chad smiled and asked "Now tell me something you've never told anyone else." Okay. I'm wearing a necklace that I don't take off," She laughed softly, teasing him.

Chad laughed with her. "C'mon, seriously? That's it? And I thought it was going to be some deep dark secret." "It's something I've never told anyone until now. Truth! Ask my friends. See, here it is!" She showed off her half-heart pendant on her neck, which led his eyes down towards her breasts. She noticed. "My face is up here!" Krista teased. She was too cute to challenge her answer.

"Thank you, Krista. I mean it." Chad said, as the song ended. "Now, it's time for your end of the bargain. Can I have your number?" Krista nodded and gave her number after they got back to their table. "Oh, and if I don't hear from you tomorrow, I'm going to assume that you won't call. Something I've told many people before." Krista winked at him. "I need to go. My ride is leaving." She kissed him on the cheek and left him speechless at the table. He watched as she moved away, her blue dress swaying with her hips. She was a sight to see coming and going He knew she was many years younger than him, but he also knew he would be calling tomorrow.

"You and my daughter looked very comfortable on the dance floor, Mr. Burton." Chad looked up to see William Carson standing there. He stood up immediately and offered his hand. "Chad Burton, it's nice to meet you, Mr. Carson."

"Likewise, Chad. I've heard that you've got a great head for retail sales," William smiled. Chad was pleased that he'd seemed to have made a good impression so far.

Chad was scrambling for something positive to say about his low-level furniture sales job, but couldn't come up with anything, so he figured vague was better. "Thank you. Business is in my blood, I guess. I enjoy my work."

"I've heard good things about your sales record, they're very impressive. I've been looking for someone who likes a challenge. Any experience in real estate?" William was straight to the point.

Chad knew that he was in a moment that might change his career forever, but he knew he had to be honest. "No, sir, but if I can sell furniture to people who were just coming to look, then I'm sure that I could sell property if I was given the chance."

William smiled, "I don't have a doubt that you could do great things. Why don't you stop by the office on Monday? We'll talk more then. Say about 10:00?"

"Of course. I'd like that." Chad said, grinning from ear to ear. This was an opportunity of a lifetime, especially considering his dead-end job at the furniture store.

"If you're going to get involved with my daughter, I'd rather have you closer! I've gotta keep an eye on you!" William joked lightly, although Chad was certain there was more than some truth to William's statement.

William

After a short meeting with William that following Monday, Chad began his training to learn the ropes. In less than a year's time he'd moved up to become one of the top realtors at Carson Realty. Chad had a head for business and a good rapport with clients which was necessary, and never failed to make a sale. William had spent some time checking up on Chad's relationship resume, which wasn't quite so spectacular.

But by this time, Chad and Krista had been seeing each other every day, and had been exclusive for close to a year, and were discussing moving in together. So when Chad asked William's permission to marry his daughter, her father had questions. What made her different, and what would stop him from being someone that liked to 'shop around' when things weren't going so well. Chad admitted to his past rocky relationships and assured him that he was serious about his daughter. Yet, William was still cautious and had questioned his daughter.

"Kris, he's a great guy, but the age difference? Can't you find any nice men your age to settle down with?" William was always skeptical about men his daughter dated.

"Dad, you like him! You even gave him a job and said that he's the best realtor you have working for you." Krista reminded him.

"I know. I just want the best for you. I want you to be happy, sweetheart!" William had always felt overprotective of Krista, especially being a single father all these years. He didn't like to think about the past, in fact, he avoided it most of the time, but he and Krista had been through difficult times. It was hard raising a girl without her mother for obvious reasons. He'd had some help from his sister, Barbara, who'd been there when Krista began her adolescent years and needed some female advice. He'd always strived to be the best father he could be, after her mother left when Krista was three years old.

He struggled through Krista's insistence that she had a sister and would to "talk to her" as if she were actually there. William felt that she was too young to understand if he were to explain the past to her. Eventually, the "sister" phase subsided, and Krista thrived throughout the years. She'd asked questions about her mother and William tried to answer them honestly, but it was difficult to avoid telling her the whole story. He hoped he'd never have to do that. He never wanted her to feel as hopeless and lost as he had for a decade. There was no reason to at this point in her life, and now she was getting married to a smart, handsome man that was older and wiser and promising to take care of her. He had no doubt that Krista could take care of herself with her career as a school counselor, but he also knew the job didn't pay as well as other careers.

She'd never had any interest in sales, real estate or anything involving business. "Dad, it's so boring! I want to help people! Sales to me equals having to deal with numbers and math, you know I hate that!" Krista had said when he suggested getting a business degree after getting into Boston College. She did attend Boston College when accepted but decided to get a degree in social work, with a minor in education. He knew there was no changing her mind. She'd inherited his stubbornness and her mother's independence.

Krista

Krista walked through the guidance main office of Johnston High School just as the final bell for class rang at school. "Good morning!" She greeted Jane, the 40-something-year-old receptionist for the guidance counselor's office, as she walked in.

"Good morning, Krista. Running a little late, huh?" Jane commented loudly, her eyes glancing up at the clock. Krista tried to ignore the usual irritation that she experienced every morning with Jane. Jane was the epitome of a secretary who obviously hated her job and was bitchy to everyone, including Krista, her fellow counselors, and the students, who referred to her as "crazy lady". Whenever her students said that, it was hard for Krista to stop herself from smiling. The name fit her more than they would ever know. With her dowdy ill-fitting skirts and jackets, short mullet-like hairdo, Jane was clearly as miserable as she treated everyone else. Krista was sure she also had a houseful of cats, named after Bible disciples.

"Just running behind, but it'll be fine." Krista replied as she walked into her office and closed the door. She loathed the woman, and really wanted to give her a sarcastic response, but why waste her time? Besides, she didn't want to start her day with a power struggle with Jane.

Krista sat down and took a swig of her coffee before glancing at her schedule for today. She was glad to see that she had an hour before she was meeting with a student. Some time to recoup was necessary. These nightmares were getting more intense and she wasn't sure how to interpret them anymore. At first, they'd been just dreams. She was able to recover and didn't wake Chad up. But lately they had become more vivid and downright scary, to the point where she was trapped on a cliff and chased by a doppelganger of herself.

Krista tried to clear her mind and began to review the next student's file. She managed to focus on reading the file when she saw something moving in her peripheral vision that made her stop. She looked to her right and at first didn't notice anything, but as she glanced down at the paper in front of her, she saw movement again and did a double take. The glass prism in the window was swinging back and forth which was strange because her office window wasn't open. Krista closed her eyes for a moment. 'It's nothing, just your imagination', she told herself. She opened them again and glanced at the window. The prism was completely still. A chill ran up Krista's spine, and she suddenly felt like she needed to get out of the room. She quickly pushed open her office door to head for the bathroom.

"Ms. Burton, Travis Jenkins is here for your 10:00 appointment," Jane announced as Krista brushed past her. Krista tried to compose herself. "I'll just be a minute. I need to use the restroom. Be right with you." Krista hoped she didn't look as frantic as she felt, and rushed to the ladies' room, splashing cold water on her face. She took a deep breath and wiped her face. 'It's like the dream, but I know I'm awake. Maybe I'm just overtired, and it'll pass.' She took another deep breath and made her way back to the office, suddenly feeling embarrassed about her abrupt departure when a student was waiting for her.

She tried her best to forget about the incident while her student was talking to her about his problems with his classes, his friends, and his parents, but her mind continued to wander. Was she going crazy? It was as if her nightmares were invading her waking hours.

Krista managed to make it through the rest of the day without any other strange occurrences, but she couldn't shake the anxiety of the morning. She knew that she wasn't seeing things; it was the same strange feeling that she had after the nightmares. She sighed and closed down her computer for the day. She picked up her coffee mug and shoved it into her bag. As she looked down at where the mug had been, she saw "KAREN" written in bright red letters where her mug had been sitting. Who the hell was Karen?

She inspected the handwriting more closely. It looked like hers, but she didn't remember writing it and it wasn't there this morning. She looked in her appointment book for the day and there was no "Karen" listed as a student that she counseled. 'I'm definitely going crazy. I did not write that!' Krista murmured to herself. She grabbed her purse and left her office. She felt frantic. Her office used to feel like a safe haven but she was having a hard time concentrating. She started to think that she was having some sort of breakdown. She sat in her car, frightened and unsure where to go or who to talk to.

She texted her best friend, Jen Whitcomb. "Crazy stuff happening. R U you around later?" Jen texted back "Pretty busy, but will talk to you end of day." She had been friends with Jen since their college days. After a few minutes, and no response from Jen, Krista knew that she was on her own for the time being. Jen was an attorney for a prestigious law firm, and since her new partnership they rarely talked because Jen was working most of the time. Krista thought about reaching out to a few other friends, but discounted that idea. Most of her friends with the exception of Jen were casual acquaintances and she didn't feel comfortable talking to any of them about this.

This was when she missed her mother the most. She loved her dad, and her husband, but this time she needed a female voice, a mother's advice, someone that loved her unconditionally. Krista had always felt the void, even though her Aunt Barbara had helped out, but it wasn't the same. Her dad just said her mother had left when she was young, but that her mother was always there with her in spirit. She'd never gotten any straight answers as to why she left except that her dad said that she'd been depressed, but he'd never understood the reason. She chose to believe him, because she didn't remember her at all. Her only memories were through pictures that were old and faded. Her mother's face always looked beautiful, yet tired, and as if she were straining to smile. Had *Krista* made her upset? Had *Krista* done something?

Her friends always had their parents. They may have been divorced, but they weren't gone from their lives, like her mom had been. When she was sixteen, she became convinced that her mother was dead, that she had committed suicide. She'd finally confessed her fears to her father and it'd taken him the better part of six months to convince her otherwise. He'd had family members corroborate that she wasn't well and she'd left on her own. Couldn't she have just divorced her father, if she was that unhappy? Her mother leaving for no reason just didn't make any sense and it made her feel worse.

Krista continued driving, opting for the side roads instead of the highway. A red flashing sign "Psychic Reading" caught her eye. She wasn't religious. She'd never bought into the after-life palm and tarot card reading. On the other hand, she had never had recurring nightmares and or seen images that no one else could see. What the hell? She figured it was worth at least checking it out before admitting herself into the nearest psychiatric unit for observation.

She took a deep breath as she opened the door, setting off a bell chime as she entered. The room seemed ethereal, with wind chimes making a silvery, almost eerie sound with the occasional breeze. Lavender-scented candles burned, giving the small room a relaxing ambiance. A small desk with a Tiffany lamp occupied one corner of the room.

"Hello, there. I stepped out of the room for a moment." Krista was startled as a young, exotic-looking girl appeared from the drapes. She was very pretty, dressed in jeans, and a button-down plaid shirt with Birkenstocks. Her dark curly hair was pulled back in a casual ponytail. She was not the typical psychic Krista had envisioned.

"Hi! Um, I was just checking out this place….." Krista began, stumbling over her words. What the hell was she doing here? Her doubts set in again.

"No problem. It's pretty usual for people to feel a little out of place at first. The girl smiled. "My name is Nadine. I work here with my aunt. She owns this place."

"Are you the psychic?" Krista questioned, still surprised at herself for coming through the door. She might as well give it a shot. Maybe it was bullshit, but it was better than sitting in a psychiatrist office and being given medication because they thought she was delusional.

Nadine smiled again. "I am, although I'm still training with my aunt. Can I help you?" Her brown eyes were friendly and inviting. "I can tell you're a skeptic about readings."

Krista blushed. "You're right. I should go. I'm sorry." She walked toward the door. What the hell was she doing here anyway?

"Wait! I should meet with you!" Nadine said before Krista could open the door.

"What? No, I don't think so. I'm just checking this out. I'm fine, really." Krista pulled on the door.

"Please. You should meet with me. I sense a presence," Nadine insisted. Krista stopped. Did she really want to go this far? What could it hurt? She didn't need to tell Chad about it. She walked back over to Nadine.

"What do you mean a 'presence?'" Krista suddenly needed to know more.

Nadine sat down behind the desk and motioned for her to sit down in the chair in front of it. Krista sat down, intrigued and scared at the same time.

"A presence means that I can feel that someone is with you, they are following you and they're trying to tell you something." Nadine answered.

"What? They're following me? Are they dangerous?" Krista suddenly felt frightened. Nadine shook her head, "I mean that someone from the spiritual world is following you. I can tell you that much. However, if you wish to have more information, I'll have to charge you the required fee."

"How much?" Krista asked.

"Fifty." Nadine answered.

Krista shook her head and walked toward the door again. Nadine followed her to her car, "You really need to pay attention to the signs.

I'm assuming the dreams are bothering you. That's why you came here."

Krista turned around as she reached for the car door. "How do you know about my dreams?"

"I only know what I see. Being psychic isn't always recognized by scientists, but it does exist. It's a gift that isn't given to most. Come back when you're ready to face the dreams. We will be here." Nadine turned around and walked back into the office.

Krista sat for what seemed an eternity in her car, debating about whether to go back in or not. Curiosity won out and she walked back in, the bell chiming once again. Nadine was sitting at the desk. She had known she'd return! Krista had no doubt about that.

Krista took out two twenties and a ten and slid them across the desk. "Okay, what do my dreams mean, Nadine?" She was already paying to hear what might be nonsense, but how could this girl know? She was more curious than frightened now. Whatever tactic Nadine used had worked this time.

"Give me your hand, Krista." Nadine asked. Krista stretched out her right hand and put it in Nadine's. She sat for a moment and traced the lines on her palm. Finally, she spoke. "Where's your sister, Krista?"

"I don't have a sister." Krista was surprised. Wow, fifty bucks for this?

"I'm sorry, but I'm getting a feeling that you do. You don't have a sister?" Nadine seemed confused. Maybe it was because she was making this up? Krista was not impressed so far.

"I'm sure I don't! I'm 28 years old and think I would know if I had a sister!" Krista was becoming upset. She remembered when she was younger and doing the "pretend sister" thing enough so that she had to go to a therapist to convince her otherwise.

"Sorry. I'm just getting an aura from a person close to you, like a sister. She is very persistent." Nadine said. "She believes you're in danger. She wants to help you."

"What kind of danger, what do you mean?" Krista leaned forward, knowing that this was likely a hoax to get her back and take more of her money, but at the same time wanted to know.

"I'm not sure. I'm not getting any more messages right now." Nadine opened her eyes.

"No more messages? What do you mean? You can't tell me anything else?!" Krista asked, almost frantically. She felt like someone had told her she won the lottery, only to tell her she was one number off.

"I'm sorry, that's the way it is sometimes," Nadine said, apologetically. "I tried to get her back but she's resistant."

"Who is being resistant?" Krista asked, anxiously.

"The person that is looking out for you, but they left for some reason. I can't get them back right now." Nadine said. She seemed frustrated by their lack of response herself.

Krista felt let down. She was dying to know more. "Okay. Thank you for your time," She picked up her purse and headed for the door.

Nadine handed her a business card. "Here. Take my card. Give me a call if you want to make an appointment."

"Thanks, I will," Krista replied through gritted teeth. She resisted the urge to demand her money back and call her a fake.

Instead, she grabbed the card, and stuffed it in her pants pocket, as she headed out to her car and hit the unlock button on her key fob. She started the car up and put it in reverse.

"There is more to find out, it just takes time," Nadine had run outside and called out as Krista pulled out of her parking space. Her voice fell on deaf ears at this point. Nadine hoped she'd be back. It was the most interesting client that she'd ever encountered. She would admit that she embellished details for some clients, but this one didn't have to give any information. It was all around her.

Chad

It was after 6pm and Chad was still at his desk, working on the final details of his next sale. He was feeling the pressure, not only from himself but from Krista's father to be the best. In the beginning, it had been a jumpstart to a career, but lately it was becoming exhausting. Was it worth it? Chad hoped so. Before they were married, he knew first-hand how much William's daughter meant to him. A knock at the door kept him from worrying any further. He didn't need to ask who was there. It was 6pm.

His secretary, Nancy walked into the room. "Mr. Burton, is there anything else you need from me?" Chad smiled. "Why yes, I think I still need you to show me the spreadsheets on our latest clients." He watched as she took off her black suit jacket and pulled the clips out of her long, dark hair that cascaded down her back.

"I don't think I can get those for you tonight, Mr. Burton." Nancy replied, while walking up to his desk. Her dark eyes were focused on him, her red lips beckoning. Her curves were accentuated by her snug red dress. "Can it wait until tomorrow?" Nancy kicked off her black heels and pulled at the skirt of her dress.

Chad gave up on resistance. "Of course. But you'll have to make up for it." Chad grinned and pulled Nancy across his desk, and yanked her dress over her head. Nancy moaned as he ripped off her underwear, anxious to be inside her. His allegiance to Krista was long gone at the moment. Nancy was a beautiful woman, sexy as hell and willing to please without any strings. She kissed him long and hard, and put her hands on his crotch. "Can I make it up to you, Mr. Burton?" Her breath was coming hard and fast.

"Why I think you are doing that, Nancy." Chad groaned and pulled down his pants, ready to get down to business, oblivious to anything or anyone else. Mind blowing sex with his secretary was something he didn't envision for himself two years ago, but when Nancy was hired 3 months ago, it was almost as if he couldn't stop himself. She was the opposite of Krista; olive skin, dark eyes, dark hair and a curvy body that some would consider slightly overweight, but it worked on her body type. Besides, she didn't demand any relationship. She seemed to understand what he wanted without strings.

It was only afterward that he felt like a traitor, a cheat. Trying to justify his actions, he also felt as though he'd paid his dues to William during working hours and deserved some 'off time' indiscretions. After all, she'd made it known when she was hired that she'd wanted this. She'd come into his office her first day, wearing a tight dress, hair down, and flirting with him. Chad always told himself that he loved Krista and his life with her, but sometimes the intensity of the commitment became too much and he couldn't help himself. He rationalized his actions by knowing that he was providing for Krista as her father wanted. As long as she didn't find out about Nancy, who was it hurting? Except that he felt horribly guilty afterwards.

Afterward, Nancy dressed, gave him a short kiss and left. "See you tomorrow," she said winking at him as she walked out the door. Chad smiled. He liked watching her leave, especially in that red dress. He preferred Krista in more feminine attire. She usually wore pants as opposed to skirts or dresses, flats rather than heels, and wore jeans and sweatshirts all weekend, everywhere, including going out to dinner. He sighed and shut down his computer, ready to leave for the day when the phone rang. He knew who was calling and grudgingly picked up. "Hey, babe," Chad was trying his best to sound happy, but knew that he wasn't coming across that way.

"Chad? Are you coming home?" Krista asked. She sounded a little worried.

"Of course I'm coming home. I was just headed out when you called." Chad insisted, irritated. He tried unsuccessfully to change the tone in his voice. He rolled his eyes. Everything had to be on her timeline now, especially lately. When he'd met Krista, she was so independent, so focused, but in the last month she was becoming clingy, almost needy. Did she suspect anything? He didn't think so. It was probably about the ongoing nightmares she was having that had made living with her a chore lately.

"Okay. I just had a really bad day and wanted to talk to you. What time will you be here?" She was insistent now.

"Is everything okay, Kris? I talked to you this morning and you were fine. You sound upset." Chad tried to check it out, suddenly feeling paranoid, and hoping that she wasn't becoming suspicious.

"I'm okay. I'll talk to you when you get home." Krista seemed to calm down, yet she still had an edge to her voice that told him otherwise. Chad knew he wasn't going to get a clue to the problem, but he assumed it didn't have to do with his evening trysts with Nancy. If she knew, she'd be down at his office. He was sure of that.

"Okay, Kris. I'll see you soon," Chad said and hung up. He grabbed his briefcase and left the office, confident that he'd left enough time between himself and Nancy leaving. As he walked through the row of cubicles to the elevator, he looked around for any employees that might be lingering. He knew he was being paranoid, but he also knew he couldn't afford for anyone to get suspicions about the affair. He'd be finished at Carson Realty. All the hard work he'd put in the past two years would be for nothing. As he reached the elevator and pressed the L for the lobby, he heard a voice. He hit open on the elevator doors, stepped out and looked around. He didn't see anyone.

"Hello, Chad." It was a female voice, soft yet decisive. It sounded familiar, like Krista and yet he knew that Krista couldn't possibly be here. He'd just hung up. She was home.

Chad turned around, looking to see where the voice was coming from, but didn't see anyone. "Yes? Who's there?" Chad was becoming nervous. Maybe someone was still here? Did they know what was going on? No answer. Chad looked around before getting back on the elevator. Once on the first floor, he ran to his car and headed home. During his drive, he was still trying to figure out where that voice came from. Curiosity won out and he called Krista from the car.

"Hey, there, you headed home?" Krista's voice sounded concerned.

"Of course, I told you I was coming home. Where did you think I was going?" Chad was relieved that she answered. There was no way she could've been at his office.

"Okay. Well *you* called *me*." Krista sounded irritated.

"I'm sorry, babe. It's been a long day. I'll see you in a few minutes, okay?" Chad knew he sounded sketchy and needed to get his shit together. She didn't seem to know anything; he was sure of it. He knew he was playing roulette with his after hours 'conferences' with Nancy and it was clear it needed to stop. He couldn't afford to have his career ruined, and he knew that it would be if William Carson knew he was having an affair. When he pulled into the driveway he remained in the car, trying to collect his thoughts. The front porch light came on, and Krista came out. She looked at him quizzically. Chad smiled, got out, and met her at the door.

Krista gave him a hug. "I'm so glad you're here. It's been a crazy day." Chad smiled, feeling relieved with his wife's reaction. He returned the hug and kissed her. "Me too. But I'm home now! I'm starving! What's for dinner?" Chad felt a tinge of guilt, as Krista led him into the kitchen and they sat down for a dinner of chicken parmesan with angel hair pasta she'd made. "So what was so crazy about your day, Kris?" Chad asked.

Krista tried to explain her morning. "It started with seeing my prism in the window at my office. It started moving by itself. Then there was a name on my calendar written down that I didn't know about. It was so strange. I can't even explain it!" Chad nodded, and tried to seem interested. The events seemed even more far-fetched than the nightmares she'd been describing. He felt himself tuning out and convinced that his wife was in need of psychiatric help.

"Kris. Honey, I really wish you would talk to someone, a professional, about this. I just don't get it." Chad tried not to sound condescending. Krista was surprised that he even made the suggestion, so she decided to tell him about her unexpected afternoon 'appointment.'

"So, I went and saw a psychic today after work. You know, just to see." Krista started to tell him about it.

"Wait, you what? Saw a psychic? Are you kidding me right now, Kris?" Chad was stunned that his wife would go as far as to see one of those whack jobs that claimed to be psychics. "You know they're not psychic, right? They're con artists, taking peoples' money, telling them bullshit based on their reaction!"

"But it wasn't like that. I went in, and was going to leave, but then she started telling me all of these things that she couldn't have known!" Krista insisted. She knew he wouldn't agree to the psychic thing, and suspected he would react this way. Why had she bothered telling him in the first place? She wished she hadn't. She could have just talked to Jen later. Jen would probably think it was nuts too, but at least she didn't have to live with Jen.

"Kris! You won't go back there! You need to promise me!" Chad became suddenly demanding, almost angry. If there was anything to the psychic nonsense, he hoped there wouldn't be mention of any extramarital affairs in their premonitions. It was starting to worry him, no matter how ridiculous he thought their practice.

"Chad, what's the problem? It wasn't expensive. I already told you that she didn't get information from me ahead of time. We only talked for 5 minutes. She followed me out after I was leaving and said I needed to listen to her!" Krista knew he'd be a little resistant, maybe tease her about it, but didn't anticipate this dramatic reaction. She felt afraid of him for the first time. It was not a feeling she wanted to have about her husband.

Chad managed to pull himself together. Of course it was ridiculous that any psychic would give his wife that information. He also knew he wasn't going to get anywhere telling her what she could and couldn't do. Krista was too independent for that, despite her recent clingy behavior. "Kris, honey, I just want you to tell me you're not going to get more advice from these crackpots that are making things up as they go along! In fact, I think it would be a good idea if you saw a professional about your dreams. Maybe there's something psychological going on........" Chad trailed off. He didn't want to say the word "psychiatrist," but they both knew what he meant.

"So you want me to see a psychiatrist?" Krista said, surprised and confused that he would make that suggestion in the first place. "Do you think I'm making this up?" She asked, trying not to sound as upset as she felt.

Chad knew he needed to tread lightly. "Kris, I know you don't want to see someone about these problems, but clearly, they are interrupting our lives. Please, I love you. Won't you just humor me and see a professional, rather than some phony psychic?"

Krista got up to clear the table and began rinsing the plates. "I guess I could see someone. I'll look into it." Krista looked back at Chad.

"Just give it a chance and we'll go from there." Chad would agree to anything at this point. He just wanted his young, innocent, agreeable wife back. Once she wasn't so consumed by these dreams, they could get back to the relaxed relationship that they'd had when they met. He gave her a kiss before going to the living room to watch TV. "I just want you to relax a little, Kris. Come sit down with me. Let's binge watch some Netflix." He patted the space on the couch next to him.

Krista nodded in agreement, but she wasn't so sure. "Ok, I'll try." She snuggled down next to him, hoping that the comedy they watched would translate into a restful sleep. However, after a few minutes the show wasn't keeping her attention. "I'm going to call my dad." She told Chad and went into the kitchen. Her dad always had a way of helping her feel settled.

William

William Carson sat down after a long day with his usual cigar and a glass of whiskey on the rocks. He turned on the TV just to have some company as he usually did. The house was so quiet since Krista moved out. He almost regretted Krista's marriage to Chad, but it was something that she wanted and he knew that he couldn't stop her regardless of what he said. She was so damn independent, just like him. He was hearing reports of his son-in-law and Nancy staying later in the evenings. It was becoming suspicious. He'd hoped that Chad would be a devoted husband to his only daughter, but was beginning to have doubts. Krista hadn't said anything to him so far, but he planned to keep an eye on Chad.

Feeling fuzzy and warm from the whiskey, William pulled out a family album and began thumbing through it. Photographs of his wife frozen in time always made him nostalgic. They'd had a few good years together before she was gone. Her bright blue eyes and blonde hair inherited by Krista made them look like sisters and as always, he couldn't turn the next page. He sighed and closed the album. 'No use living in the past,' William told himself, although this was a nightly ritual for him. He'd never even contemplated another serious relationship after Maria. She'd been his soul mate and he knew there wouldn't be anyone else for him.

The phone rang, interrupting his thoughts. It was Krista, and he was thankful that he still had his daughter. "Dad, I need to ask you something." She sounded upset.

"What's going on, Kris?" He was suddenly pulled out of his melancholy world.

"I don't know. I'm just ...just confused, I guess. I've been having some strange dreams lately. They're scary, and I wasn't sure what to do." Krista blurted out in a tirade. She didn't want to burden her dad with this, but Chad seemed to think she was being a drama queen and her best friend, Jen, still hadn't texted her back.

"Kris, you're just stressed." William assured her. "You're not crazy. Crazy doesn't run in the family." He tried to joke, but Krista wasn't laughing.

"Dad, I'm being serious! I'm having these dreams and seeing things when I'm awake and I don't know what to do anymore!" She sounded frantic.

"Kris, you just need some rest. You're probably just having more intense dreams because I think you take your work home with you." William tried to reassure her.

"I know, dad, but it's starting to get to Chad and it he seems like he's angry with me most of the time. I don't know what to do. He wants me to see a psychiatrist!"

"Why would he want you to do that?" William became concerned. He was immediately on the defensive for his daughter. His concerns about his son-in-law were mounting.

"Because I went to meet with a psychic today and I told Chad about it. He was upset and said that I should see a professional." Krista sniffed, still upset that her husband thought she was delusional.

A psychic? What was Krista thinking? What did they say? William was stumped for words for a moment.

"Dad, did you hear what I said? I saw a psychic today. Chad thinks I'm being duped and that I should see a psychiatrist. What do you think?" Krista valued her father's opinion as always. If he thought she needed to seek out professional help, then she would take that into serious consideration.

William took a minute to think about his answer. It was like a whirlwind in his head about the past, first Maria, and now Krista. "No, honey, I don't. You've been having some dreams. Okay, everyone has them. But why did you want to see a psychic?" He was suddenly worried, and had to agree with Chad on this.

"It was just a strange day, dad. There was a prism on my window that was swinging around and then some name on my calendar that was in my handwriting, but I know I didn't write it....." Krista faded off, as she realized she did sound kind of ridiculous. "You know what, I'm sorry I bothered you. I'm probably just tired, that's all."

"What? A prism in the window? A name? It was probably a name of one of the students you were going to see, Kris." William tried to rationalize, as usual. It was what he did best and while she found it annoying sometimes, this time she was thankful. "Thanks dad. You always have a way of bringing me back to reality."

"So what did the psychic have to say?" He couldn't help but ask. Curiosity was getting the best of him.

"I thought you didn't believe in that, dad." Krista kidded him. "She basically recognized that I had some stress in my life, which isn't hard to guess. She did say something strange, though. She tried to convince me that I have a sister. I left after that, because I knew she was full of it." Krista tried to joke about it.

There was silence on the other end. "Dad, are you still there?" Krista asked

"Yes, I'm here. I'm just wondering why anyone would say that." William answered, struggling to keep his voice calm. He didn't like where this conversation was headed so he felt it better to talk to her tomorrow. "Honey, I'm tired, can we talk more tomorrow?"

"Sure dad. I'll talk to you tomorrow. Love you."

"Love you too, Kris." She looked up at the clock. It was 7:30. She couldn't ever remember her father going to bed before 10:00. "It's 7:30, dad. Are you feeling okay? You're not starting to be like grandpa.

Up at 4:00am and in bed at 7:00? You're a little too young for that."
She laughed.

"I'm not that young, but definitely no grandpa hours for me yet. I just need to relax and catch up on the new season of Survivor. I have a bunch of them to watch." William used it as an excuse.

"You're still watching that? Okay, tell Jeff I said, it's time to end the show and move on! Talk to you soon. Good night!" Krista said.

"Sleep well, Kris. Talk to you soon." William said. His mind was suddenly spinning with Krista's psychic telling her about having a sister. How could they have known? On a whim, William dialed the number for Johnston detective division. "Detective division, McCaffrey speaking." William recognized his name from years ago. "Hey, Andrew, it's William Carson. Can you get me the number for Detective Sumner? I know he's been retired for a few years. Just need a number, please." William turned back to his photos and poured himself another whiskey. "I'll check for you, Mr. Carson." Andrew said.

Andrew McCaffrey came back a few minutes later. It was not good news. "Mr. Carson, I'm sorry to say that I contacted his home number and his wife informed me that he is in the hospital and unable to take phone calls." William took in a breath, surprised at the news. Dave Sumner was fairly young, only 45 years old, and never took a sick day in his life. Damn! He wasn't sure where to turn now.

"I'm sorry to hear that. I hope that he's okay." He didn't press for details. Andrew probably didn't get any.

"Is there anything *I* can help you with, Mr. Carson?" William opened his mouth to say yes, but decided against it. Andrew McCaffrey wouldn't know anything and William didn't want anyone digging around into old files. Dave Sumner was the only detective that he trusted.

"That's okay. I'll check with his wife in the morning. Thank you." William said. He didn't want to bother Dave's wife at this time of night. But he made a mental note to call Maureen Sumner in the morning. Hopefully it wasn't anything serious.

Krista

After the talk with her father, Krista felt better about her visit to the psychic. After starting the dishwasher, she went to the living room where the Netflix show was still on. But Chad wasn't in the living room.

"Chad?" She called out. He was probably changing into his 'comfy clothes,' referring to pajama pants and his Patriots sweatshirt that she would sometimes have to sneak into the laundry because he wore it so often. No answer. "Chad? Are you upstairs?" Krista called out again. After waiting a minute or so, she made her way upstairs. "Chad?" She could hear his voice coming from his office. He was speaking quietly and she couldn't make out the words. She started to feel guilty, as though she were spying, but couldn't help herself as she perched right outside the door.

"Yes, I know. I asked you not to call me at night. I can't really talk, you know?" Chad's voice was low and quiet. He was on his cell phone, something that he rarely did when he was in his home office. Unlike most people, Chad insisted on having a landline in his office, because he didn't want clients having access to his cell. Krista peered around the corner to find him pacing behind his cedar desk that he insisted on buying. He glanced in her direction. Krista felt her suspicions growing, so she decided to walk into the room, just as he said, "Okay, I know!

47

But you understand what my position is in this situation." As soon as he saw his wife, Chad's quiet tone changed to his businesslike voice and his cheeks flushed pink. "Yes, sir, I understand. I'll talk with you tomorrow." Chad ended the call.

"Hey, what's up, honey? I just got off a call from work. Damn bankers! I had to set up a wine and dine to get everything right." Chad said casually, as he began walking out of the room, putting a hand on her back to usher her out. Krista followed his lead and headed downstairs with him, but wasn't convinced. Not in the least. "Who were you talking to?"

Chad seemed flustered but regrouped quickly. "I just told you! Bank executives! I'm trying to put together a deal on this million - dollar home in Charlestown for a potential buyer!"

"But why did you say that you couldn't talk at night? Why weren't you on your office landline? Krista fired her questions at him. She knew he was lying and wanted the truth, but given his resistance, she wasn't sure she would get it this time.

Chad ran his fingers though his hair. Krista could tell that he was stalling. It was a standard Chad move if he didn't know what to say or do to buy him time. "I knew you were having a rough day, and didn't want to be stuck on the phone with work stuff. I wanted to be here for you." Chad was playing his empathy card, but she wasn't buying it.

Krista knew better. "Chad, I don't know what's going on here. I can tell you that I don't believe you." She walked away, feeling on edge. "I think I'll head up to bed now. Good night."

"Krista! What are you doing? What are you talking about?" Chad made a valiant attempt at defending himself, but she wouldn't budge. Not today. After a few minutes of trying to appeal to his wife, he was frustrated. "Okay, fine. Sleep well then." He said, knowing he was fighting a losing battle at this point. Damn! Why did Nancy have to keep calling? He knew his wife had overheard at least part of the conversation. Krista might not be behaving like herself, but she wasn't stupid.

She heard every word and with every word, he just pushed himself further from where he was trying to be. Krista lay silent then impulsively dialed her friend, Jen, hoping she would pick up. After three rings, she finally did. "Jen, it's Kris. Sorry to call so late."

"Hey there, I was headed to bed, but what's going on?" Jen yawned sounding less than interested.

"Chad had one of his late nights again. I'm just so tired of it, Jen. I know there's something going on with him and his assistant. Don't tell me I'm nuts, just go with it okay?"

"Okay, Kris, I get it. He's been working late, she's there, but do you have any proof? Jen asked.

"What do you mean 'proof'?"

"I mean, have you caught him in a lie? Have you caught them together? Does he seem different?" Jen asked.

"Well, tonight I overheard him talking to someone on the phone that seemed strange. He said 'I told you not to call here at night' and suddenly ended the call when I walked into the room." Krista said.

"Okay, that's kind of strange. But, maybe he really was working?" Jen offered, but her response lacked conviction and Krista knew it. "Thanks, Jen. I appreciate the vote of confidence, but I know you and what you really think."

"You got me. I'm just trying to be positive though." Jen admitted. She yawned again. She was obviously tired and wanting to go to bed.

"By the way, I saw a psychic today." Krista informed her friend.

"What? What on earth made you do that?" Jen acted as though Krista had signed up for the next trip on the space shuttle.

"Some weird stuff happened at work today. A prism in my office was moving in front of a closed window, as if there was a breeze. Then a name was written down on my calendar that I know I didn't write." Krista said. As soon as she said the words she realized how insignificant it sounded to other people. But it wasn't to her. Not with these dreams she was having.

"Okay..." Jen said, not sounding convinced that these events required a trip to a psychic.

"Just bear with me. She insisted that I have a sister. I know, it sounds like a Twilight Zone episode, right? But she seemed as though she knew what she was talking about. She said there was a presence. She said that this presence was trying to help me." Krista insisted.

"Kris, seriously? You don't really buy that crap do you? They want you to pay the money to fill your head full of nonsense that they make up!" Jen's disgust for any kind of psychic advice was clear. Her response was the same as Chad's. "You need to chill out. We need to schedule a girls' vacation soon!"

Krista suddenly felt less anxious after Jen's advice hit home. "You're right, Jen. Let's schedule something soon, ok? Sorry to bother you so late. Call me later this week."

"Definitely! I'm thinking Jamaica or some other island where we just soak up sun and drink exotic drinks all day! And maybe look at some hot guys too! Look, no touch!" Jen laughed. She was happily married to Clay, a guy she'd met in law school. They continued the small talk and vague plans and Krista hung up. She shut down her phone and was fast asleep within a few minutes.

* * * * * *

The light through the window woke Krista up. Shit! What time was it? Her phone which was her alarm was completely turned off. She glanced at the clock on the end table. 8:00! She was due at the school in 30 minutes! She jumped out of the bed and ran for the shower. "Thanks for waking me up!" Krista yelled in the direction of the master bedroom, as she got into the spray of the hot water. She'd never gotten ready for work so fast in her life. By 8:30, she was pulling out of the driveway and noticed that Chad's BMW was already gone. 'Well that explains why he never said anything back! What an asshole for not waking me!'

Krista's anger about the obvious lie last night began to bubble over, as she drove quickly to the school and ended up being only 15 minutes late. Crazy Jane was ready and waiting, making her comments without fail. "Running late again?" Jane shook her head with a smirk on her face. Krista resisted the urge to tell her where to go, ignored her, and kept walking into her office, slamming the door behind her.

Krista plopped down in her chair, head in her hands and rubbed her eyes. Coffee! 'I need coffee!' In her rush to get to work, she'd forgotten her usual stop by Dunkin Donuts for her toasted almond coffee and now she was feeling it. Not just the lack of caffeine but the feeling of the warm Styrofoam cup in her hand was the boost she needed for the morning.

The ringing of her phone forced her to answer. "Yes?" Krista tried her best not to sound irritated as she felt.

"Your 9:00 appointment is here. Steve Stanton." Jane's voice was curt. Krista managed to keep her cool and replied, "Fine. I'll be out in a minute."

Krista rummaged around her file cabinet until she found Steve's file. She was flustered and hated that she was so late that there wasn't time to look it over. In fact, she had no idea why this student was here. 'Guess I'm flying blind on this one!' She grabbed the file and pulled, but it wouldn't budge. Frantically pulling at the file, she realized that there was something stuck in the back of the cabinet, causing it to jam. She put her hand all the way to the back and pulled out a small pocket sized photo album. "What the hell?" Krista said out loud. She opened it to find only one photo. It was a picture of an attractive woman with dark blonde hair, with two blonde, curly haired toddlers, probably no more than two years old, sitting on some rocks near the ocean. The woman was laughing and the little girls were on either side of her, hugging her with their small plump arms wrapped around her neck. The little girls looked very similar, almost like twins. It was clearly an older picture. There was no time stamp on the back, and the picture was beginning to yellow around the edges. Krista was still studying the picture for details when the phone rang again. She put the photo album in her purse and picked up the phone.

"Mrs. Burton, your student is still waiting!" Jane was in rare form today. Krista swore the woman lived to annoy her. "Yes, I'm coming." Krista replied through gritted teeth. She grabbed the file and opened the door.

"Steve Stanton?" A tall gangly boy with a 'man' bun and dressed in a baggy pair of jeans that were threatening to fall down stood up and followed Krista into her office

The next hour was spent with Krista trying to focus, but only half -listening to the student's problems. She felt horrible that she wasn't on her game, but she couldn't forget that picture. 'What was it doing there? Who was in the photo? 'Her thoughts wandered as the student in front of her continued to talk.'

"So what do you think I should do, Mrs. Burton?" Steve asked. His lanky 6'4" frame would be an asset to any basketball court, but Steve had no coordination. His many tryouts convinced everyone, including his overbearing parents, that Steve wasn't athletic.

Krista tried to recall what they were talking about, but couldn't. She realized in that moment that she really needed to focus. This wasn't fair to her students. What had they been talking about? Oh, yes, something about his classes being too easy for him, and needing more challenging classes for his GPA.

"I think you should enroll in the advanced biology and college algebra. It seems like you're ready for that challenge." Krista offered, crossing her fingers that she'd gotten it right.

Steve smiled. "Thank you so much, Mrs. Burton! I was hoping you'd say that! I can't wait to start these classes next semester!"

Krista returned his smile. "Great! Glad I could help!" She breathed a sigh of relief as he exited her office. She pulled the album out of her purse, and studied the picture again. Who were these people and why was it in her desk? She could recognize that it most likely was a picture taken in Rhode Island. She could see what looked like the Pell Bridge connecting Newport and Jamestown in the distance.

Chad

As Chad walked into the reception area, Nancy gave her usual come-hither smile. 'Not today, Nancy,' he thought as he gave her a nod and continued toward his office. Krista was obviously onto his after-hours conduct and he knew that if her father found out, he was done. Nancy looked upset, but he didn't care. What mattered was William's opinion, and staying on good terms with his father-in-law. He only hoped that Krista hadn't already called him with her suspicions about his affair.

As he opened the door to his office, he was shocked to see William sitting in one of the chairs in front of his desk. "Good morning!" Chad managed, surprised and confused to see his boss waiting for him.

"Good morning, Chad. Running a little late today?" William asked. He was calm, but Chad could tell there was more.

Chad glanced at his watch. It was 8:45. He wasn't late. "Well, I try to get here at 9:00, so actually, that makes me early." He smiled although he was terrified. Did Kris call him today? Did he know? He felt anxious and sweat began to drip from his armpits and hoped that it wouldn't soak through his suit jacket. He set his briefcase next to his desk and hoped his boss didn't see his hands shaking.

"I'm kidding, Chad!" William smiled, which took Chad's anxiety down a notch. "I just needed to talk to you about the Charlestown property. They're ready to wheel and deal with us, so I wanted to check in with you, make sure you were up to speed on this. This is a big sale for us, as I'm sure you know."

"Of course, it's a huge deal for the agency. I'm right on top of it!" Chad inwardly sighed in relief, and felt as though the world had just lifted up and given him a gift. As long as William wasn't here to discuss Krista, he would work as many hours as needed to make sure this deal went through.

"Fill me in on what your objectives are, where you're planning to go with this, considering their initial offer." William was all business and in the next few hours, Chad was able to prove to his boss/father-in-law that he was worth keeping on the payroll.

At the end of the two-hour meeting, William changed gears suddenly. "How're things with Kris? She seems kind of stressed out lately."

"She is stressed. There are a lot of new students, needing a lot of help, you know." Chad was vague. He didn't want to talk about his wife, not now. Not here.

"She's just very dedicated. She always has been. She sets out to make something work out and she won't stop until it does. That's my kiddo." William replied. "Has she been sleeping okay? She looked tired the last time I saw her."

Chad paused. What was he getting at anyway? Did he know about the affair? "She seems to be." He decided to keep it short and simple. "Great!" William smiled and nodded. "Good to know. She's in good hands!" He paused before grasping Chad's hand. "I'm really lucky, you know. She's my only daughter, my life. I'm glad she has a loving husband that can be there for her."

"I'm there for her, William. You know that." Chad said evenly, avoiding direct eye contact. His guilt was setting in.

"Yes, that's what you've told me many times, Chad." William replied, walking out of the office. "Take care of my daughter, Chad. She's all I have," William said before he walked out the door. Chad gulped and straightened his tie. "You've got it, sir. Of course I will." Chad noticed that he stopped to talk to Nancy on his way out. 'Oh, shit! What!' Chad was becoming paranoid. What if Nancy said something? What if she said something about their affair because she was upset with him? He suddenly realized that he'd put his whole career on the line with this affair. What the hell was he thinking? He needed to do some damage control and soon.

"Is everything all right, Mr. Burton?" Nancy had left her desk and was standing a few feet behind him. Chad could feel the hairs on his neck stand up. He had to tell her it was over and that he could trust that she wouldn't talk about it. To *anyone.*

Chad turned around and smiled, "Everything's great, Nancy. I really need to get back to work. Mr. Carson wants this sale to go forward soon. I'm going to need you to contact the housing inspectors and attorneys in regards to the Charlestown property." His tone was kind, yet all business. He needed to let her down easy and he'd need to come up with a plan to cut ties for good.

Nancy was clearly upset by his cold and stoic attitude, but knew better than to ask questions during business hours. "Of course, Mr. Burton, I'll work on those contacts right away." She held his gaze for a moment. Chad smiled and turned his attention to the documents on his desk. Nancy walked away without another word, and Chad breathed a sigh of relief and went back to his office, more determined than ever to finish up the closing on the Charlestown house. No more distractions, he promised himself.

The phone rang, interrupting his thoughts. "Shit! Are you kidding me?" Chad said out loud. He picked up, anticipating Nancy or Krista to be on the other end. Either one was promised to bring potential drama he didn't need. "This is Chad Burton," he answered, trying to sound as cheerful as he could.

"Hello, Mr. Burton, I was hoping you could help me. I've heard a lot of great things about you and I'm trying to sell my property on Block Island." The woman on the phone had a wispy, southern quality to her voice.

"Well, I hope I can be of help. Why don't I have you schedule an appointment with my assistant, so that we can discuss the details?

Chad's tone changed immediately. He was all business and more than interested. Homes on Block Island were usually worth millions.

"Actually, I was hoping that you could meet me out here, at the house. I think the house speaks for itself." The woman seemed eager to sell. Chad never went on a house tour without a meeting to discuss price, any problems with the property, and invoices on any renovations done to the property.

Chad began, "Ma'am, our standard practice is to have an initial appointment at our offices to discuss the property, value, any renovations,"

"I'm sorry. I'm not used to selling property." The woman's voice broke and she sounded stressed.

Chad softened his tone. He knew this was a realtor's dream. "What's your name, ma'am?"

"My name is Caroline. Caroline Ahearn. I'm sorry for my presumption that you would come to meet with me at the home. I'm not really good at this sort of thing." Caroline apologized again.

Chad was intrigued by the name. Ahearn, where had he heard that name before? Ahearn? Suddenly, it came it him. He'd read about Stanley Ahearn. He was a well known director, winner of many awards, and bought a home on Block Island a few years ago. Shit! This must be his wife?

"It's nice to talk with you, Mrs. Ahearn. I'd be happy to come out and meet with you. What is a good time for you?" Chad knew it was worth bending the rules this time. After all, it wasn't every day he was on the phone with the wife of a well-known director. Chad wondered why Stanley himself wasn't calling to get his home on the market.

"Are you free tomorrow? I've got some time around 1:00." Caroline sounded relieved. Chad looked through his schedule for tomorrow. The schedule was completely booked, but he knew he could move his afternoon appointments around for the following day. After all, it wasn't everyday that he was asked to help sell a famous director's home on Block Island! William was going to be ecstatic!

"1:00 it is, Mrs. Ahearn. I'll catch the 11:30 ferry." Chad said, trying to keep his voice professional. Silently, he wanted to scream 'Yes!' This was an amazing opportunity!

"Thank you so much, Mr. Burton. I appreciate it." Caroline's southern accent was much more pronounced this time. Chad began to wonder if her husband had any idea that she was trying to sell this property. She gave him the address and her phone number before hanging up.

Chad sat in his chair for a moment, trying to take it all in. He was going to be Stanley Ahearn's realtor! "Hell, yeah!" He yelled out loud. Nancy heard him and came running in. "Mr. Burton, is everything okay?" She opened the door to Chad jumping up and down like a kid that had just won his first baseball game.

"Nancy! Yes! Everything is okay! In fact, it's great!" Chad smiled. Then he realized he needed to call William. "I need to call Mr. Carson, Nancy. I'll talk to you later, okay?"

Nancy nodded. She looked confused as she walked back to her desk. She'd started getting the message from Chad about their fling. She smiled to herself, knowing that she had ammunition if it was needed and continued on with her paperwork.

Krista

She walked in the front door, and took a deep breath. They hadn't talked about the drama last night and she was still wondering where she stood. She'd caught him on the phone, and had a suspicion that he was cheating on her. Considering that, should she even bother to tell Chad about the photo album that she'd found in her desk? Would he still think she was crazy? She'd put it in her purse. She just needed the right moment to bring it up. As she came into the kitchen, she was greeted with the familiar smells of a rich tomato sauce. Chad was at the stove and turned to her. He was smiling and wearing her pink apron. Despite her suspicions and her strange day, she couldn't help but smile. Her anger toward him disappeared for the moment.

"What's going on here, Chef Emeril?" She said jokingly.

"Hey, honey! Thought I'd cook for you for a change! We need to celebrate!" Chad smiled as he tossed the cooked pasta into the marinara sauce that he'd bought at the store. "Now, I know I took some shortcuts, but I did add some of my own flavors!" He laughed at the dubious look on her face as she glanced at the skillet of sauce and pasta.

Krista smiled. "So what *are* those flavors?" She was giving him a hard time, but he knew she was kidding.

"I added white wine, garlic and oregano. So now it's homemade!" Chad laughed. "I had a little help from Emeril, I must confess. He provided the sauce and I brought the love." He grabbed her and gave her a huge bear hug. "Oh, Kris! This is a great day! I can't wait to tell you about it!" Krista felt excited for him, despite the confusing find in her file cabinet and mysterious phone call the night before.

"Great! I could use some good news right about now." Krista returned his hug and gave him a quick kiss. Chad shook his head. "I need to finish dinner and set the table, so go relax in the living room."

"Are you sure you don't want any help?" Krista pointed to the sputtering pot of pasta and sauce on the stove. "Oh, shit! Guess I should turn that down! "Now, you can go relax, Kris. I promise I won't burn the house down!" He gave her a kiss, a glass of red wine, and a light shove toward the living room. "I'll be done in a few minutes."

"Okay, okay!" Krista threw up her hands. "I'm gonna trust you on this one!" She winked and retreated to the living room and turned on the TV. She couldn't concentrate as she flipped through the channels, and finally settling on a cooking reality show that looked as mindless as she felt. The photo album and Chad's phone call kept running through her head. 'It looks familiar, but I didn't put it there. Who was Chad talking to? 'I've told you not to call me at night'. Who had he been talking to last night? "Dinner is ready!" Chad announced. He hadn't lost steam from his initial excitement since she walked though the door. Krista was intrigued. She walked into the dining room to a table complete with place settings and lit candles. "I'm impressed!" She was being honest. Chad had some cooking skills, but had never made her a dinner like this before. A serving bowl of angel hair pasta and red sauce was in the center, along with a salad of spinach and grape tomatoes with parmesan. Chad grinned. "I'd hoped you would be! Now, if you will do me the honor." He pulled out the chair for her.

"It looks great. Thank you." Krista was still trying to understand the meaning behind this sudden attention to detail. She had a feeling it had to do with his cryptic conversation she'd overheard last night but she wasn't going to bring it up just now. 'Let him spoil me and he can sweat it out.' She decided not to bring it up, at least not right away.

"So I guess you're wondering what all this is about? What are we celebrating?" Chad was bursting at the seams. She hadn't seen him like this, well, since they first started dating.

"Chad. Please, have out with it already! You're about to combust!" Krista teased him.

"Well, today I got a phone call, totally out of the blue! I can't even believe it myself!" Chad was giddy. "It was......you'll never believe this.....Stanley Ahearn's wife!" He watched for her reaction, expecting as much excitement as he had felt.

"Stanley Ahearn? I'm sorry, honey, that name isn't familiar to me." Krista said gently. The way Chad was acting, it was like the President of the United States had called. Chad's face fell. "From the way you said his name, he must be someone important!" She said brightly. Chad's face lit up again.

"Krista! Are you serious? He's only one of the biggest directors in Hollywood! I can't believe you didn't recognize the name!" Chad's tone was almost chastising.

"Sorry, not familiar with the Hollywood scene. You're the one that watches 'E' every night!" Krista said, suddenly feeling as though she was ignorant for not knowing. "So what's the news?" She changed back to the subject at hand.

"Stanley Ahern's wife, Caroline, called. She wants to sell their home on Block Island! What a great opportunity! The house has to be worth millions!" Chad was almost jumping out of his chair. Krista could almost see the actual dollar signs above his head as he spoke.

"That's great!" Krista replied. Money wasn't overly important to her. But then again, she'd never lacked for anything growing up. She understood her husband's need to be financially stable.

"Honey, do you know what this means if I sell this property? We're well on our way to being able to do whatever we want. You won't have to work. We'll be able to finally take vacations more often. Maybe we could start planning to start a family, especially if you don't have to work." Chad's eyes were lit up by that possibility. Krista could tell he was imagining a yacht, a huge mansion, a vacation home in Italy; the list went on. She was also realistic.

"Chad, it sounds like a great opportunity. But you need to keep things in perspective, okay?" Krista served herself some pasta and took a bite. "This is amazing!" The pasta was slightly over-cooked, but she wanted to change the subject.

Chad was quiet for a moment. He dove into his pasta dinner, but clearly couldn't wait to talk more about this new business venture. After a few bites, he put down his fork and continued. "Kris, aren't you happy, excited? I mean, this could be huge for us! This would be good advertising for your dad's business!"

"It's great, honey! Really! I'm excited for you. I just have a lot on my mind. I had something else strange happen today." Krista could tell that Chad was bummed that she wasn't more excited about the potential sale of the Block Island mansion.

Chad sighed. "Okay, Kris. What is it?" He sounded annoyed with her and he tried unsuccessfully not to roll his eyes. "I reached into one of my desk drawers and found this," Krista pulled out the photo album, and pushed it across the table. Chad was quiet for a moment, as he looked and then pushed it back to her. "Ok. So it's a picture of a woman and some kids somewhere near the ocean. What about it?" Chad didn't understand why his wife was so upset with this.

"Why was it in MY desk? Who are these people and why did I just suddenly find this in my desk?" Krista knew her voice was getting louder, but she was so frustrated that he didn't understand why she was upset. She'd worked at the school for close to 5 years. This wasn't there yesterday; she was sure of it.

Chad groaned. "Kris, is this going to be an all night conversation? It's a picture! Someone probably left it, and then it was in the back of your drawer all this time!" He was trying not to sound as irritated as he felt.

Krista knew that he wasn't going to understand, so she decided it was better to drop the subject. "Ok. I just wanted to let you know what was going on. We can talk about it later." Her face fell and she took another bite of pasta. Her voice was as calm as she could manage and he looked surprised.

"You okay, Kris?"

"Yes, I'm fine. This obviously isn't the time to talk about this. I'll figure it out."

Krista couldn't help with the last dig. It ticked her off that he wouldn't even take the time to talk about the photo. Actually, it wasn't just the picture, it was last night's mystery phone call that was bugging her too but she knew this wasn't the time to bring that up.

"Let me clean up here. Thank you for cooking! It was really nice of you." She gave him a kiss and brought the plates to the sink to clean up. She busied herself with the process but her thoughts wandered to the picture. Someone had to have put it there!

Afterwards, she tried to get interested in some reality show that Chad was watching, but couldn't. "I'm going to bed."

"It's only 9:00, Kris! I was hoping we could ...you know..." He winked playfully. Krista couldn't be less in the mood, but instead of telling her husband what she really thought, she gave him a kiss.

"Sorry. I'm really tired and I've been late for work a few times this week. Crazy Jane will report me if I show up late again, I just know it." Krista wasn't lying. The bitch probably would. Besides, she needed to relax and try not to think about today.

Chad looked disappointed that his plan of a romantic evening was a fail, but quickly recovered when his football game began. "G'night, honey," he called up the stairs. Krista got into their king sized bed and pulled the covers up. 'Thank god for sleep. I really need this day to be over.' Krista thought as she drifted off.

Krista was standing at the edge of the familiar cliff, where the waves of the ocean were churning. She felt as though someone was watching her, but turned around to find no one. She backed up and made her way through the trees. As the woods cleared, a huge house was in clear view. She continued walking toward the house when she heard a child-like voice. "It's okay. I won't let anyone hurt you. Keep going." She looked around but again she couldn't see anybody there. The voice seemed to be coming from all around her. "Keep going. Go in the house. You need to go in." She was scared, but she felt compelled to continue to the huge front doors with old fashioned door- knockers.

The doors opened by themselves as she approached, and Krista backed away in fear. "I'm scared. I don't want to go in." She said out loud.

"No one can hurt you right now. You're safe. I'm here with you." The surrounding voice assured her.

Krista looked wildly around. "Where are you? Who are you? Why am I here?"

"I'm here with you. I'm Karen. I'm here to help you. Help you find out the truth." Krista could tell it was a little girl. "Karen? Who are you Karen? Why am I here? "

There was a childish giggle. "I'm here to show you who I am. I'm here to help you. Go ahead." Krista cautiously walked through the open doors. The elaborate vestibule showcased a winding staircase that seemed to stretch for miles upwards. She didn't feel fear as she walked up the stairs covered with a regal red carpet. At the top of the stairs, she felt compelled to go to the right and continued down the hall. Old gas lamps flickered, dimly lighting the way. She came to the second room on the right and felt herself being drawn to go in. She turned the knob and was about to open the door when she felt someone shaking her shoulder, "Kris? Kris! Wake up!"

Krista opened her eyes to Chad staring at her. "Honey, are you okay? You were walking around the room, mumbling. When I asked you what you were saying, you just stared at me!"

"I guess I was dreaming again. I was in this old mansion, and some little girl was talking to me." Krista felt disoriented, and rubbed her eyes. It was all still so real. Chad was right. She had been up walking around. She was in fact in front of their bedroom closet. "What am I doing here?" She suddenly shivered, scared. Despite the nightmares, she'd never gotten up and walked in her sleep. Chad embraced her. "Honey, you've been stressed at work, no wonder you keep having bad dreams. I'm sorry that I've been working late. I'll try to be here more often." Chad kissed the top of her head. "I love you, you know that, right?"

"Yes I know. Did you find me here?" Krista was groggy, still getting her bearings. The experience made her feel out of control, and more anxious than ever. Chad held her in a hug.

"It's okay, Kris. Maybe it's time to see someone about these dreams. I know we've talked about this before, but I really mean it. You really need to see someone. Promise? Please spend the time to find someone tomorrow and schedule an appointment."

"Fine. I'll see someone. But if I don't feel comfortable, I won't continue with them okay?" Krista was tired, willing to agree to anything just to go back to sleep.

"Agreed. Please call and find someone tomorrow." Chad breathed a sigh of relief. His mind was trying to focus on the Block Island property. "Get back in bed, babe." Krista slid back into bed for the night, rustling around with the sheets and pillows to get comfortable.

"Babe, can you please turn on the TV? I need some background noise." Krista knew her husband hated having the TV on when he was going to bed, but at this point, she knew she needed the distraction to actually get back to sleep after the nightmare.

Chad sighed, but relented. "I'll put on Threes Company just for you." He turned on the sleep timer on the TV, knowing she'd be asleep in minutes. He just hoped she wouldn't sleepwalk again. He was stressed enough about tomorrow.

Chad

Chad wasn't a morning person by any stretch, but when the alarm went off at 5:30, he was up and getting ready to go. He had an appointment at 8:30 with another important client. He needed to have enough time to drive down to Point Judith to catch the 11 o'clock ferry to Block Island. As he put on his usual suit and tie, he glanced down at Krista, still sound asleep. He felt a wave of guilt about his attitude toward her dreams, and his affair with Nancy. He was lucky to have Krista in his life. From now on, he was going to start listening to her. He screwed up with this affair with Nancy. Although Krista hadn't said anything, she was suspicious, he could tell. He wasn't sure what to make of the sleep-walking episode last night, but it scared him. He hoped that Kris would follow through and seek help. He made mental note to look up some counselors later as he gave her a light kiss on her cheek. He whispered, "See you later, babe." Chad headed out for what he hoped would be the start to the bigger and better things to come.

His 8:30 appointment was late and Chad was pacing his office when William came in. "What's going on here, Chad? You okay?" William could see that he was on edge.

"I'm fine, just that my 8:30 client is running a little late, that's all." Chad tried to sit down, but then got back up after a few seconds and continued to walk back and forth.

"It seems like you're worked up about that Block Island account this afternoon." William could see that his son-in-law had his eyes on that prize, and it was almost too good to be true.

Chad sighed and nodded. "I guess so. I just want it to go well. I'm kind of nervous to be honest." He hated to admit it, but amidst the excitement he was questioning his own abilities to get the job done right.

"Yes, I know. It's written all over your face, Chad. I'm so glad you got this opportunity, but let me warn you. Stanley Ahearn owns this property, not his wife. Be careful. Don't go into detail. You don't want Ahearn coming back with his high-paid attorneys saying that he wasn't aware that his wife was trying to sell, got it? That kind of publicity could hurt the agency." William had been skeptical about the phone call from Ahearn's wife ever since Chad called with the news. He knew Stanley. Something didn't sit right with him. It was too easy. But then again, Stanley Ahearn was also known to be eccentric and unconventional. He was unpredictable.

Chad nodded. "I got this. No details, just conversation. I'll take a look around the property. Maybe get an idea of a price range?" He was starting to question himself again.

"Let her lead on what the property is worth. Don't suggest, just follow. Take notes, and make sure that you pay attention to what's positive about the property. "William advised. He was almost as on edge as Chad, but he remained outwardly calm. This was potentially a huge account and it could make them millions. On the other hand, if there was a deal and it went wrong, it could cost them their reputation.

The phone rang. "Mr. Burton, your 8:30 is here." Nancy said. It was now 8:47. "I got this. Trust me." Chad said. He was up and running with his late appointment, determined to succeed. William watched and shook his head. He only hoped that he'd be able to make the 11:00 ferry to Block Island. It would be a close call.

As it turned out, the first appointment was a wash. The couple didn't like the first property right away, and there wasn't time to show them another, so Chad had to reschedule. He had an hour to get to Point Judith and catch the Block Island ferry for his 1:00 with the Ahearn property.

It was a good day to be on the ferry. It wasn't too windy and it was sunny and warm for September. The water wasn't too choppy and it was after Labor Day, so there were fewer tourists on board. They docked and Chad was pulling off in his car at 12:30, earlier than expected. He turned on his GPS to get to the house on Mohegan Bluffs, and was surprised to find a signal. Not that he really needed directions; the mansion could be seen from a mile away.

Overlooking the ocean and only a few hundred feet from the bluffs, the property was an impressive sight to see. The initial specs he'd received boasted 6,500 square feet, 6 bedrooms, 4 bathrooms, a gym and a pool besides the 5 acres of land. It definitely wasn't your average home found on the mainland, especially with the location. As Chad pulled up the circular driveway, he was amazed by the landscaping. Perfectly trimmed hedges surrounded the entrance. Colorful waves of Rosa Rugosa roses lined the stone-crusted path to the stairs leading to the wrap-around porch. "Wow!" He said the word out loud as he walked up the stairs and rang the doorbell. "Guess I should've been a Hollywood director!"

The door opened and a lovely blonde woman with bright blue eyes and a small petite figure greeted him. "You must be Mr. Burton." She had a quiet, calming effect on him as she reached out to shake his hand. Chad returned her handshake, surprised at how young she looked. He was expecting a much older-looking woman. Someone who was bordering on elderly, with graying hair, an outfit straight out of the Golden Girls and a strict attitude. But Caroline Ahearn was the complete opposite. She was dressed in white cropped pants with a blue blouse that matched her eyes. She looked as though she were headed out for a casual lunch with friends.

"Chad Burton. Mrs. Ahearn, it's a pleasure to meet you." He shook her slender hand, once he'd gotten over his initial shock at how wrong he was about this woman.

"You seem surprised, Mr. Burton. Did you think I was an old lady?" Caroline laughed good-naturedly. "I'd like to think that being almost 49 years old isn't really old. I'm just getting better with age."

"Not at all, Mrs. Ahearn. I'm very impressed with your home."

"Please, call me Caroline. Mrs. Ahearn is way too formal." She insisted. "Should we start with the tour?" She turned and Chad followed her down the hall. He was mesmerized by the sparkling crystals hanging from the chandelier.

"Absolutely! Mrs—I mean, Caroline, your house is a dream. I see many buyers looking at this property!" Chad was impressed with both the property *and* Caroline. This woman was classy, put-together and very attractive. No wonder a man with Stanley's status and notoriety had married her.

Caroline laughed. "Thank you, Mr. Burton. I'd like to think that I've made this house what it is today. I do love this house." She added.

"Please call me Chad." He was not accustomed to being on a first name basis, but if she was insistent, then he was all for informality.

"Okay, Chad." Caroline's smile and cerulean blue eyes were similar to Krista's; the kind of eyes that were noticed from across a room and stood out. She continued through the foyer to the living room. Chad was almost speechless. The décor was impressive. The eighteenth century furnishings were updated with sheer pale pink drapes and brightened by egg-shell colored walls. It made the room seem comfortable in contrast with the antique furnishings. There was a massive stone fireplace with a gold-framed portrait of a solemn-faced man dressed in 15th century attire. "That's an original painting of Giovanni da Verranzzano." Caroline told Chad as he admired the portrait. "Verranzzano was the first to discover Block Island back in

1524. Stanley *had* to have it. He claims that his love for it was for historical reasons. Personally, I believe he wanted it because it's rare and expensive." She laughed softly. They continued through the sunlit kitchen with a Viking stove and double ovens, a 16-foot black marble island and a quaint breakfast nook off in the corner. The ceiling to floor windows had a sliding glass door that led to the porch. "I love being here in the morning. The light helps me wake up!" Caroline joked. "I swear I need sunscreen in here!"

Chad nodded in agreement. "I can see why! But it's amazing! Just what you need to start your day!"

They started up the grand staircase straight out of The Sound of Music and into the first bedroom. The room was decked out in pink including the drapes, the quilts on the double beds, the decorative pillows, the desk with an 18th century chair and the contrast of a large TV in the middle of the room. "What a nice room, I'm sure your children love it!" He commented.

Caroline hesitated for a moment, but continued walking toward the next room. "Yes." She said simply. Chad could sense something was wrong but said nothing. 'Maybe she doesn't like talking about her family because of Stanley's status,' he thought. He followed her through the next several bedrooms, all of which were beautifully decorated.

The master bedroom was the last room and Chad was almost thankful. Caroline continued her silence and, it was becoming awkward. He admired the cherry-wood king bed and accessories and continued through to the attached bathroom. He was in the midst of examining the glass encased shower big enough for ten people when he heard a sound. He came back out and saw Caroline turning over a picture on the bedside table and walking out of the room. He couldn't help but wonder about the picture and out of curiosity, he picked it up. It was a picture of a young woman wearing sunglasses with two little blonde girls that appeared to be twins. Suddenly, he felt like he couldn't breathe. He'd seen this picture before, but couldn't remember where. "Chad, are you coming?" Caroline called out to him and he put it back down, chalking it up to déjà vu. "I'm right behind you."

Chad knew he needed to get his act together. She wasn't just some ditz with a director husband and a credit card with no limit. Caroline Ahearn was sharp. He caught up to her by the staircase and followed her outside to the pool area. "Now this is one of my favorite places," Caroline smiled. A real smile this time. Chad could understand why she loved it. The large kidney- shaped pool with enough lounge chairs for a party and the landscaping of wild pink roses, and both blue and purple hydrangea bushes. There was a large hot tub area off the pool and a curtained cabana completed the perfect setting. "I can understand why it's your favorite place. It's absolutely stunning, Caroline." Chad answered. The fragrance from the flowers blowing in from the ocean breeze was pleasant, and the view of the cliffs was a photographer's dream. It was postcard perfect.

Caroline walked over toward the tree line outside the pool area. "This is actually my favorite place." Chad followed her and suddenly he was looking at the ocean over the cliffs. He peered over the side of the cliff, with nothing between him and a 200 foot drop to the Atlantic Ocean. "Wow! That is amazing! What a view!" He pulled back, feeling uncomfortable being that close without a barrier preventing him from going over.

It was as if Caroline could read his mind. "Yes, it's a bit of a drop there. I've been meaning to get some kind of a barrier or fence, but I was too focused on the interior and unfortunately, this area was neglected in the process." Caroline shrugged. "If a family with young children decides to buy, they would need to put up a fence, that's for sure!"

Chad nodded, "I agree, but it's still a spectacular view and has great selling points." Caroline smiled, "Thank you. I do love this house. It's just become too much for me. Stanley is gone much of the time and I have all this room." She spread her arms out, and looked wistful. "I have all this room and no one but myself and the housekeeper living here. It's a waste of space for me, I think. Stanley is in agreement. He knows that I'm meeting with you and gave me his price."

Chad was thankful that she'd mentioned Stanley was in agreement about selling. That was something William had been worried about. He nodded. "Let's go back to the house and we'll discuss it over some cappuccinos." Caroline suggested as they made their way back to the house.

"Sounds great." Chad agreed. He contemplated bringing up that little-girl designed bedroom, but knew it wasn't his place. But that picture? He must have been mistaken. Krista's paranoid behaviors must be getting to him. Back in the kitchen area, Caroline served up cappuccinos as they discussed the asking price. When Caroline told him the initial asking price, Chad was shocked. The price for a mansion on Block Island was so low, he couldn't believe it at first. Only a little over a million for this entire estate. $1,200,000 to be exact. Unreal.

"Are you sure about this number, Caroline? Stanley is in agreement?" Chad asked. He wasn't accustomed to advising clients about raising the price of their home. In fact, it had never happened before. Usually, his clients were asking a hell of a lot more than anyone would ever dream of paying. But in this case, the price was low. Questionably low. He knew that would be what potential buyers would be asking.

"Yes. He is. In fact, he's the one that set the price. I'm not involved with the business side of this. I just take care of the house, decorate it, live in it, but I don't get to set the price." Caroline said sharply, losing her soft demeanor for a moment.

Chad cleared his throat. "Caroline, I don't mean any disrespect toward you, the house, or the price for that matter. It's a matter of answering questions for clients that might have questions. That's all."

Caroline's expression softened. "I'm sorry. I understand that's part of your job. It's just been....well, difficult."

"Difficult? Are you referring to anything structural, or problems with the house itself?" Chad was confused.

"No. Not problems with the house in terms of structure, repair, nothing like that." Caroline looked out the window toward the view of the bluffs and ocean. She had a troubled look on her face that Chad found vaguely familiar, even though he'd never met her before. That picture in the master bedroom was still on his mind as well. "What has been difficult?" Chad blurted out then realized he was prying. "I'm sorry, Caroline. I didn't mean to put you on the spot."

"Mr. Burton,...Chad. It's difficult because it's so hard to explain to anyone. Stanley and I have owned this house many years. Fifteen years, in fact. I love this house, more than any that my husband owns. I love it here. The summers are beautiful. We tend to go south to our home in the Caribbean or Florida for the winter. It's just too cold here, you know?" Caroline paused and Chad nodded, knowing full well what New England winters were like, especially on Block Island. Block Island winters didn't get the amount of snow as on the mainland, but between the chilly temperatures and the wind, it was brutal at times.

"It's peaceful. No one bothers us, because the tourists aren't allowed on our property. Stanley isn't here much of the time, you know. Most of his time is in LA, doing what he loves." She laughed then. "He does his job so well that he needs to be there most of the time. I don't like Hollywood very much. Too busy, too many people. I love it here." She repeated.

"Why is it so difficult to explain, Caroline?" Chad didn't expect this novel length answer, although intriguing to find out about their life.

Caroline slowly moved her eyes to him from the window. "Strange things have been happening in this house over the past year. There really isn't any explanation. In fact, Stanley probably thinks I'm crazy, so I stopped telling him after the first few times because he laughed. I hear a voice sometimes and there's no one there. Clocks change time without anyone changing them. I've been seeing a young girl at night walking around the grounds; she stands at the cliffs. When I go outside, no one is there. I know this sounds crazy, but I can't take the stress anymore, so I insisted that Stanley sell this house. So the long answer to your question is that we want to sell immediately. That's the reason for selling at a low price."

Chad took in what she had to say. A few weeks ago, he'd think she was crazy, but given Krista's latest experiences and strange dreams "I can understand how stressful that must be for you, Caroline." He nodded.

"Really? How so?" Caroline took his response as literal, which took him by surprise. He didn't want to get into a discussion about Krista and her random strange "events".

"Oh, just some strange things have been happening with my wife lately. I think she's just stressed about work. She's having some strange dreams, but nothing like you're describing." Chad tried to sound casual, even though their lives seemed to be unraveling because of how Krista was reacting.

"Sometimes dreams can seem very real." Caroline was serious as she spoke. "I believe that dreams are trying to tell us something, giving us a message sometimes."

Chad cleared his throat, feeling suddenly at a loss for words. He would have loved to spend the rest of the day talking to her but didn't want to disclose more about his own troubles, however tempting. "Well, Caroline, I think that it's a more than fair price and I'm sure I can have some potential buyers soon enough." He knew she wanted more detail about Krista's dreams, but this was business and definitely no time to discuss his wife's recent night terrors.

"Oh of course! I'm sorry I've been carrying on with my own worries." Caroline said. The conversation turned to moving forward with selling the property; coming back to take pictures, followed by a listing and holding an open house. Chad looked at his watch. It was almost 3:00!

"Caroline, I need to get going if I'm going to catch the 3:30 ferry back! I'm going to talk to the CEO about the property and call you within a few days about a date and time to take some pictures and get it listed." Chad wished he could just set up a time, but he wanted advisement from William on this property. He wasn't accustomed to taking on this type of property sale without his involvement.

"It was a pleasure to meet you, Chad. I look forward to hearing from you soon. It is a beautiful home. I'll miss it." Caroline smiled, but she seemed wistful and almost sad.

"It is an amazing home, Caroline. We'll find someone who'll take good care of it." Chad shook her hand and headed to his car, hoping he wasn't too late for the ferry. He heaved a sigh of relief as he just made the ferry. He couldn't shake an uneasy feeling that he'd gotten from that house, and Caroline. She was comforting, and kind, yet there was an underlying sense of melancholy. That picture in the bedroom was still bothering him; he knew he'd seen it before, but where?

Suddenly, he remembered where. It was identical to the picture Krista found in her desk.

Krista

After an intense day of constant crisis at school, Krista headed home. Her head ached from being tired. Apparently sleepwalking was in fact not really sleeping. Chad's car was in the driveway and she breathed a sigh of relief, although she wasn't sure if she was glad to see him, or just to have someone home in order to feel safe. Their relationship had been so up and down these days. The one thing she was curious about was his meeting at the Ahearn property. She knew how much this meant to him and to her father. She couldn't help but wonder about that house. As she opened the door she was greeted with a huge hug from her husband. Surprised, she returned his hug.

"What's this all about? I'm assuming things went okay today!" She laughed after Chad let her go. The intimacy and closeness was something she'd missed.

"It was better than just okay! They're selling for way below the value and the house is amazing! You'd have to see it to believe it!" Chad was ecstatic. "Kris, you should see this place! It's so beautiful! I'd love to live there myself! The house, the views, the landscape! Just unbelievable!" Chad went on about the house for another few minutes.

"Good! I'm glad it was worth the trip." Krista tried to be enthusiastic for her husband, but she was tired and her head was throbbing as a result. She was not one that did well on very little sleep.

"Kris, if I can sell this place, the commission will be huge!" Chad embraced her again and could see that she was holding back. Something was wrong. Inwardly, he groaned. She was still upset about the picture she'd found.

"Kris, what's wrong? Aren't you happy? You do realize that if I sell this house, we're going to be doing well!" He was hoping that this new opportunity would help her get out of the funk she was in lately.

"I'm fine. Really!" Krista insisted. Chad remembered the photo he'd seen on the Ahearn's nightstand identical to the one Kris had shown him. He was unsure if he should share this with his wife, especially when she was so emotionally distraught already.

"Kris, it was probably just there from the last person that had your desk long before you. You're overthinking this." Chad decided to go with his first reaction and not tell her. She was already anxious and between the sleepwalking episode, and nightmares, he wasn't sure how she'd react. He didn't want to find out tonight.

Krista knew better than to rain on Chad's parade today. After all, he stood to make a substantial commission off the Block Island house "I'm sure you're right. I'm just stressed." She relented, but her mind wouldn't let it go. After the dishes were done and the kitchen was cleaned up, she announced that she was going upstairs. Chad was busy

86

watching football. "Okay, babe, I'll see you when I come to bed." He replied over his shoulder as she headed upstairs with the photo she'd found in hand.

As she looked closer at the picture, she noticed that the two little girls were almost identical; in fact, they looked like twins. Their smiling faces, curly blonde hair and blue eyes were the same. The only difference was what they were wearing. She couldn't help wondering who these children were, how old they were now or where their mother was. The picture of the woman wasn't as clear. She was wearing sunglasses and the camera had caught her moving to the side, but she could see blonde curls that were the same as the little girls. She sighed as she put the photo down, feeling envious of the two unknown little girls who had a mother. She'd always wished for hers to come back.

She fell asleep almost immediately and found herself inside a mansion with a winding staircase. The only light came from an old-fashioned gaslight at the top of the stairs. She felt frightened. She wanted to go back, but the girl from her previous dreams was at the top of the stairs, encouraging her. "It's okay, Krista. I'm here. I can help you."

"What do you want? Why am I here?" She asked. "Who are you?"

"I'm here. Come up the stairs." The voice commanded. Krista slowly moved up the staircase toward the girl, but she could no longer see her. "I'm here, now where are you?" Krista said, starting to panic. No answer.

"Where are you?" Krista yelled. Suddenly, the lights came on in a room down the hall and she walked toward it, nervous about what she would find. As she entered the room, she saw nothing but a child's music box on the floor in an otherwise empty room. "Open it." The voice commanded.

Krista took a deep breath and began opening the box. As the lid opened, there was a flash of lightening and she backed away, screaming. Arms were holding her, but she tried to get away. "No, No!"

"Kris! It's me! You're dreaming. Wake up." She recognized Chad's voice and realized that she'd had another nightmare.

"Chad? Am I still dreaming?" She wasn't sure what was real anymore.

"No, you're not. I'm here, holding you. Let's go back upstairs, okay?" Chad's voice wavered.

"I thought I was upstairs. Didn't I just go upstairs?"

"Honey, you came downstairs. You were sleepwalking again. You were talking to someone. You were looking through the DVD cabinet, like you were looking for something. Let me bring you back up to bed." Chad was really concerned.

"I did? I'm sorry. I don't remember what I was looking for." Krista managed. She was so tired, and still half asleep. She only wanted to get back to that house and find out what was in that box. She allowed Chad to assist her back to bed. "Honey?"

Chad pulled the covers over her as Krista curled up in bed. "What, Kris?"

"I'm afraid. What if I sleepwalk again? What if you're asleep and don't find me? What if I walk out of the house?" Krista began to cry as she realized that she was truly at the mercy of these nightmares and what she was doing while she was sleeping.

Chad gave his wife a big hug. "Sweetheart, we're going to figure this out, I promise. I won't let anything happen to you. Tomorrow, we'll find someone for you to talk to and find a solution, okay?" He didn't want to admit it, but her sleepwalking and nightmares were scary to him too. "Maybe you should stay home tomorrow. You can get some rest and we'll find someone that you can talk to." He suggested. He wasn't sure she was capable of going to work tomorrow. Besides, the night wasn't over and he was concerned that she might very well sleepwalk again.

Krista groaned. "I wish I could call out, but I've got back to back appointments tomorrow. Besides, I've been late so many times in the past week. Crazy Jane is going to get me in trouble with the principal." She tried to joke, but it was true. She had been late many times, and although Jane was only a receptionist, she wouldn't hesitate to bring it to Principal Martin's attention. She'd had it out for Krista since her first day.

"Well, get some sleep. I'll be up for awhile. Don't worry, honey. I'll be watching out for you tonight." Chad gave her a kiss and turned off the light. He couldn't get his mind off that picture that was face down that he'd seen on the Ahearn nightstand and he was certain that it was the same picture Krista had found in her desk. This couldn't be a coincidence. He decided to do his own detective work and headed to the internet.

Chad

As he sat at his computer, Chad realized he had no idea what exactly he expected to find about a random picture that had somehow made its way into his wife's desk at work and at a client's home on Block Island? He decided to do a search on 'Caroline Ahearn' and go from there. What came up was very limited. Apparently, Caroline really did prefer privacy. She was very much out of the limelight of her husband's career and out of public view. The only hits he got was a "LinkedIn" and a Facebook page, that brought up at least ten 'Caroline Ahearns' none of which belonged to the Caroline Ahearn for which he wanted. Even searching on Wikipedia under Stanley's name didn't give any indication of Caroline, including their marriage. He found this strange but chalked it up to Stanley being a very private person (so he'd heard).

He glanced over at the clock near the computer and realized it was almost 2:00am. 'Need to get some sleep,' he thought, and then realized that he hadn't called William since seeing the Ahearn property. He groaned and shut the computer down, forcing himself to climb into bed. His mind was still racing. Between the house, the quirky coincidence of the picture and Krista's sleepwalking, he couldn't shut it down. He lay in bed for what seemed hours before he drifted off.

He awoke to Krista's voice urging him to wake up. "Honey, it's almost 7:30! Shouldn't you be getting up?"

Disoriented, he sat up in bed. "What? I thought the alarm was set for 6:30! I wanted to get an early start today." Grumbling, he got out of bed and headed for the shower. Krista was already dressed and ready to head out to work. Finally realizing that she'd been up for at least an hour, he was upset that she didn't wake him up.

"Seriously Kris? Is there a reason you didn't wake me up before 7:30?!" Chad said loudly as he turned off the shower. No answer. "Kris!" He tried again.

"What? I'm right here." Krista was coming up the stairs and stood outside the bathroom. She knew he was probably mad at her for not waking him, but was well aware of what time he'd finally come to bed. She figured he needed to sleep.

"Never mind. Just make sure there's a travel mug of coffee to go. I'm running late." Chad decided against chastising his wife. He knew she meant well allowing him to sleep longer. But he also knew that he needed to get to the office and talk to William as soon as possible.

"Okay. I'm sorry I let you sleep. You just seemed so tired." Krista's voice became faint as she went back downstairs.

"I am tired." Chad whispered. But there was no time to be tired now. He got himself ready and within 15 minutes was headed out to the office with the travel mug of coffee he'd requested. His energy was renewed as he neared the office, excited to share the news about the Ahearn property with his boss.

William

William had been at his desk since 7:00am. It was his usual routine, and today he was particularly anxious since he hadn't heard from Chad about the Block Island property. He spun his chair around to face the window. He was 10 floors up, and he crept up to the edge of the ceiling to floor window, and took a step back. He'd always been scared of heights, no matter what the situation. It made him think of Maria and her fearlessness of heights. She'd always been the one to encourage him to get on a plane, go to the top of Empire State Building, go up in the St. Louis arch. It made him miss her all over again, even more so than he already did everyday. Tears rolled down his face and he wiped them away. He knew that he needed to get it together as he glanced at his watch. Chad should be walking in soon and he was looking forward to hearing about the Ahearn property. The area was a gold mine in terms of realty, but he couldn't kid himself that the interest in the property was more personal than business.

At 8:30, Chad made his appearance and was immediately in his office. "Chad. You're running late today! What gives?" William was joking. His son-in-law's track record was impeccable and he knew if he was late, it was because he'd been working late the night before.

Chad grinned. He knew William was kidding, but also knew that he was anxious to hear about the Ahearn property. "Sorry. I was up late and Kris thought I needed more sleep. You know the drill." William nodded. "Yeah, I know. And she'd be right."

"The property is spectacular. No problems with needing updates, no structural issues according to Mrs. Ahearn, and the views are to die for." Chad began. He knew his description was inadequate of what he'd seen at the Ahearn property but it was a start. "And here's the thing. Stanley Ahearn wasn't there. His wife, Caroline gave me the tour, stated the price and said Stanley approved it!" When Chad told him the price, William almost fell over. The price was way below the value and he questioned it.

"They could get a lot more for that! A lot! There must be something wrong with it." William's concern echoed what Chad had thought initially.

"I thought that too. I questioned her about it, getting confirmation that Stanley approved it. She says that he did and that it needs to be sold. She seemed as though she was in a hurry. Her explanation was very strange. She said she kept seeing a young girl on the cliff near the house that bothers her and convinced Stanley to sell at this price. It's a pretty strange explanation. But then again, the people with money are usually the most eccentric, right?" Chad joked.

William was silent. His face looked sad, almost as if he were about to break down in tears. Chad was confused. "Bill? What do you think?" He'd never seen his father in law this speechless. He waved his hand in front of his face. "Bill? You okay?"

"Yes, I'm fine." William finally responded. But his demeanor was less than fine. He turned to the window.

Chad continued on, "So I was hoping we can get this listed as soon as possible. Someone is definitely going to jump on this!" His enthusiasm was palpable.

William turned back to Chad as if he'd snapped back into reality. "It's an amazing property, Chad. If this sale goes through, it'll be huge for this agency. You've done well with this. Well done!" Yet behind his eyes, Chad could sense a feeling of discontent, sadness even. Definitely not like him.

"Bill, you sure everything's okay? I mean, you don't seem like yourself today. Is there something I should know about this property?" Chad knew he might be overstepping his bounds with his father-in-law, but he also knew him well enough that his behavior was definitely out of character. This potential sale was huge for the agency, yet he was melancholy, almost nostalgic, and seemed to be forcing excitement about this sale.

William nodded, but his mind was off in other directions. Chad's statement about the woman seeing a 'young girl' near the cliffs had his attention. Who was this Caroline Ahearn anyway?

"I'm sure. Just curious about the wife that apparently is selling this house. What's her story? What's she like?" Mrs. Ahearn was clearly someone her husband trusted if she was selling at this price.

"She's....well, she's not what I expected. A nice looking lady, blonde, petite, dresses nicely. She doesn't look a day over 40, although she's got to be older. I was expecting a 70- year -old spinster," Chad admitted. "As far as her story, I tried some online research last night and didn't come up with anything about Caroline Ahearn, including that she's married to Stanley. She confirmed that Stanley has agreed to the list price so what's the problem?"

William took a deep breath. "I know she said that, but I still believe that we should talk to Stanley prior to any buyers seeing the property. I'm sure Mrs. Ahearn's name is on the mortgage, but we still should talk with him directly."

Chad squirmed. "Are you suggesting that I contact him in Los Angeles? Mrs. Ahearn told me that he's working on another film there. She's isn't sure when he'll be back."

William shook his head. "No, Chad. You did fine. I think I'll contact Mr. Ahearn myself. I really want this to go through, but I feel more comfortable talking to both parties."

Chad breathed a sigh of relief. "Thank you so much, Bill. I'm not sure I'm up to that at this point!" He definitely wasn't. He was tired and had his hands full with Kris and her sleepwalking and her dreams. He wasn't prepared to wheel and deal with a Hollywood director that was in the middle of a film in California.

After Chad had left the office, William sat back in his chair for a moment. One of the few pictures he had of Maria was still in viewing range on his bookshelf, slightly hidden by other books. After she was gone, he'd left it on his desk but as the years went by, he knew he needed to move on and that meant moving her picture. Thing is, he'd never really moved on. He'd never remarried because he'd never gotten to know anyone else. He'd moved the picture after a million comments about how he should start dating and moving on. But he never had. Now he pulled the picture from its hiding place. He saw her blonde hair flying in the wind and in the background was the bluffs from Block Island. As he wiped a tear, he dialed his secretary, Cindy. "Get me Stanley Ahearn in Hollywood."

"Mr. Carson? Do you mean Hollywood, California?" Cindy clarified, intrigued about why her employer was someone in Hollywood.

"Yes. I want you to find a number to speak to Mr. Stanley Ahearn in Hollywood, California." William insisted.

"Yes, sir. I'll find the number right away." Cindy responded quickly. William was a great boss, and he was respectful, paid her a decent salary. If he seemed off the wall at times, she was willing to go with it.

Krista

There wasn't enough coffee to get through this day. Krista groaned as she pulled into the school parking lot and dutifully made her way into the building. After last night, she hadn't been able to go back to sleep and it was wearing on her. She wasn't late, though. That was something less to think about this morning. As she walked past Jane's desk, she almost laughed as Jane looked at her, surprised that she was early.

"What a surprise! You're early today!" Jane in her usual fashion, masking a dig behind an ordinary comment.

Krista stopped. This woman had been giving her shit for the past year and she was tired. Tired of the nightmares, tired of being afraid to sleep, tired of sleepwalking, and tired of Jane. She'd tried being nice, but she'd had it.

"Yes. Thank you for pointing that out. Your announcements of everyone's arrivals aren't really part of your job description though, are they?" Krista smiled sweetly at the tweed-suited secretary, went into her office and shut the door. She felt better already. If she wanted to tell the principal about her recent tardiness, Krista no longer cared.

She took a deep breath and looked at her calendar for the day. It was booked, as she knew it would be and assured herself that today would be okay. 'No more photos showing up, no more swinging prisms, I'm fine.' Krista whispered to herself.

The day went by, student after student and before she knew it, it was 4:00. No word from Chad, which was surprising, and also worried her. She picked up the phone and dialed his cell. No answer. She decided to leave a message just so he didn't worry. "Hey, babe, it's me. It was long day, but nothing weird happened. I'll see you at home. Love you."

She picked up her purse and keys at 4:30 to head out for the day and clicked the key fob to her car as she approached. As she pulled down the sun visor, something fell out onto the passenger seat. "Damn it! I need to move that insurance card to the glove box!" Krista was irritated as she moved to retrieve it. But it wasn't a card. She picked up an old, yellowed piece of a newspaper article. Her hands suddenly shaking, she closed her eyes for a moment. What the hell was this doing in her car? How did this get there? She looked around frantically, scanning the parking lot. All she could see was other staff getting into their cars. She looked closer at the yellowed article.

"Family Tragedy After Three Year-Old Killed". There was a small picture of a mangled car, another of rescue personnel, and another blurred photo of police officers behind yellow tape reading "Do Not Cross". The date on the article was September 9 1991.

'A three- year- old has been killed this evening in Narragansett as a result of a head on collision. Facts are unclear at this time, but it appears that the driver of a vehicle driving down the wrong way on Rt. 1 hit the vehicle almost head on. Rescue crews were on the scene as someone called in soon after the accident. The passengers were two adults and two children. Rescue and police responded, but were unable to save one of the children. She died at the scene. Names have been withheld pending family notification.'

Krista dropped the article in her lap, frozen for a moment. What the hell was this doing in her car visor? A sick joke? Who could have put this there? With shaking hands, she picked up her cell and dialed her father's office number. It went straight to voice mail. She almost put down the phone without leaving a message but at the last second said "Dad, it's me. You need to call me right away. Please!" She clicked the off button and sat for a moment, trying to think straight. Desperate to talk to someone, she dialed Chad's number again in hope that he would pick up. When he didn't, she hung up in frustration. "Shit! Now what?" She sat for a few moments, head in her hands and trying to get a grip on her emotions. She took a deep breath. 'Relax, just relax. Start the car and go home. Chad will have answers when you get home,' she told herself. She pulled out of her parking space quickly and headed for home.

Halfway home, Chad called her back. She hit the Bluetooth button on her car. "Chad? Are you on your way home?" She asked in a panicky voice. No answer.

"Chad? Are you there?" Krista's voice went up an octave. Why wasn't he answering?

"Hello, Krista." It was a female voice that answered finally. "Sorry that I had to answer, but Chad has been somewhat delayed, shall we say." She laughed vindictively at the last comment. Krista slammed on the brakes and quickly moved her car to stop on the side of the road.

"I know this is an unexpected call, I'm sure you're in the middle of a panic attack or whatever right now. But you need to get it together, Krista." The voice on the other end was oozing evil.

Krista finally regained her ability to speak, "Who are you? What do you want? Where is Chad?" Her hands gripped the wheel so tightly, her knuckles were turning white. What if they kidnapped Chad? Her mind was running wild now.

The woman on the other end laughed. "Why he's fine. He's having a drink at the bar as we speak, perfectly fine and unaware that I am using his phone. Relax. Now I'm assuming that you saw that article in your car a few minutes ago and that's why you called him so desperately a few minutes ago. What do you think he can do? Can he change what happened?"

"What do you mean? What happened?" Krista tried to steady her voice, but she could feel bile start to rise in her throat.

"You saw the article. What do you think?" The woman was relentless and goading her now.

"I think you're a sick piece of shit and I'm calling the cops!" Krista yelled and hung up without thinking. She instinctively reached out to dial her phone again, but then realized that they probably were ahead of her, whoever it was. She sat for a few minutes, trying to take in what just happened. What would happen if she called back? She instinctively dialed Chad's number again. It rang twice and then someone picked up.

"You've got some nerve calling me from Chad's phone, you bitch! I'll find out who you are!" Krista's fear turned to anger.

"Kris? Kris? What? What's going on?" Chad's voice came across, concerned, confused.

"Chad? Chad, it's you, thank god! Some woman just answered your phone a few minutes ago and she was awful and threatening me and, and …where the hell are you?"

"Kris, what's wrong with you? Seriously? I'm at the Oyster Bar on Federal Hill having a few drinks, some appetizers, you know the drill. Clients are here." Chad sounded annoyed and felt more than done with her drama in the past few weeks. "Kris, this paranoia really needs to stop. You knew I would be here tonight."

"Yes, I knew that! What I didn't know is that you are associated with a crazy woman who called me from your phone threatening me. She also planted some horrible article about a car accident 1991!"

"What are you talking about Kris? I'm not here with anyone! I promise. The only people here are Steve and Joe! I swear! You can come down here and see for yourself!"

Krista was confused and fuming. "Fine! I'll see you in 15 minutes! Make sure you're still there!" She clicked off on the phone and headed out to Federal Hill. Her mind was scrambling around, trying to pinpoint who that woman could be. She knew there weren't many women in Chad's office to begin with so it should be easy to narrow down. Nancy, his secretary, and some girl from accounting whose name Krista couldn't remember. 'I'll catch whoever it is, and then Chad will know that I'm not crazy or imagining things!' Krista was determined to find out who took his phone and called her whether he knew she did it or not. Maybe Chad was in on it? Krista wasn't sure about anything anymore. She was beginning to question trusting her own husband and starting to think maybe he was right. Maybe she did need to see a psychiatrist. Or maybe that psychic woman was onto something.

William

"**M**r. Carson, I have that number that you requested. Would you like me to put you through now?" Cindy asked through the intercom to William's office. William was sitting at his desk, preparing himself for this call. It would definitely change everything and he wasn't sure he was prepared, but it needed to be done. He took a deep breath.

"Yes, thank you, Cindy. I'll be ready for the call." He tried to steady his voice and cleared his throat. She patched him through and soon the ring of the line started. He felt his hands start to sweat, as he awaited the answer on the other line. But maybe Stanley wouldn't answer? William was half- hoping he wouldn't.

"Mr. Ahearn's office. May I help you?" A curt female voice answered, as if she was bothered by the phone call.

William cleared his throat again. "Yes, may I speak with Stanley Ahearn please?"

"May I ask who's calling?" Her voice was condescending.

William bristled with her attitude and decided to play the power game. "Tell him it's William Carson. He knows who I am. Please put me through immediately." His tone was polite, but strict and made it clear he would not tolerate 'he's out of town' games with a receptionist.

"Yes, Mr. Carson, one moment and I'll connect you." The woman changed her tune.

The phone switched over and rang three times. "Ahearn here," Stanley's voice came across brash and arrogant, just as William remembered it.

"Stan? It's Bill Carson here. How're you?" William figured he'd start out with niceties and move on from there.

"Bill? How the hell are you? It's good to hear from you after all these years. It's been awhile." Ahearn's voice sounded less than thrilled to hear from him. William wasn't surprised in the least.

"I'm great, can't complain! How are things in Hollywood? Still selling dreams?" William replied sarcastically, but pretty sure that would pass by Stan. He had always been a narcissist, and clearly that had not changed.

"What else does anyone else in this town do anyway, right?" Stanley's reply sounded bored, yet kind of accurate. William couldn't imagine living in that environment.

William rolled his eyes. "So let me get to the point of this call. You are aware that your wife, Caroline is selling your Block Island property for less than it's valued?" He waited for an ear-splitting outcry from Stanley.

"Yes, it's a little below what I'd like to sell it for, but my wife wants to sell it. She's insisted. My wife insists that she 'see's things'. It's just too much for her. Plus, the traveling to get there is a pain, pretty much from wherever I'm traveling." Stanley replied as if he were talking about a beach house he rented for the week.

"That's what I wanted to hear, Stan. I was just checking with you. My associate met with your wife today. I was just surprised with the price." William said calmly, still skeptical.

"What's with the paranoia today, Bill? We go way back, right?" Stanley made it sound like they were old college frat brothers from way back. Nothing could be further from the truth. "In a way, yes. That's why I'm calling. Just to make sure the price has your approval." William tried to remain formal. "By the way, what do you mean by your wife 'see's' things?"

Stanley laughed, "She thinks she sees this kid near the cliff or in the house that she claims appears and disappears out of nowhere. I think she's just bored and needs to get a hobby!" His un-empathic description of what his wife was upset about in the house made William wonder why any woman would marry this man. Such arrogance!

William's head was whirling. "Stan, do you mind if I come out and check out the house myself? I mean, I'd like to make sure you get the best deal."

"No problem, Bill. Just let my wife know when you're coming out. If you let me know in advance, I'll try and be there. It'd be great to catch up with you again!" Stanley was slurring his words, and William was pretty sure he wouldn't remember much of this conversation, but he had his confirmation.

"I'd like to do that sometime soon." William was surprised that he was agreeable.

"By, the way, Bill, have you told Krista about what happened?" Stanley asked.

William was speechless for a moment, not expecting this conversation. Now he had to clear his throat. "No, I haven't and I don't want anyone else talking to her about it either, know what I mean?" His voice took on an edge that he used when he meant business.

"What's the matter, Bill, afraid the truth might hurt?" Stan was taunting him now.

"Let's just say that Kris is fine the way things are, there's no need for her to know anything, especially now. Leave her out of this!" William raised his voice, irritated that Stan would even bring her up.

"Fine. No problem! Just leave it all alone. No need to come out to the property, it's all on the up and up. I'd hate to have your daughter find out the truth, especially from complete strangers after all."

William gritted his teeth. After all this time, he still had to contend with ghosts from the past. "Ok. You have my word. I'll let my associate proceed with the deal."

"Sounds like a plan, Bill. You're thinking straight now. Let's just put the past behind us and move on. Hey, anytime you want to get ahead in your real estate business, you let me know. I'll hook you up with some celebs that are looking!" Stan sounded like an infomercial now. He laughed. "Hey, it's been great talking with you, Bill, but I'm late for a meeting." Stan said

"Later, Stan." William signed off, glad to be done with this call.

Chad

He'd been hanging out, having a few drinks with co workers. Kris had called, hysterical, claiming that someone had called her from his phone, an article in the car about some accident and now she was on her way to meet him. He was less than ecstatic for her arrival. Her antics at home were one thing. But he only hoped that she could keep it together in front of his co-workers.

Krista called again to let him know that she was pulling into the valet of the Oyster Bar. "I'm here. The valet is parking my car. I'll see you in a minute!"

Chad tried to regroup and think straight. He had a feeling his night out was about to be officially over. Actually, it was more like a celebratory drinking fest. He had his fair share of tequila shots, along with a few beers and was feeling no pain. He definitely wasn't in any shape to deal with Krista's antics tonight. "Ok, babe, see you inside." He frantically tried to get himself together and ordered a glass of water. As if that would help his buzz at this point, but at least it would benefit him when Krista arrived. Besides, he did need it! He looked around to see if there was anyone that might be a potential suspect to Krista's accusations. Joe, Steve, and another few people from administration were there. Nancy had been there, but he didn't see her anywhere now. He secretly said a prayer. Kris had never liked her, and he was always worried that she'd figure things out when things were going down with her. Kris wouldn't hesitate for a second to accuse her of the alleged phone call if she were here.

Krista walked in a minute later. Her face looked pale, and streaked with faint stains of running mascara. Her usual hairstyle of perfectly waved hair was up in a sloppy pony tail. She spotted him and gave him a big hug, even snuggling her head into his chest, something she hadn't done in a long time. Her shoulders shook, and he realized she was sobbing. "Kris, honey, what's wrong? I know you told me about some woman picking up the phone, but maybe she just dialed the wrong number. I'm here, I'm fine." Chad struggled against the fuzziness from the shots of tequila earlier.

Krista's mood turned from sad to rage within seconds. She pulled away from him. "Are you serious? Did you hear anything I said to you? She called FROM YOUR PHONE! It came up as your number. No, it wasn't imagined, or made up and I don't need a fucking psychiatrist to tell me that! But, since you seem to have all the answers, please let me know! Because I would love to know what other answers you have, besides that some bitch that was here called from your phone, then picked it up when I called back!" Krista's voice was getting louder and Chad knew he was in trouble. "By the way, whoever she *is* left this in my car!" Krista pulled out the article and attempted to throw it at him. It fell to the floor and Chad managed to retrieve it before someone stepped on it. He glanced at it. She was right, this was pretty creepy.

"Kris, okay! I get it! We need to talk about this! How about we go home now? Let's go." Chad attempted to usher Krista out of the restaurant. Suddenly, Nancy emerged from the ladies' room. She spotted Chad and Krista and made her way over. "Chad, I was hoping we'd get a chance to talk about that new Block Island deal. She glanced over Krista. "Oh hi, Krista, good to see you," She extended her hand. Krista looked at her like she was the demon, and for a split second, Chad was sure she would go on a tirade, but Krista rolled her eyes, turned and walked away. "Okay…" Nancy withdrew her hand and attempted to continue on with her 'shop-talk', but Chad interrupted.

"Nancy, I really have to go. We'll discuss this tomorrow at the office."

"But, Chad, we really need to nail down the details. Please, we're on a deadline with this…" Nancy pleaded.

"I said no. I'm taking my wife home. We can talk about this tomorrow in the office." Chad's tone was low, but strict and non-negotiable. 'Why is she all of a sudden interested in talking about business now?' Chad wondered.

Nancy finally backed down. "Of course, Chad, I mean, Mr. Burton." His formalities made her feel, and look awkward. But this wasn't the place or the time to talk to him about the place in his life that she wanted. Since Krista hadn't been drinking, Chad conceded to her driving them home in her car, and he asked the valet to allow his car to remain for the evening and would pick it up in the morning.

"No problem, sir." The valet attendant responded politely as Chad handed him a fifty-dollar bill as a tip.

It was the longest drive home with Krista. She hadn't said a word, but Chad knew that she was like a hornet, ready for attack, yet she was silent, almost statue-like the entire trip home. She hadn't moved or said a word. She just stared out the window. As they pulled up to their driveway, Chad finally tried. "Kris…honey…I know this has been a tough night for you. Please talk to me."

Krista turned toward him for the first time since she got in the car, "I would start by telling me the truth for once. I'm sure you haven't been for awhile." With that, she got out of the car, slamming the door behind her, and headed to the house.

Chad got out and followed her, knowing that this was going to be a long night. He thought about calling Bill as that always seemed to be a safety net when Kris was upset. But he was tired of relying on Bill to make things happen. Bill was always there for Kris, always took her side. There wasn't much chance in this case. He'd wait until tomorrow to bring it up. Hopefully, he'd find a way to smooth things over before then, but the look Krista gave him at the restaurant made him feel unsure about anything in their relationship anymore.

Krista

Nancy's presence at that restaurant made her blood boil. She was almost certain that Nancy was the person on Chad's phone threatening her and Chad's insistence that she wasn't involved pissed her off more. She had a suspicion that there was some kind of flirtation going on between the two of them before, but now she was certain. Maybe they hadn't done anything. She had no proof, but it was the way Nancy approached him. It was how she looked at Chad that made Krista positive that she was right about Nancy's motives.

When they reached home, she was in no mood to talk. He'd wanted to talk to her, but she told him that he wasn't telling the truth about Nancy and their relationship. Chad followed her into the house, insisting that they needed to talk. "Kris, please talk to me!"

"Not going to happen right now. I'd like to go inside, soak in a tub and sleep. I don't want to talk to you right now." Krista managed to keep her voice calm and even, despite how much she wanted to scream her frustration about what happened tonight. As she walked to the front door and stuck her key in, she suddenly felt empowered. She was done being nice about everything and sick of being played. She was sure that Nancy or someone that Chad knew was responsible for that article and phone call. "By the way, why don't you actually read that article that she planted in my damn car? Maybe that will convince you that I'm not making this up!"

"Kris, wait!" Chad's voice faded as she closed the door and headed up the stairs. She was no longer sure who he was anymore, or who he associated with. She proceeded to fill up the tub with hot water and her favorite bath wash scented with lavender. As she sunk down into the fragranced water, she took a deep breath. 'I'm not crazy. This really happened.' Krista was sure that someone was out to get her. There was a knock on the door. "Kris, can I come in for a minute?" Chad's voice was pleading. She sighed, "Ok, for a minute." Then she had another thought. "Bring your phone in here with you."

"What? Why?" Chad sounded confused.

"Let me see your phone. I'm going to prove to you that someone called from your phone." Krista was insistent.

"Ok, I'll be right back." Chad agreed. His footsteps headed back down the stairs and up again. "I've got it. Can I come in now?"

"I guess." Krista was still fuming, but the bath was relaxing enough to keep her from jumping up and scratching his eyes out which was what she felt like doing earlier. Actually, Nancy, then Chad, both of them on her shit list. "Here's my phone. Look at it. I checked. There aren't any calls from this phone at the time you said someone called you from my phone. But look for yourself." Chad's expression resembled a little boy being chastised by his mother.

"Let me see it. She probably deleted it!" Krista was determined to prove that she wasn't making this up. Chad was still looking at her like she was a nutcase. She grabbed the phone after wiping off her wet soapy hands. She scrolled through the recent calls. Chad was right. Although the calls from this evening were close together from the woman and Chad, the woman's call wasn't there. Chad's was. "What the hell? I told you, she must have deleted it!" Krista stood up, and grabbed a towel. "I swear it was from your phone, Chad!"

"Kris, I know. You told me that many times now. But it's not there." Chad felt defeated. She was not backing down.

"Can't you check with Verizon? I'm sure they can look up deleted calls!" Krista refused to give up. There must be some record of this call, somewhere, even if it had been deleted from his recent calls. Chad nodded. "I'll check with them in the morning."

"No! Check with them now!" Krista's voice was close to hysterical again. Chad pulled her into his arms, hoping to calm her down. "Kris, it's almost midnight. Let's go to bed. We both need our sleep. We'll sort this out in the morning. Okay?"

Krista was feeling exhausted, and nodded. "Okay. Let's go to bed. You're right. It's too late to figure this out." She conceded and allowed Chad to usher her to the bedroom. She pulled on her favorite sweats and t-shirt and slipped under the covers. "Good night, I'm going to bed." She told Chad and turned over on her side. He didn't protest, but gave her a kiss on the cheek. "Love you, sweetheart. I'm sorry that this evening was such a mess. I'll check with Verizon tomorrow about the phone call. I'll come to bed soon, just going to brush my teeth and read a few emails." Krista simply nodded, and faded off into the welcoming sleep.

She was suddenly in an office building. The bright fluorescent lights were overbearing, and the blue cubicles were endless. She was standing in front of huge windows that went from floor to ceiling and looked down. There was nothing below except clouds and fog covering up whatever ground was below. "Hello? Is anyone here?" She heard heels clicking on the tile floor and knew she had to follow them. Maybe they could lead her out of this place. The clicking stopped as they got into the elevator. Krista stepped in and looked over. A blonde woman with a black skirt and suit jacket, her hair up in a perfect knot stood there, staring straight ahead. "You need to go to the lobby. You need to get out of here, Krista!" The woman turned to face her. Krista suddenly froze. What do you want? Stay away from me!" Krista backed up against the wall of the elevator that seemed to go on endlessly.

"I'm here to help you, Krista. You're in danger. They're getting closer. You need help." The woman held out her hand. "Let me help you, let me help you......" The voice continued on and on.

"Get away from me! I don't know you!" Krista was panicking, ready for the elevator to stop so she could get away, but it kept moving. In fact, it seemed to be speeding up. "What's going on? Why isn't this elevator stopping? Stop!!!!" She screamed. Someone was grabbing her shoulders, shaking her. "No!" Krista went to her throat, determined to keep her away. She was squeezing and hoping that she would let her get away! Suddenly, she heard a male voice, shouting her name. She sat straight up in bed, her arms around his neck, clinging, suffocating.

"Kris! Stop! What are you doing?" Chad was wrestling away from her grasp. She looked at him, sitting straight up in bed and her arms wrapped around his neck. He had a look of terror on his face, as though someone were trying to hurt him.

"Chad?" She shook her head, still trying to figure out if she was in a dream or reality. Maybe he was in on it, trying to drive her insane. He did want her to see a psychiatrist and didn't believe the incidents she'd told him about. Chad was sitting away from her, with a look of disbelief on his face. "Kris? Are you awake now?" He tentatively touched her arm, and pulled back, afraid she would still be in her crazy dream state.

"What? Why are you asking me that? What happened?" Krista had never felt so confused. Her husband was acting as though he was afraid of her and was as far away from her as possible on their bed.

"Kris, you were trying to choke me! You were dreaming! Or at least I hope you were! I don't know what's up with these dreams, but I need to get some sleep!" He grabbed his pillow, stormed out of the room and rummaged through the hall closet for a blanket.

"Chad! Wait! Don't leave me! Nancy is after me!" Krista begged, as he ran out of the room. No answer, but she could hear him downstairs, opening the refrigerator, grabbing something and slamming it shut again. She desperately wanted to run after him, explain what was going on, but she knew he wouldn't believe her. He was right. The eerie feeling left from that dream was still with her and she couldn't brush it off as she had in the past. She felt it now even when she was awake. "Chad?" She ran down the stairs and found him on the living room couch with a blanket. No answer. "Chad?"

Chad finally poked his head out of the blanket. "I'm sorry, Kris. I just have a big day tomorrow. We can talk tomorrow. I need to get some sleep, ok?" She nodded and he turned his back to her.

Krista's first impulse was to continue to insist on conversation, but she knew it would only make things worse. Instead, she gave him a kiss and said good night. It was clear that maybe he was right; she needed to see someone, knowing it wasn't a psychiatrist.

William

He'd thought long and hard about this day. The day when he'd finally have to deal with Stanley again and he hadn't changed. Stanley was still the blackmailing, money-grubbing ass that he had always been. He had every reason to believe that he would contact Krista and give her information that would send her over the edge at this point. He knew that something was going on at that Mohegan Bluffs estate, and wished that he could go out there, lay eyes on this Caroline and the house for himself, but also knew Stanley was as good as his word about Krista. He couldn't risk that. Once again, Stanley had gotten him right where he wanted him. He had to depend on Chad to do this deal on his own, in person, but William had a feeling that something was going wrong in that house. Why else would they be selling and why for such a low price? Stanley himself had even said that his wife was seeing a presence there.

Suddenly, he had an idea. Maybe crazy, but it was worth trying. He sat down at the computer and googled 'Maria Evans Carson'. As tough as it was to look up his deceased wife, he needed to be reminded about what was at stake with his daughter and why he couldn't interfere with Stanley's instructions to stay away. What came up was an article about the initial disappearance of Maria. An article he'd read very long ago, caused him so much pain, that he swore he'd never read it again. But here he was.

January 20, 1992- Providence Journal

There was a report about a woman missing by William Carson who had last seen his wife, Maria Evans Carson January 19th. Carson reported that he had woken up in the morning to find her and some of her belongings missing. According to Mr. Carson, they had been going through 'some tough times' with the recent death of their daughter, but he was certain that they were getting through it and that she wouldn't have left without warning. The police have put out an all points bulletin on Maria Carson. If anyone has information regarding Mrs. Carson, please contact Providence police.

William felt the tears sliding down his face. Not just because of the police investigating him as a suspect, or that he had to be interrogated and fingerprinted. He was finally cleared after 3 months of the bullshit.

It had been a long time since he'd first read this, but now it was as if he had lost her all over again. If only she had shared with him how much she hurt. Maybe he could've helped more, done more. But he had been bogged down with the accusations and the investigation following the accident, and ended up with Krista spending most of her time at his parent's house. He still could remember how awful it was, waiting for police to arrest him, and waiting to be free from the horrible turn of events that caused his family to eventually fall apart despite his efforts, when all he wanted was his family back.

But he knew that if he could do anything to help Krista, he would make sure no one told her about what happened. She was already stressed, and she didn't need to worry about the past. He knew how she would react; and although she was a strong young woman, he didn't want to risk her happiness. He'd need to find out more about this Caroline Ahearn, who'd come up as a ghost on the web with Chad and his own searches. He suddenly recalled his conversation with Stanley. Why didn't he want him to come to the house? Stanley was even making veiled threats if he came there. He knew he'd need to do some digging. He'd keep his word about not coming to the house, but he never said he wasn't going to find out more about his wife. Stanley was hiding something. William was sure of it.

He decided to try and contact Detective Sumner again. He'd been the detective working on Maria's case when she'd first disappeared. He knew he'd been in the hospital a few weeks ago, but maybe he was back to work by now. He dialed the Providence police department and asked for Detective Sumner. "May I ask who's calling?" The receptionist asked.

"This is William Carson. I tried to contact him a few weeks ago, but I was told he was hospitalized."

"One moment, sir." The receptionist put him on hold for what seemed like eternity. When someone came back on the line, it wasn't Sumner. "This is Detective Scott. How can I help you Mr. Carson?"

Why the hell wasn't anyone giving him contact with Sumner? "Hello, Detective, my name's William Carson. I was calling to speak to Detective Sumner in regard to a case that he worked on for me in the past." Why the run around? William suddenly didn't have a good feeling about this.

"Mr. Carson, I'm sorry to inform you that Detective Sumner passed away a few days after being admitted to the hospital." Detective Scott's said gravely.

"What? Oh my god. I'm so sorry to hear that! What happened?" William was shocked, and felt so sorry for his family. He'd gotten to know Dave somewhat during the investigation and he had a family; a lovely wife and two daughters.

"It was an accident. He was on a family vacation and he fell off a boat that they had chartered to Martha's Vineyard. They were able to get him out of the water, but he never regained consciousness. He'd been underwater for too long." Scott sounded upset while giving him the information.

"He was a very nice man, very helpful to me many years ago. Again, please give my condolences to his family." William was truly sorry. He knew only too well how it was for someone to just disappear.

"Thank you, Mr. Carson. Is there anything else I can do for?" Scott questioned.

"Actually, yes, there is. Could you please pull the file for Maria Carson? I just want to see it. She's my wife that disappeared 24 years ago, but I'd like to look at it. Dave Sumner was the detective assigned to it." William crossed his fingers.

"That shouldn't be a problem, Mr. Carson. I could have it ready for you in a few days." Scott replied earnestly. Detective Scott was truly devastated by Dave's death. He had been his mentor. He was curious about a case that Dave had. Clearly it hadn't been resolved.

"Thank you so much, Detective Scott. I really appreciate it." William was shocked that they were actually going to help him.

"No problem, Mr. Carson. He was a mentor of mine. I'd like to think that if I can help, it would be like Dave helping you out. I'll call you when the file is ready for review." Detective Scott advised.

"Thank you again." William gave him his home, cell and office numbers and hung up with mixed emotions. He was still trying to wrap his head around Sumner's death. He looked online and sure enough, there it was. David Sumner had been on a ferry headed to Martha's Vineyard when he had either jumped or been pushed overboard. He was found and brought to the hospital. Three days later, he was taken off life support due to lack of brain activity. At the end of the article, "Maureen Sumner is still convinced that this wasn't an accident. There is an ongoing investigation for cause of death."

Chad

The morning sun woke him. Chad sat up and looked frantically at the clock. It was 6:05. He lay back, sighing relief that he wasn't late. He checked his phone for text messages and emails. There were at least 6 texts from Nancy.

12:30am-"Hi, hope you got home okay." 3:30: "Are you okay, haven't heard from you." 4:00: "Are you home? Let me know!" "4:15: "Hello?" 4:30: "Chad, seriously, I'm worried." 5:00: "I'm calling you if you don't come to the office tomorrow."

Chad felt like throwing his phone out the window. She really was nuts! He had never regretted anything more than getting involved in a fling with this semi-attractive bimbo that may have just cost him his marriage. He immediately deleted the messages and walked into the kitchen to make coffee. He was definitely going to need it today. It was too early to call William, but he intended to speak to him later about potentially replacing Nancy.

Suddenly, he remembered the article Krista had thrown at him and rummaged through his coat pockets, hoping it hadn't fallen out. Luckily, it was still in his coat pocket, crumpled up, and he grabbed it. As he read it carefully, he realized that Kris had a right to be upset. No wonder! And the phone call that came afterwards that they couldn't confirm? He knew that he had to make this right with Kris. He needed her to know that he believed her. They couldn't prove that it was Nancy, but clearly someone wanted Krista to see this article. Nancy was at the restaurant and could have had the opportunity to call her from his phone. He remembered leaving it on the table when he used the restroom. Who else would do that?

He knew Kris needed to be up by 6:30, so he went upstairs, hoping that she wouldn't still be upset with him. She was sleeping soundly when he walked into the room. He watched her for a moment, realizing that he'd promised this woman to take care of her. Her face was half covered by her pillow, and she had her left foot sticking out of the blanket. He smiled to himself. Some things never changed. He liked to call her feet sticking out of the blanket her 'trademark' and even joked with her about being the first to be out the door if they had a fight.

"Kris? Honey, its time to get up," Chad gently shook her shoulders and gave her a side hug. Krista moved her head from the pillow. "Chad?" She answered sleepily.

"Hi, sweetheart. I'm sorry for last night. From now on, I'm going to listen to you, okay?" Chad brushed a lock of blond hair out of her face. He only hoped that she wouldn't continue to hold a grudge. Krista sat up and wiped her eyes. "What time is it?"

"It's almost 6:30."

"I need to get up. I need to get to work!" Krista was frantically throwing off the blankets and headed for the shower. As she headed to the bathroom, Chad followed his wife. "Kris, you have plenty of time. Finish your shower and I'll make breakfast." Krista didn't reply.

"Kris? Did you hear me?"

"I did, Chad. Thanks. I'll be down soon." Krista's voice was quiet, but he was glad that she at least had responded to him.

"Take your time. I'll have breakfast ready soon." Chad said, and headed downstairs to start his cooking duties. He wasn't sure of what he was doing, but how hard was it to fry some eggs and make toast?

After almost a carton of eggs and a pile of burnt toast, he had to give credit to Kris. Aside from that pasta dinner he'd managed a few weeks ago, he was never good at cooking. Especially eggs! He'd managed to find a bit of shell in every single one that he'd attempted to fry. Finally, he found a package of Hot Pocket breakfast sandwiches in the freezer. He quickly read the microwave directions and threw them in, praying that they'd be edible. When the timer stopped, he cut them up and found some cut up cantaloupe in the fridge and threw them on the plate. "Kris?" He called to her upstairs.

"I'm coming." She responded and trudged down the stairs. Chad was shocked at her appearance. She looked tired, even after her shower, and was dressed in her yoga pants and a ratty sweatshirt. "What's wrong? Are you sick?"

"I'm so tired. I don't know what's wrong with me. I thought I slept well but I'm so tired." Her face looked almost gray.

"You look exhausted, honey." Chad suddenly felt horrible about leaving his wife to sleep on the couch. Krista nodded, "I don't know what's going on with me. I'm just feeling out of it. I think I'm going to have to call out today." Her voice sounded almost robotic.

He went to her and felt her forehead. She felt cool, in fact, her forehead was ice-cold. "Kris, I'll call the school for you. You need to stay home and rest today. Okay?"

She looked at him, but that eerie look in her eyes from when he woke her up was staring back at him again. He felt a shiver go up his spine just looking at her. "Sure, that'd be great. Thank you, honey." Before he could respond, she turned around and walked back up the stairs.

Chad was confused. Something was really wrong with Krista and explaining her behavior right now to anyone would make him sound like a lunatic, but she seemed completely in some kind of trance. He decided to go back upstairs and try again. She was lying down on her back with her eyes closed. "Kris, honey, can you hear me? Wake up!" No response. He shook her shoulders. "Kris! Please, let me know that you're okay. I'm not leaving until I know that you're okay."

Her eye fluttered open. "Chad, I'm fine. I'm just really tired. She wants so much from me. I'm just so tired." Her voice was lethargic, almost unrecognizable.

"Honey, who's making you so tired? What's wrong? Let me help you!" Chad was freaked out by his wife's reference to "her".

"I don't know who she is. She keeps talking to me. She shows me things. I'm so tired. Why doesn't she go away?" Krista's eyes opened now, but seemed to be focused on an object on the wall. It was a random art piece that Kris had picked up at an auction.

"What does she look like, Kris?" Chad asked wondering if she was even lucid enough. Maybe she was really going crazy after all?

"She looks like me. She looks just like me." Kris responded. "Just like the dreams, she looks just like me."

Krista

She remembered last night's events; the article, the random phone call and meeting Chad at the bar. Beyond that, she just remembered Chad waking her up. She felt strange. Her mind was foggy and she'd never felt so confused or tired in her life. It was as if someone was literally draining her physically. She knew that she'd dreamt again. Her "clone" was still near her, she could feel it. As if someone was drawing her in, making her move, making decisions for her. She'd tried to get up for work, but had no energy to even figure out what to wear, and put on something that was comfortable instead. Even as she was getting dressed, she knew that she couldn't wear this to work. 'What am I doing?' She asked herself, but she couldn't fight against the fatigue and it won out.

Chad had been so sweet, attempting breakfast, being attentive. The anger about Nancy being at the restaurant and her involvement with the phone call had disappeared, almost as if it hadn't happened. Usually, she'd be pissed for days, but now it seemed like nothing. She hoped he wasn't upset with her strange behavior. She was feeling like a shell of herself and it scared her. As she returned to bed, she remembered the psychic she'd seen last week. Maybe she still had the card and began rummaging around the room, hoping to find it. What had she been wearing that day? Suddenly, she saw the blue dress pants she remembered wearing that day. She grabbed the pockets and there was the card. "Nadine--Medium and Psychic Reader-" 401-546-7568. Thank god! Krista suddenly felt some hope. How ironic that just a week ago, she couldn't wait to leave the shop, and now here she was scrounging around her room for her card. She needed to call her right away. She listened for Chad's movements downstairs. She could hear him talking on the phone and decided to stand at the top of the stairs to investigate. He should have left for work already.

"Yes, she's not well. I'm not sure." She could hear Chad saying on the phone. "Yes, I know, she's stressed. I know. I'm not sure what to do. I do need to work on that Block Island property. Okay." A minute passed while Chad continued to talk to her father. That much Krista could get from this. "Okay, I'll come in. But someone needs to check on her. Okay, Bill, I'll let her know that you'll be coming by before I leave." Chad hung up the phone.

So her dad would be checking up on her today. She formed a plan to call him to stall the 'checking in' timeline. She needed to schedule an appointment with Nadine today to shed some light on what these nightmares meant. She ran back to the bedroom and got under the covers just in time for Chad coming up the stairs. "Kris? I'm going to go into the office just for a few hours, but your dad is going to check in on you. Are you okay?" Chad's voice sounded unusually panicked. "I called the school and let them know you were sick and going to be out today."

Krista turned over and reached out a hand to her husband, "Thanks. I appreciate it. I'm sure I'll be fine. What time did dad say he would come?" Chad gave her a kiss on the cheek. "He didn't say. He just said he'd stop in." Krista gave him a kiss back. "Okay, so that means whenever. That's fine. I'm just going to get some rest. I'm sure I'll feel better after I rest."

"You're just stressed Kris. These dreams are probably just a result of what happened last night. I promise you, I'll find out what happened with that phone call. We'll figure this out, okay?" Chad seemed reluctant to leave.

"I'm sure it's just stress. If I don't feel better tomorrow, I'll see my doctor, okay?" Krista didn't want him to worry any longer. Just go already! She knew who she needed to see.

"Okay, honey, call me if you need anything!" Chad gave her a final hug and left. Krista returned his hug. "I'm just going to get some sleep. Love you." She gave him a kiss goodbye and laid back down, shutting her eyes.

She heard his footsteps down the stairs and the door slammed shut. She got out of bed. First, she needed to take care of her dad stopping by. She grabbed her cell from the charger in the living room and dialed her father. It rang several times, and went to voicemail. What the hell? Her dad always picked up. She decided to try again, thinking he might be on another call. This time he picked up.

"Dad? It's me." Kris kept her tone light, in hopes that he wouldn't worry.

"Kris, how're you doing, sweetheart? Chad said you weren't feeling well. I was just going to come over and check on you." Her father's voice sounded concerned. Krista felt horrible for deceiving him right now, but knew that she needed to find out what was behind the nightmares and sleepwalking, and also knew that he wouldn't understand the way she was going about it.

"I'm fine, dad. Just stressed and really tired. I'll be okay. You don't need to come by today. I'll just rest, maybe watch some crappy reality TV shows and feel better tomorrow."

"Are you sure? I can always drop by with some good take out from Luigi's, you know." Her father offered, sounding less anxious.

"I promise. And Luigis' sounds great! But not at 9am! Maybe this evening?" Krista wanted to make sure she had enough time to see Nadine.

"Okay, Kris. But call if you need anything. I'll come by after work, around 5." He sounded less upset and willing to wait on stopping by.

"I will, dad. Promise. I love you. See you tonight." Krista hoped that would make him feel better and not stop by. If he did and she wasn't here, that would just lead to more questions. Questions she couldn't answer right now, but she hoped Nadine would be true to her word and give her the answers. She pulled out the card and dialed the number, hoping someone would answer. She was starting to lose hope when suddenly a young woman's voice answered. "Hello?"

"Hello. Is this Nadine?"

"Yes, who is this is?" A girl answered sleepily.

"I'm so sorry if I woke you up. My name is Krista. I was in your um…..shop about a week ago and you gave me your card. I wanted to make an appointment, if that's possible." Krista suddenly realized it was still early, only 8:30. It was too early to be calling anyone. "Oh, yes, I remember you. Yours was a very intriguing reading." Nadine's voice sounded more awake. "It was your sister that was trying to contact you."

"Yes, you kept saying I had a sister. So I wanted to get an appointment to meet with you again. Do you have any time to see me today?" Krista crossed her fingers.

"Um, I'm pretty booked up for the next week, Krista." Nadine yawned, obviously still waking up.

"It really can't wait. I'll pay extra! I need to see you today if at all possible." Krista was desperate.

"Ok, I'll see what I can do. Can you come in around 1:30? It'll have to be a 30- minute session, but I can squeeze you in." Nadine assured her.

"Perfect. Thank you so much! I'll see you then!" Krista felt relieved already, although she wasn't sure why. Just last week, she thought Nadine was nuts. Now here she was begging for an appointment. But then again, her life had been turned upside down with these nightmares and strange occurrences without explanations that added up. She went back to her bedroom and retrieved the photo of the woman and the two girls that she'd put in her jewelry box for safe keeping. 'What does this mean? Who are you?' She wondered.

William

As he arrived at the office, William decided to make a plan. Chad would need to go back out to the Ahearn property. He wished he could go out there himself, but he would keep his word to Stanley that he'd keep away. He understood on some level, given his history with Stanley, but there was something that Stanley didn't want him to know. He was sure of it. But he also knew that Stanley was always true to his word about following through with threats. He couldn't afford to play with those odds. This was not a time to upset Krista when she was already struggling.

Chad was passing by on the way to his own office, and William motioned him in. "Morning, Chad. I hope you slept well last night because I've got a lot to discuss today." He sat down in his chair. "Bill, what's going on?" Chad remained standing. He hoped it wasn't too intense, as his night was the opposite. He might have gotten three hours, in between tossing and turning, and checking on Kris.

"Have a seat, please, Chad." William was all serious and business. His face was solemn, lacking his usual jovial attitude, and Chad knew that something serious was going on.

"Bill, what's going on? Did something happen?" Chad was worried that he'd somehow screwed up a transaction with one of his sales. Or worse, he'd gotten wind about his indiscretions with Nancy.

"Chad, relax. It's nothing like that. It's just that…well… I need for you to go back out to the Ahearn property. I want you to be the one to work on, and finalize on this sale. You're the best man for the job."

Chad breathed a sigh of relief. He was worried he was getting scolded or fired by the way William had approached him. "Of course, Bill. I'll do it all and run everything by you before I do it. Thank you! I appreciate the opportunity!"

"There's something else. I want you to find out all you can about Caroline Ahearn. I did speak to Stanley, and he's in agreement with the price. However, I'm wondering about her."

"Actually, Bill, I did try. After I went to the property I did a search on her. Nothing much comes up. There wasn't anything. There was no trace of her on Facebook, Twitter, or Linked In, and nothing in the news about her in relation to her husband. She's like a ghost as far as the internet is concerned." Chad informed him. Bill shook his head and spun his chair around to face the window without saying a word.

"Bill? What's going on? You know I'll do anything I can to help this sale go through," Chad had never seen William so emotional or out of sorts like this.

William spun back around to face Chad, his face looking determined. "No, I'm fine. I just think you'll be the best person to handle this sale. I only have one request from you for the next time you go out there to take photos. I want you to get a picture of Caroline."

"Uh, okay. I guess. But why?" Chad was confused. He was sure that she was the sort of woman that didn't want her picture taken by a realtor, given that her husband was famous.

William nodded his head. "Good point. But I have my reasons. I can't explain them to you right now, but I do. It doesn't have to be a posed photo. It could be random, when she's not suspecting it. Just get her in the background while you're taking pictures of the house. You'll have opportunities. I mean, you could always ask her, but if she says no, and I suspect she will, then you'll look like you're trying to be sneaky if she catches you after the fact. Just do this for me, please." William's explanation didn't clear anything up, except that he wanted a picture of Caroline. But he needed to know. He needed to know what this mysterious Caroline Ahearn looked like.

"No problem, I can do that. I'll figure it out. I'll schedule another appointment today, and let you know when it is." Chad assured him. He had all kinds of questions that he definitely wasn't asking today, especially with William's strange behavior.

"Thanks, Chad. You'll do well. I'm sure of it." William stood up and gave him a pat on the shoulder. "I can always trust you." As he walked Chad out of his office, he couldn't help but feel that he'd hired a spy. He couldn't help himself. Stanley didn't want him to come there. Why? He needed to know if it was something to do with Caroline. Maybe she knew something that he needed to know, or maybe she was hiding from something or someone. What she had said to Chad about a young girl in the house and on the cliff only made him more curious about this woman.

He was feeling nostalgic and searched through his desk until he finally found the photo in a frame that said "Family" on the top of it. It was a picture of Maria and his girls. He looked at it for a long time before putting it away again. He knew he couldn't have it on his desk. It was too much for him to even see again, let alone have on his desk to see everyday.

Chad

He was headed back to his desk, still concerned about William's random request about getting a picture of Caroline, 'He still didn't understand, but at the end of the day, Bill was still his boss. He'd do his best, no matter how creepy it seemed. Between Kris and Bill's strange behaviors, he was starting to wonder if HE was the one with issues. What if it was him that was really over thinking this? 'No, this is really strange,' Chad reminded himself.

Just as he sat down, Nancy showed up. "Mr. Burton, I need to talk to you." She was dressed in a prim collared dress, which was very unlike her. She usually wore low cut blouses or overly tight dresses that were on the cusp of being inappropriate, but not so much that human resources could lay claim to an issue.

"Yes Nancy? What's going on?" He kept his gaze on his computer screen to avoid eye contact, fearing more flirtation that he needed to dodge.

"I need to give my notice. I've been offered another position at another company." Nancy was smiling smugly and looked as though she were expecting some kind of reaction from him.

"I'm glad that you're giving a notice, Nancy. I'm assuming you'll be leaving us in two weeks?" Chad kept his facial expression calm, which was easy because he actually felt relieved. At least he didn't need to deal with her trying to continue on with their affair, or talk to William about replacing her. Nancy seemed oblivious to him for the first time and smiled contently, as though she were the one that had the upper hand. He was again reminded of how completely inappropriate this woman could be.

"Actually, I'm not. I'm leaving now. I can start tomorrow at my new job. I'm sorry that I'm not able to give more notice but they wanted me to start right away. It's a great opportunity, so I didn't want to turn it down. I'm very sorry." Nancy's attitude was anything but sorry, and the words came out as if they were rehearsed. She gave him another half- smile that said 'Too bad, your loss.'

Chad took a deep breath. This was going to put him in a huge bind over the next few days. The time it would take to put out a job announcement for her position and in the interim, have no one to type up necessary documents would be almost impossible. "I'm interested to know why you've decided not to give at least some kind of notice, Nancy. Even a week would be helpful. I'm sure your new employer would understand the necessity to hire a replacement?" Chad said evenly, but he was beyond irritated. It was almost as if she were doing this on purpose, just to spite him because he'd been ignoring her obvious attempts to rekindle their 'indiscretions.'

Nancy fiddled with her watch for a moment, but no remorse crossed her face. "Chad, I've liked working for you. It's been great, but I need to move on. I know that I'll have much better opportunity to move up in this company. And quite frankly, you haven't given me what I was promised when I started here." She laughed. "Actually, you've done the opposite. The closer I came to getting to what I wanted, the more you kept me from it. So no, I'm not going to explain to them that YOU need more time. Too bad, you should've played by my rules. You lose this time." Nancy picked up her purse and gave him the finger as she headed toward the door. "You don't finish what you start. It's all about the planning and the know-how. That's your problem! Good luck with that crazy wife of yours!" She was laughing, as she walked out the door, letting it slam shut.

Chad sat at his desk, still trying to take in what happened in the last few minutes. Now, he had no secretary, and he needed to sell this Block Island property. On top of it, William wanted pictures of the owner that he was supposed to get 'at random' as he was positive Caroline was not going to pose for a picture. When William suggested him asking, he knew immediately that he wouldn't do it. It was a gut feeling, but he knew that she'd never agree to a picture and he understood. She was the wife of someone famous, and she'd learned not to trust anyone, as well she should. Shit! First thing, he needed a new secretary to type up necessary documents, answer phone calls, and basically keep him afloat in this mess! He went out to the main reception office in hopes that maybe one of them knew someone that needed a job.

He approached the front desk receptionist. "Hey, Sabrina, do you know anyone that needs a secretary job?" He was trying to be casual despite his desperation. She smiled at him but motioned to her headset. She was on the phone. "Okay, sorry, Mr. Burton, I was on the phone. Actually, I do know someone. My cousin is looking for an administrative position. I can give her a call if you want. She has some experience."

"Some experience? Does she have any knowledge of real estate transactions?" Chad was desperate, but not enough to hire a completely green secretary that he would need to baby sit. Sabrina shook her head. "Actually, that's the only experience she's had. I'll let her know you're looking for someone if you want."

"Yes, that would be great. Thank you. Have her email her resume to me immediately if she's interested." Chad wasn't expecting anything, but it was worth a try. He wasn't sad to see Nancy leave, but she'd done it with absolutely no notice and he was now stuck. He only hoped that her departure meant keeping their brief affair quiet.

He went back to his office, head in his hands. He dialed Williams' extension to inform him about Nancy's departure. Bill picked up on the first ring. "Nancy's leaving us. She told me just now and left. No notice, so now what?" Chad couldn't help his rising panic.

"No problem, I'll get Kate from Human Resources to fill in for now. She's great and can help out." William didn't sound stressed about the situation. Chad was amazed at how he could just solve a problem that quickly.

"Thanks so much, Bill. I'm working up the details on that Block Island property and getting ready to schedule an appointment as soon as possible. Are you sure you aren't going?" Chad was still wondering about William's hesitance on going to the Ahearn property with him. He was tempted to tell him about the picture that Caroline had in her room and its resemblance to the picture that Krista found in her desk, but decided against it. There was enough going on, and William was acting almost as strange as Krista lately.

"No, I'm busy here. I trust you. Don't forget that picture though, Chad." William reminded him again. Chad agreed. "I won't. This deal is as good as done, trust me." Chad assured him. He still didn't get it, but he would do what his boss told him to do.

Krista

She decided to go in to work after all. Chad had called her out, but, Krista felt almost guilty about it, like it was a deep dark secret. She didn't need anyone, especially Jane, questioning her calling out sick. Besides, she needed to stay busy until her appointment, and she found herself pacing at home. She knew her dad wasn't going to check in on her until this evening.

As she went through the front office to her own, she noticed Jane's desk was empty today. She found it strange because she couldn't remember a day when Jane wasn't there. She greeted the receptionist.

" Hi Marcy, where's Jane today?" Krista asked casually, secretly hoping someone had kidnapped her. 'Probably wouldn't bother, she'd just bitch at them until they let her go or killed her.' Krista smiled at the thought of Jane being in that situation.

"Actually, Jane gave her notice. Not much of one, though. She came in this morning and gave her notice and left. Not even considered a notice, if you ask me By the way, what are you doing here?" Marcy seemed taken off guard that she was here today. "Your husband called and said you were sick"

"I wasn't feeling well earlier, but I had some appointments that I didn't want to reschedule today." Krista said.

"Well, I wish all employees were like you and actually cared about their job. Some of them obviously don't!" She replied in reference to Jane's sudden departure.

"I'm sorry." Krista tried to sound authentic, as she *wasn't* sorry that Jane left. She actually was sorry for Marcy. Now Marcy would have to deal with all the extra paperwork. But as for Jane, good riddance!

"Not as sorry as I am. I sure wasn't a fan of hers, but I know it's going to be hell until they hire someone to replace her!" Marcy didn't hide her disgust about the way Jane treated people.

"I'm sure someone will be hired soon. In the mean time, don't worry about me. I'll schedule my appointments and take my own calls." Krista knew that it wouldn't help much since there were 5 other people that Marcy supported as an administrative assistant. She went to open her office door.

"Thanks, Kris. I appreciate it. You know, you're not as bad as Jane said you were."

Krista spun around, keys in hand. "What did she say?"

"I mean, well, uh, Jane, she just said some things about you sometimes. They weren't good." Marcy was uncomfortable, but Krista was insistent on finding out what was said. Anything negative could mean a reprimand from the principal, and she was worried about what this bitch had spread around. "She said that you were a 'little rich bitch' and that you got this job because of your father. She also said you slept around with other staff. She complained to the principal that you were late. Look, Krista, I know this isn't true and I'm sorry I'm telling you this, but you can't tell anyone that I told you what she said. She told me that she would ruin my life because I overheard her one day on the phone. She was saying horrible things that I overheard, and she realized it after the fact. Please don't say that I told you, okay?"

Krista was dying to know what else Marcy had overheard, but her frightened face told her it wasn't a good idea. Not now anyway. After all, Jane was a huge pain, not only to Krista, but to other staff. Marcy had no reason to make this up. Clearly, Jane was not only a bitch, but a vengeful one at that. Krista was sure she could go through the DSM and find a laundry list of diagnoses for Jane.

"Marcy, it's okay. I understand, really. She was never nice to me anyway. I won't tell anyone, I promise. You'll be fine." She gave Marcy a side hug. Marcy returned the hug, and smiled. "Thanks, Krista. I appreciate it." She sounded genuine.

Krista opened her office door. "What the hell!" The sight inside was unbelievable. Her pictures and wall hangings were torn down. Her files were thrown all over the room and her trash can had bee dumped upside down, with its' contents sitting in a pile next to it. "Marcy!" Krista called out, still trying to wrap her head around the mess.

"What's going on?" Marcy rushed into her office and held her hand to her mouth in disbelieve. 'What the hell? Who could have done this?

I swear no one has been here since I came in this morning!" Marcy was clearly shaken.

"I know, Marcy, it's not your fault. I'm pretty sure I know who's responsible for this!" Krista bolted to the door and headed straight for the principal's office. She pushed through the door and was greeted by his elderly secretary, Mrs. Jenkins. The woman had to have been there for as long as anyone could remember and had a reputation for being bitchy. "Yes?" Mrs. Jenkins pushed her bifocals back up on her nose and glared at Krista as though she'd just ruined her morning for coming in the door. Her thinning hair was gray, and apparently she made no attempt to cover up the bald spots. She was heavy and wore a muumuu type dress with a pattern that resembled a 1970's curtain pattern. As Krista came closer she tried not to wrinkle her nose at the scent of moth balls. They reminded her of an unfriendly version of Mrs. Roper from Three's Company.

"Hello, Mrs. Jenkins. I'd like to see Mr. Samuels immediately. It's urgent." Krista said firmly. Mrs. Jenkins scowled and looked down at her calendar for a moment. "Did you have an appointment?"

Krista sighed. She knew this would be a battle. "No, I did not. But there's been an incident in my office and I need to talk with him immediately."

"Ms. Burton, you don't have an appointment and Mr. Samuels is busy right now. You'll have to schedule a time to meet with him, just like everyone else." She replied curtly. Just like everyone else? Krista felt her pulse rising and she was already ticked off. Someone had just destroyed her office!

"Mrs. Jenkins, I need to see Mr. Samuels now! My office was destroyed by someone and I need to let him know!" Krista raised her voice. She wasn't going to be pushed around by some rude secretary that was rude to everyone on the planet because she needed to retire. She moved closer to the woman's desk to let her know she wasn't leaving.

Mrs. Jenkins scowled at her again, but picked up the phone to call him. "Yes, Mr. Samuels. I know you're busy," She glared at Krista as she spoke. "Yes, I'll show her in."

"You can go on in. But next time, you need to make an appointment!" Mrs. Jenkins said in a condescending tone.

"Oh, thanks, you've been SO helpful," Krista said sarcastically. She was done with being bullied by these people at work. Mrs. Jenkins just gave her another scowl and turned her back on Krista. Just then, Mr. Samuels opened his door. "Ms. Burton? Come on in." Charles Samuels also had a laid back attitude and today was no different. "Have a seat. What's going on?" He asked as casually as if he were asking her how her weekend was.

Krista described how her office was ransacked this morning, with the principal nodding here and there. "Mr. Samuels, I really have a feeling that Jane was behind this. She did leave her position here without notice, I might add! Maybe she wanted to get back at employees that worked here." Krista was careful with her words, knowing that Mr. Samuels was very politically correct.

Mr. Samuels sat back in his chair with a grim look on his face. "You know, Ms. Burton, I know you do a great job here. I've heard some good things. I've also heard that you've been late for work in the past several weeks. While I understand that people are late because of traffic and what not, I see that you've been late 8 times in the past month. Is there something going on?" Krista was correct that Jane had been reporting her and she struggled to keep a nonchalant look on her face.

"Who gave you this tally of alleged late days?" Krista asked, hoping he would give Jane away as the snitch.

"It's doesn't matter. And furthermore, it's not just about you being late. I'm concerned about your well being. That's why I was asking." Mr. Samuels replied.

"I'm fine. I've had some doctor's appointments. That's all." Krista lied and decided to change to the subject at hand. "Mr. Samuels, someone destroyed my office between yesterday and today. I suspect that it's someone who has keys to the school and to the office!" Krista stood up. She was tired of people trying to push this issue to the side.

"Okay, Ms. Burton. I'll have the security staff conduct a search at your office. I'd like you to be present so that you can validate if anything is missing."

"No! I want the police contacted and I want them to do an investigation. I've got a good idea of who destroyed my office and I'll happily give a name, even if you want to keep it quiet." Krista was sure that it was Jane that had done this, or at least hired someone to do it. Mr. Samuels looked uncertain, so Krista decided she'd had enough. "Mr. Samuels, I'm positive that someone destroyed my office on purpose. If you aren't going to have the police investigate, I'll notify the superintendent!" Krista's voice became louder. "Are you threatening me, Ms. Burton?" Mr. Samuels asked. His tone turned from condescending to accusatory.

"Of course not! I'm just advocating for my rights as an employee of this school district! My personal office has been violated and as I recall the policy is to conduct an investigation to determine the persons responsible." Krista was quick to recite. She knew he'd be pulling that 'are you threatening me' card sooner or later. She'd worked at the school long enough to know that Mr. Samuels was quick to brush anything that might be a problem under the rug, rather than deal with it. She also knew the 'security' staff he mentioned usually spent their time getting high on their lunch breaks.

"Well, then, I will contact the local police right now and we'll get started," Mr. Samuels replied reluctantly. "I'm very sorry that this happened, Ms. Burton." Krista nodded, but was sure that he meant he was very sorry that he had just been forced to deal with this.

"Fine, thank you for your time," Krista tried to keep the sarcasm out her voice. She bit back some choice words that she wanted to say and walked out of his office. As far as she was concerned, Mr. Samuels and his bitch of a secretary could go to hell.

The morning dragged on. The police showed up, as promised. They went through her office looking for any evidence of who might have done this. Krista gave them Jane's name and the police took down the information, although she was sure nothing would come of it. "Ms. Burton, is there anything that you can think of that someone would be looking for in your office?" One of the officers asked. He at least seemed somewhat interested in the case.

Krista began to shake her head, then remembered the photo that she'd found. "I found a strange photo album the other day that someone put behind my files in the cabinet. I don't know why it was there. I took it home, so maybe they were looking for it? Do you want to see it?" Krista asked.

"It might be helpful and possibly give us something to go on. Are there surveillance cameras in this office?" He asked.

"Good question. Apparently there should be!" Krista said. "You'd have to ask Mr. Samuels about that. If there aren't, there should be!"

"Thank you, Ms. Burton. I'll check on that. I'm Officer Brad Wilson, by the way." He offered his hand. Krista shook his hand. "Thank you, Officer. I'm glad someone doesn't think I'm overreacting to this. I appreciate you speaking with him. He doesn't seem to be taking this seriously." Krista wasn't into bashing her boss, but it was true. If he wanted to take it to the school board, she'd be ready. "I'll get you that picture tomorrow morning if that's okay."

"That would be fine. Just bring it down to the police department and ask for me, okay?" Officer Wilson said. After the officer left, Krista returned to her office and started cleaning up the mess. She couldn't even begin to imagine what the person (probably Jane) was looking for. As she was putting her office back together, Mr. Samuels knocked on the open door. "May I come in?"

"Sure." She wished she could tell him where to go. Krista waited for his tirade.

"Krista, I'm very sorry about this happening." He looked around the office and finally got a good look at the damage and how messed up this really was. "I am too." Krista kept her response to a minimum, as she continued to pick up her files and put them back in her desk. She didn't want to say anything she'd regret.

"I just want to let you know that I'll stay in touch with police about this situation." Mr. Samuels continued on. "We'll find out who did this and make sure it doesn't happen again." Krista nodded.

"Well, you might want to start with Jane as a person of interest. I'm almost positive she had something to do with this. Keep in mind she left today after giving her five-minute notice. But I've already told you that." Krista replied as she continued the clean-up. She was too upset to be around anyone at this point. She looked up at the clock. It was 1:15. "I've got an appointment to go to. I'll talk with you later."

Krista grabbed her purse and jacket to leave for her appointment with Nadine. There was no way she was going to miss it.

Chad

After a crazy morning with Nancy quitting, Chad dove into his work. His first call was to Caroline Ahearn to schedule another appointment with her. He felt uneasy, especially since he knew his boss's instructions were to get a picture of her. Caroline picked up on the second ring. "Hello, Chad. It's good to hear from you so soon." Her voice was warm and soothing.

"Caroline, it's good to speak with you again too. I was calling to schedule another appointment, see if we can get things moving with your property. I'd like to come out and take some pictures to prepare to list the house and get ready for an open house. When are you available?" Chad answered.

"You know me from being here already. I'm pretty open for anytime!" Caroline laughed.

"Is this afternoon too soon? I don't have any afternoon appointments and I could get out there about 3:00 depending on the ferry schedule." Chad didn't want to waste any time. He looked at the clock. It was 1:25. "Actually, let me try to catch the 3:00 ferry. I'll take the high speed that will take about half an hour and be there by 4:00 at the latest. Does that work for you?"

"Um…. Yes, I think that would be fine." Caroline seemed conflicted, but agreed.

"Are you sure it's not too short notice? I can schedule another time." Chad sensed that she sounded hesitant.

"It's fine, really. I'd rather get the house on the market sooner than later." Caroline said.

"See you soon, then." Chad hung up and quickly looked up the ferry schedule. There was one leaving at 2:30. He grabbed his briefcase and headed out. On his way through the reception area, he called out, "Nancy—I mean Kate!" The young red-haired receptionist nodded and smiled. He'd been so busy he'd almost forgotten that Nancy was gone. "Kate, I'm going to the Block Island property so I won't be back in the office today. Please take messages if anyone needs to talk to me. Thank you!" Chad felt sorry for her. She was thrown into this position at the last minute. But he was glad that Nancy was gone. She had been a time bomb, holding him hostage because of his bad decisions. He swore to himself that he would never give in to temptation again. He wanted his relationship with Krista to get back on track.

He jumped into his car and headed to Point Judith to catch the 2:30 ferry to Block Island. He was worried about the time. From Warwick to Point Judith was at least 30 minutes unless he stepped on it. He couldn't help thinking of Nancy and her decision to just leave with no notice, and it made him worry even more. Why did she leave so suddenly? Chad tried to rationalize with himself that she just found another job and left. But leaving without some kind of notice was bizarre. In his brief discussions with her during their after hour trysts, Nancy had mentioned how she didn't have anyone in her life, including her parents. She even mentioned how much she missed her parents and when he had asked about them, she explained that they had been in a terrible accident and were deceased. She never talked about the details, but she always seemed angry when she mentioned them. He just hoped she wouldn't spill details of their affair. He wasn't sure how he or Krista could begin to repair that, especially now.

He finally reached Point Judith with just enough time to get on the ferry. He breathed a sigh of relief as the boat was pulling away from the dock. He knew he could nail down this sale. He was secretly planning a get away for him and Krista once the property sold and he was able to take some time off. They'd had a couple of rough months and were ready for a vacation. He looked out to the sea, as the ferry sped away, toward what he hoped would be their ticket to more money and freedom.

As the ferry docked, Chad got back in his car, ready to head to Mohegan Bluffs as soon as he could. It was 3:15. It looked like he could make it to the property by 3:30. He called Caroline to let her know that he was almost there. The phone rang several times and went to voicemail. 'Maybe she was outside and didn't hear the phone,' he thought. As soon as he was given the go ahead from the ferry crew, he sped off toward the Ahearn property at Mohegan Bluffs. At 3:30 on the dot, Chad pulled up to the mansion that still took his breath away. He parked his car in the circular driveway and rang the doorbell.

He heard several voices in the house and suddenly the door opened. His mouth gaped open when Nancy, or someone who looked exactly like her, opened the door. "Nancy?" Chad managed to ask. "What are you doing here?"

"Nancy? I'm sorry. You have me confused with someone else. My name is Amanda. Amanda Ahearn. Can I help you?" The woman in front of him was Nancy. He was sure of it. The curly dark hair, the curves, the dark eyes and her exotic features were all too familiar. She had a satisfied smirk on her face that told him he was right. What the hell?

"I'm sorry. You just look like someone I know." Chad managed to regain his composure. He was sure it was Nancy, but he wasn't going to argue with her. He couldn't lose this potential sale because of a secretary that used her alias for working at Carson Reality. Why the hell would she do that when she was part of the Ahearn fortune?

"No, problem, I get that all the time." Nancy-Amanda tossed her head. Combining her names was the best way for Chad to remember who she really was. "Is Mrs. Ahearn here? We had an appointment."

"Why, yes, she is. I'll let her know that you're here. Please come on in, Mr. Burton." She replied sweetly and winked at him. Chad swallowed hard. This was going to be the most interesting home visit of his real estate career and of his life as ' Nancy-Amanda' invited him in and closed the door.

"I don't believe I introduced myself. How did you know my name?" Chad was curious to how she was going to get away with this one.

Nancy-Amanda was silent for moment and he could almost see the wheels turning. "Caroline let me know that someone named Mr. Burton was coming to see the house. I assumed that was you." She seemed triumphant with her quick response, but Chad wasn't buying it.

"Yeah, right." Chad said. "I know who you are."

Krista

She made it to her appointment with Nadine right on time despite the drama from her morning. As she parked her car, she was feeling anxious, unsure about what she was doing here, but what the hell. It was better than a psychiatrist telling her she was having a mental breakdown and at this point, that was the last thing she needed to hear. As soon as she arrived, Nadine appeared, "Hello, Krista. How are you today?" She had the same youthful look about her; casual dress, ponytail and her Birkenstocks.

"I'm fine. Just interested in what you have to tell me, I guess," Krista said nervously. Nadine smiled reassuringly. "No pressure here, just learning new information, relax, ok?" Krista nodded, "Ok. Thanks."

Nadine smiled. "Well, let's get started. I'm already sensing some energy from you." Krista wasn't surprised by that. 'She'd have to be completely oblivious not to notice my anxiety', Krista thought to herself. Nadine guided her to a nearby room with low lighting and a faint lavender scent. She placed a set of cards in front of her. "Okay, Krista, I want you to shuffle these cards and while you're doing that, think of yourself, your life, anything that is troubling you. Krista did as she asked and then placed them down. Nadine picked up the first card, and began to set them down in a cross like sequence. "I see that

159

you're stressed. There are many things in your life confusing and upsetting to you right now."

"That's an understatement!" Krista said wryly.

Nadine began placing down more cards. She stopped for a moment. "What's the matter?" Krista asked, feeling her palms and armpits getting damp again. She was glad she didn't forget her deodorant today.

"Hold on, Krista." Nadine closed her eyes and sat back in her chair for seemed like an eternity.

"Nadine? Is everything okay?" Krista's anxiety kicked into high gear. 'Maybe this wasn't a good idea after all. What if this girl was having some kind of a medical emergency? Oh my god.' Just as Krista was ready to offer to call for help, Nadine sat back up.

"Krista, someone is trying to help you. Do you have a sister?" Nadine asked. Krista remembered her asking this the last time she was here. In fact, she'd followed her out the door announcing that.

"No, like I said last time. I don't." Krista insisted. What was with this sister thing?

"She's insistent. She's trying to help. She's saying 'don't be afraid of me. I won't hurt you. I'm trying to help you.'" Nadine looked straight at her. Krista had a flashback of being on a cliff and someone calling her name. Then she remembered last night's dream where she saw and heard the little girl and was about to open the gold box. The voice was telling her she was there to help her.

"I...I think I can see this person in my dreams. I've been having nightmares, and sleepwalking. She looks identical to me. It's almost as if she knows me." Krista felt like she was babbling nonsense now, but that was how it was coming back to her. "What's her name?" Krista wanted to know.

"Karen. Her name is Karen." Nadine nodded as she spoke. "She says she's your sister and that you're in danger of people that are trying to hide the truth."

"Karen! That was the name on my calendar that day." Krista remembered. Was it her? "How do I have a sister that I don't know about?"

Nadine was silent for a moment and pulled out more cards that Krista had no idea what they meant. After a minute or so, she asked again. "Nadine, how is this person my sister? I grew up without any siblings!" She was feeling suddenly weak and shaky. Nadine put her hand up, "Krista, please just wait a few moments." She continued with the cards and looking past Krista as if she were seeing someone behind her. Krista turned around just to see. Nope. Not that she could see anyway.

Finally, Nadine spoke about the meaning of the cards, and why she was looking behind Krista. "There was some kind of an accident, Krista, a long time ago. You did have a sister. A twin sister. You were both very young, likely less than four years old. She's always been here with you."

Krista was stunned. What? Why would her father keep this from her? This couldn't be true. He would never do that! "This is hard to believe to be honest, Nadine. I'm not criticizing you, or your abilities, but there is no way my father would've kept this from me." Then she remembered the article that someone had put in her car; the article about the car accident and the child who died. "That article! That was the accident that killed her!" Krista said suddenly.

Nadine nodded. "She did die in an accident. Krista's face became pale, as Nadine continued. "Krista, I understand this is hard to hear. Again, I'm only repeating what I see and hear. This is who has been trying to contact you all this time. All your dreams are a way of Karen contacting you. It's very rare that entities can make a physical presence."

Krista remembered the writing on the calendar, the picture in the file and the phone call, the article put in her car. "So, let me get this straight. There was an accident, I have a twin sister that talks to me and follows me through dreams. However, she can't write down names on a calendar, put articles in my car, put a picture in my file cabinet or make prank phone calls?"

Nadine nodded. "When people pass, they become an entity, a soul that has no physical presence. There are a few rare cases, of course, where there are some that are able to make physical contact and create what you've described. Karen didn't do what you've described. It's very difficult for them to do so, and must have a specific purpose, not just to play tricks on someone. Most souls will reach out within dreams or sometimes with a brief vision, but nothing like what you see in most horror movies. It's more complicated than that. Trust me. Karen is not responsible for those events." Nadine looked behind Krista just then and nodded her head in response to something.

"Was that her? Is she here?" Krista asked and turned around instinctively. Of course no one was there. Not that she could see her anyway. Doubt crept in again, but Krista knew that there was a reason for these dreams. They were ongoing, night after night. And this girl was identical to her, so if what Nadine said was true about Karen being her twin, this made sense. Krista felt somewhat comforted to know that there wasn't a ghost running around writing on calendars and putting photos in desks. But *someone* was doing it. It was someone that was very alive and trying to make her look like she was having a mental breakdown.

"Yes. She is here. I can't see her, but I can hear what she's saying." Nadine nodded. "She's saying that you're in danger, as well as your mother and your father."

"My mother? What about my mother? Is my mother alive? Really?" Krista stood up quickly without thinking. "My mother?" Nadine motioned for her to sit down. Krista sat back down, shaking. "I can't believe that she's mentioning my mother!"

Nadine nodded again. "Try to stay seated, Krista. It helps with the energy and I do want to help you. Karen does as well."

Krista nodded, in shock about what she'd heard. "My mother's alive?" She spoke in a whisper. All these years she was led to believe that her mother passed away after leaving her and her father. Nadine nodded again. "She is, but she's in danger, as are you. That's probably why Karen has made her presence known after all these years. She wants to help you. She wants to help all of you."

Krista tried to take all this in for a moment. She was hopeful and excited that her mother was still alive. The next minute the hope turned to anger, then sadness; her mother failing to reach out to her, and her father failing to tell her about her twin sister. She felt tears running down her face but she brushed them away. "Anything else I should know?" Krista asked. What else had her father been hiding from her?

Nadine nodded. "Karen has always been watching over you. She says that she was there with you when you were still a child. She remembers having pretend parties and talking to you. She wants to know if you remember."

Krista nodded, tears still running down her face. She knew. She remembered having tea parties with her, and talking to someone when she was little. She remembered now. It was Karen. Her father assumed it was an 'imaginary friend' but it was really Karen. She no longer had doubts and believed in what Nadine was saying to her. She'd always felt something was missing in her life and now she knew why. "Tell her I'm sorry I didn't remember her because I was too young, but I know now. She's my sister. Tell her I wish I'd known her. Tell her I wish she was still here with me." Tears were falling in streams down Krista's face. It was overwhelming for someone to confirm what she'd probably known all along, at least as a child.

Nadine nodded. "She knows. She's with you. She wants you to know that. She's always with you. She wants you to keep moving on with your life. That's why she's here."

Krista collected herself and wiped the tears away. "Thank you so much, Nadine. This has been so helpful today."

Nadine smiled. "I'm so glad you came back. Not for business, but because Karen was really a strong presence the first time you were here. That's why I was insistent on talking to you. You're lucky, you know."

"How can I possibly be lucky?" Krista asked her. She'd just found out that she had a twin sister that had died when they were so young, she didn't remember. Her father lied to her about her sister. She was grateful that her mother was alive, but why did she leave and not come back?

"Most people don't have someone watching out for them or warning them." Nadine advised. "You *are* lucky. If you dream about her, let her lead you. Don't be afraid anymore."

Krista nodded after a moment. "You're right. Thank you so much for seeing me on short notice, Nadine." She handed her a hundred-dollar bill even though the session was only supposed to be fifty. "I appreciate you fitting me in today, Nadine. I'm sure I'll be back." Krista gave her a slight hug and left.

Chad

After Nancy-Amanda led him into the front hallway, Chad stood uncomfortably, waiting for the host he was expecting. Caroline. After a few seconds of standing there, he called out, "Is Caroline here? I had an appointment with her this afternoon." Nancy-Amanda was in the kitchen, and supposedly let Caroline know that he was here.

"Oh, yes, she's upstairs. She'll be down in a moment." Nancy-Amanda assured him. She hadn't said a word to him, except to excuse herself to make coffee. He felt so uncomfortable; he was ready to jump out of his skin. He was positive she was Nancy, which was obviously an alias, and had just quit her job this morning. For a brief moment, he considered running out the door, taking the next ferry back and insisting that William assign another realtor on the property. Just then, Caroline appeared at the top of the stairs. "Hello, Chad, how're you?" She looked completely different from last week. Her hair was longer than he remembered, and she was wearing some kind of shapeless dress that made her look so much older than she actually was. Her eyes lacked the warmth from their last meeting. Chad could tell something wasn't right, but greeted her as if nothing was wrong.

"Chad, you've met my stepdaughter, Amanda?" Caroline asked.

"Yes, I have." Chad answered, although he wanted to add that she looked identical to his former secretary named Nancy that quit her job this morning. He hoped to minimize his time here today, as he was feeling exceptionally awkward.

"Caroline, could we go ahead and go through the house again and get specific details about what you want to take with you upon the sale of this property? I also need to take some pictures to go forward with listing the house." He figured it was best if he stuck to the usual protocol. The easy rapport of the last visit here was gone. It was as if Caroline was a completely different person than she was the first time he met with her. Nancy-Amanda's presence was not helpful either. He felt as though he was being stalked.

"Absolutely, let's start in the kitchen." Caroline showed the way and as Chad followed her, he noted that Nancy-Amanda did as well. He was getting annoyed already and there were so many other rooms to go through. "Caroline, could I speak with you a moment?" Chad asked suddenly. He intended to suggest that her stepdaughter allow them to finish the tour by themselves.

"Of course, Chad." Caroline smiled but Chad could sense that she was tense, on edge, and her voice sounded as if she were choosing her words carefully. Nancy-Amanda tried to follow but Caroline held up her hand. "Amanda, please. Let me speak with Chad on my own. I'm quite capable of having my own conversations." Nancy-Amanda looked irritated, but she backed off as they moved into another room.

As soon as she assumed Amanda was out of earshot, she turned her attention to him.

"Chad, I'm so sorry that she's here. She's Stanley's daughter and she showed up unexpectedly today. Try to forget that she's here." Caroline advised.

"Does she live here?" Chad was confused. It must have been a long commute to Carson Reality during the time she worked there, if that was the case.

"Oh no! Amanda never comes here, unless she's throwing a party. She's only here when she wants to be. She's usually traveling around partying with her celebrity friends. She showed up this morning out of nowhere." Caroline seemed less annoyed than would be expected to Chad. "She works sometimes, but then leaves and Stanley places her somewhere else, hoping she'll start making him proud. I think she will someday" The last statement seemed like an afterthought.

"Is she throwing a party tonight?" Chad had to ask. Otherwise, why would she be here? It was too much of a coincidence for her to happen to be here at the same time as he was coming to help sell the house.

Caroline shook her head. "No, I think it's because she's spying on us. She found out we were planning to sell and she's against it. She loves coming here to throw her private parties. I do love it here, though." She seemed almost dreamy and cautious about selling now, almost backtracking. She suddenly snapped back, as if she'd just forgotten the rehearsed lines of her part in a play. "Just focus on the house." Caroline whispered to him, yet seemed preoccupied with Nancy-Amanda's presence, almost as if she were being judged on a performance.

"Fine, Caroline. Let's move onto the bedrooms upstairs," Chad said. Caroline's strange demeanor was starting to make him wonder, but he knew he needed to keep calm. If Nancy-Amanda was trying to hide her anger about her father selling this property, she wasn't doing a good job. He could see her facial expressions of contempt reflecting in the mirror across from them. He almost wanted to laugh. The fact that he was dealing with a former secretary, who was an imposter and was in fact, Stanley Ahearn's daughter was completely ridiculous to him. What else could happen today? He took many pictures of every room at several angles, but could never get one of Caroline in view.

Caroline led him upstairs to the master bedroom. "Here's the master bedroom. As you can see there's a master bath off the bedroom," Caroline's commentary continued. Chad tried to stay focused and take notes. However, he was well aware that Nancy-Amanda was following them and couldn't remember being more uncomfortable. After over an hour of touring the entire house, Chad asked to move outside, more to get away from the suffocating feeling he had with Nancy-Amanda following them than anything else. With the knowledge that she was following, he was even more careful of what he and Caroline discussed.

Caroline led him to the pool area, then to the cliffs that made this house even more valuable. As he and Caroline looked over the cliffs, he couldn't remember anything as beautiful as seeing the view of the ocean crashing down. Although he wasn't a professional photographer, the pictures he took with William's expensive Nikon captured the beauty of the landscape. "As I said before, it's a fantastic property, Caroline. I believe many people will be interested. If you want to officially put it on the market, I will do so tomorrow." Chad advised her. "Do you mind if I take a picture of the house from this view?" He asked hoping he would be able to fulfill his boss's request to get a picture of Caroline.

"Sure!" Caroline agreed, until he asked her to be in the background. "I don't think so. I'd rather not." Caroline declined. Somehow she'd managed to not be in any of the photos he'd taken so far.

"Oh, Caroline, it would be a great picture! After all, this is your house. You've worked hard to make it look this amazing!" Chad tried his best. But Caroline turned away, as he tried to take her picture.

"I'd rather not. I'm sorry, Chad. Stanley's always in the spotlight. I've been there before. It's not my thing." Her face suddenly took on a menacing expression that he caught before she quickly looked away.

"I understand, Caroline. No problem." Chad would just explain to William he'd tried, but she had really made it impossible, especially with Nancy-Amanda following them every step of the way.

Suddenly Amanda appeared from behind a tree in the distance. "If you want to take pictures of someone, I'll volunteer!" She came out suddenly. Chad masked his disgust for her. "No, that's okay. I've taken enough for today."

Nancy-Amanda was not having no for an answer. "Oh, c'mon. Just one. Look, I'll pose with my step-mom." She tried to put her arm around Caroline, who removed her arm and moved away. "Amanda, please, that's enough."

"Okay, well, just one of me. I insist." Nancy-Amanda over posed like an amateur for Cover Girl and Chad took the obligatory picture just to get her to shut up. He could tell how upset Caroline was with her behavior. It made him sick that he'd ever had anything to do with this horrible woman. Chad had an instinct that something wasn't right with Caroline, but couldn't put his finger on it. Maybe it was Nancy-Amanda's presence that would explain why Caroline's appearance and demeanor was so different? He wasn't sure.

"Okay, I think we have enough to put this on the market, Caroline," Chad let her know as they left the cliffs and moved back inside. "I'm sure we'll have many offers very soon. It's a beautiful property and the price is beyond reasonable." Chad could feel Nancy-Amanda breathing down his neck as he spoke. She'd never been out of earshot the entire time; he was sure of that.

"Thank you so much for coming out again, Chad. You've been very helpful." Caroline said politely, but lacking the genuine friendliness from his last visit.

"Thank you for letting me come here on such short notice, Caroline. These photos will be helpful in putting your property on the market. Please don't hesitate to contact me at the office. I'll give you my cell number as well." Chad gave her a card with both numbers. "Take care now. I'll be in touch in the next week once your property is listed."

He turned to walk out the door when Amanda followed him and stood in front of him. "Seriously, Chad, you have no idea who you're dealing with, do you?"

Chad ignored her and headed to his car. He was not talking to this woman who was obviously a complete lunatic. She continued to follow him to his car. "Trust me, Chad. I know everything about you and that crazy wife of yours. You'd better be careful, because you have no idea what I can do! You'd better not put this property up for sale if you know what's good for you and your wife!" She shouted, as he got in his car, started the engine and sped away as fast as possible. As he looked in the rearview mirror, he could see her still yelling. Clearly, this Amanda had some power if her father was Stanley. He wondered if William had any idea about her. He was starting to feel scared, really scared, for himself and Kris. If she was Stanley's daughter, she likely had powerful connections, and he had no doubt that she was capable of anything. She was the epitome of evil.

William

He was just finishing up with a staff meeting when he received a text from Chad. "Please call me when you can." He finished the meeting quickly and excused himself to his office. He immediately dialed Chad's cell.

"How'd it go? Did you get a picture?" He was eager for some news.

"I think you'd better brace yourself, William. Things just got a whole lot more complicated." Chad said, still trying to wrap his head around the situation at hand.

"Brace myself? For what?" William suddenly felt a cold chill. If Chad couldn't handle this sale, something was really wrong.

"This is going to sound nuts, but I swear, it's true. Nancy was there when I got to the property, William! She was using an alias here all along. She's really Amanda Ahearn!" Chad started with that before he went on. "Did you know that Stanley had a daughter?"

"No, honestly, I didn't! If I'd know that, I would've never had employed her here, that's for sure!" William had to sit down in his chair. "What happened?" He was sure this wasn't going to be pretty. Just when he thought he was done with Stanley and his bullshit!

"She followed me and Caroline around the entire time, as if she were spying. Caroline acted very uncomfortable, unlike the last time I was at the house. Clearly, Amanda's presence was upsetting to her. Amanda doesn't want the property to be sold. She told me that in so many words before I left. She's a scary person, William. She made vague threats toward Kris and I if the property was listed." He left out the part about his brief affair with her. Who knew what William would do if he found out, although Chad had suspicions that it was only a matter of time before that was revealed. It was an added reason for being so on edge about today.

"What did she say, specifically?" William asked. He was almost beside himself. He knew Stanley was a tyrant, but he was shocked that he was now allowing his children to intimidate and threaten people.

"She said, 'you'd better not sell this property if you know what's good for you. I know everything about you and that crazy wife of yours.' The look in her eyes, Bill. It was the look of someone who has no conscience. Seriously, I'm really worried. I'm also worried about Caroline. She was a totally different person than last week. She seemed intimidated by this woman. I wasn't able to get a picture of her, by the way. Amanda was following us around the entire time. I even asked her and she said no. I'm sorry, I did try. Given the situation, I felt it best not to push. Like I said, Amanda's presence was almost too creepy to describe."

William took a deep breath. He was somewhat aware that Stanley had children, but that was long ago and he assumed that they were in their respective mother's custody. But then again, that was a long time ago. How could he have missed that with Nancy? In his defense, he'd never seen pictures or met her, even as a child. He had no idea what she looked like.

"Chad, I'm so sorry that you had to deal with that. Let's talk when you get here and we can decide what to do from here. I certainly am not going to put you and Kris in danger because of this property. We may need to back off for now and see what happens. Maybe I need to talk with Stanley again. Apparently, he doesn't share his daughter's admiration for the property." He tried his best at a joke, but he was still stunned that he'd employed Stanley's daughter who was an imposter and he had no idea if she had corrupted any of his computer files, or had contact with any clients. He'd need to hire a professional computer tech to make sure she didn't infiltrate any ongoing transactions. The bitch! It figured, though. Stanley was a piece of work himself. The apple didn't fall far from the tree.

"What do you want me to do, Bill?" Chad was anxious. He was trying so hard but this was a roadblock at this point.

"Just come back home. We'll have to talk about this. Don't contact Caroline again until we talk. If she happens to call, tell her that you'll have to get back to her. We've gotta think about his one." William advised.

"Ok, Bill. Again, I'm sorry I couldn't get the picture you wanted, but I couldn't." Chad felt bad, because he knew that was important to him for reasons he didn't know.

"Chad, you did well. I'm glad you kept your wits about you and didn't push the issue. Good job escaping this Amanda person as well. I know she was a pain in the ass as Nancy. Guess we can't say she's any better with a different name, right?" William added jokingly.

"Thanks, Bill. I'll be back shortly. I'm going to check in with Kris at the house before I come back to the office, though.

"Good thinking! See you soon." William hung up. So Stanley had one of his kids staking out his business now. Unbelievable! He really was relentless. He was sure this wasn't the end of putting roadblocks up for him. Stanley never forgot anything and now he had his grown child involved. He was tempted to just forget about the property, but a part of him was drawn to it. He had always loved going to Block Island with Maria while they were dating and he knew how much she loved the cliffs. No, not giving up just yet. Maybe another call to Stanley was in order to find out what his game was now.

He dialed direct this time. William wasn't bothering with the secretary. He had his cell phone. It rang three times and went to voicemail. "Stan, It's Bill. Listen, I need to talk with you about your property. My agent went out today and your daughter was there. She made it clear that she doesn't want the house to be sold and made some vague threats toward my employee. Please call me back, so we can discuss this. Thanks." William hung up, still seething that this daughter of his had been in his employ under an alias.

He picked up the phone again and called the only person who would be able to come into his business and detect any problems or viruses in his software at the business. Ray Hanson had been just a kid in the neighborhood when he met him. He delivered the paper every day, and was like clock-work, paper delivered at 6:00am every day. He was a couple years older than Krista and although they went to the same school, they didn't know each other except for his paper route. When Ray was accepted to MIT, William gave him a generous check as a high school graduation gift. He had never forgotten William and had always said "if you need me, Mr. Carson, I'm here for you." They'd kept in touch briefly over the years when Ray came to visit his parents, but he'd never had to call on him for help. Until now.

"Hello?" A man with deep voice answered the phone. William only hoped it was still the same number from several years ago.

"Hello, may I speak to Ray Hanson, please?" William asked. He wasn't sure if it was Ray.

"This is Ray. Who's calling?"

"Hi, Ray, this is William Carson. Do you remember me?" William crossed his fingers that he did. It hadn't been that long had it? He was desperate.

"Hey, Mr. Carson, how are you? It's so great to hear from you!" Ray said.

"I'm great for the most part! I can't complain. How're you doing? Where are you living now, Ray?"

"I'm in Austin. I guess once you're in Texas, you don't come back, right?" Ray laughed.

"I bet you miss the winter's here in New England." William joked.

"I have to say no, but I do miss the season changes, for sure." Ray acknowledged.

William knew he needed to get past the niceties and move on. "So, Ray I'm calling because there's been a potential security breach at my office. To get to the point, one of the administrative persons was found to be....I'll just call it, potentially vindictive in regards to the company and quit suddenly, giving no notice. I'm concerned that she may have created viruses in our computer systems here involving confidentiality breaches that could cause problems. I was hoping that you might have time to come up and help us out, maybe find out if she did anything. I'd pay you for your time of course." William added.

"No problem, Mr. Carson. I was actually coming up to visit this weekend, so I could swing by and check it out. Would that work for you?"

William was completely surprised. He was anticipating a few weeks, but not in the next few days. "Absolutely, Ray. Are you sure? I mean it's Thursday. That's not much time to plan for this."

"It's fine, Mr. Carson. I fly in tomorrow, so I could come by on Saturday morning if that works for you?" Ray sounded upbeat. "Thank you so much, Ray, I really appreciate this!" William said.

"By the way, how is Krista?" Ray asked.

"She's doing well. She's been married for a few years now, working as a school counselor. Yeah, she's doing very well."

'That's great for her. Good to know she's doing well." Ray sounded as though he were disappointed. William couldn't help but remember how much he hoped that Krista and Ray would've taken an interest in each other. He knew Ray had always had a crush on Krista.

"I'll tell her you said hello." William acknowledged politely. He needed to get off the phone. "So Ray, can I expect you this Saturday? Just meet me at the office."

"I'll see you there! About 10:00?" Ray suggested. William agreed. He was just hoping that he didn't have to share this with the rest of his staff, including Chad.

"I'll see you then." William hung up the phone feeling less anxious. He knew that Ray was an honest guy. If Stanley's daughter had messed with the computer system or breached any confidentiality, he'd find it.

Krista

Krista wasn't sure how to feel as she left Nadine's. She was so conflicted; angry, yet sad. There were so many people involved that she wasn't sure how to feel about each one of them. As she got behind the wheel, she sat for a moment. She looked at her phone and noticed that she had three texts from Jennifer from the past few days that she'd never responded to. She suddenly felt like a horrible friend for not responding and immediately dialed her number instead of texting. She anticipated Jen not picking up and was surprised when she heard her friend's voice. "Kris? Oh, my god! I'm so glad you called! I was worried about you!" Jen's voice sounded upset.

"I'm so sorry, Jen. Things have been crazy this week. You don't even know." Krista went on to fill her in on the latest including the file picture, the cryptic phone call at Chad's office party and the complete destroying of her office, along with the receptionist quitting the same day. After almost twenty minutes of nonstop relaying everything that had happened, Krista felt exhausted. "Sorry to dump that on you all at once, Jen, but that's why I've been a ghost for the past week. What do you think?"

"I don't know what to think. What are you doing about it?" Jen wanted to know. She knew Krista was susceptible to being duped because she was so caring.

"I just visited that psychic again. I feel so confused, angry, and everything in between. She says that I had a twin sister, Karen, that died when we were little and that my dreams are her letting me know that I'm in danger and she's trying to protect me." Krista tried to condense it into the short version.

"Are you serious? Kris, c'mon now. I know you better than that! Are you going to believe some psychic?" Jen's reaction was shocking to Krista. They were usually on the same page.

Krista felt her anger boil over and lost it. "What? How dare you say that to me? You're supposed to be my friend. Are you trying to insist that I'm crazy, like everyone else? Well, I believe her. The dreams are real, Jen, whether you believe me or not!"

"I'm sorry, Kris. Really, I am. I didn't know that the dreams were that disruptive. I just don't understand why you're seeing a psychic about these things. Wouldn't it be better to see a psychiatrist? Or even a hypnotist?" Jen's tone was sincere as she tried to calm down her friend.

"No. I feel like I have the truth for once. No, I don't want to see a doctor that's going to push medications that I don't need!" Krista insisted. "I need to go. I have to call Chad. He had his visit at the Block Island property today. I'll talk to you later." She hung up without waiting for Jen's response. She was tired of people thinking she was being dramatic about the dreams. They were impacting her waking life in a negative way.

Although she was almost home, she dialed Chad's number. He answered on the first ring. "Hi, honey, I was just going to call you. Are you home?" Chad asked.

"Almost there. I'm curious about the Ahearn house visit today. How'd thing's go?" Krista decided to wait until she was home to tell him about her psychic visit today. She wasn't looking forward to it.

"I'll tell you about it when I get home, okay?" Chad sounded upset. Krista's heart sank. She was hoping one of them would have good news.

"Okay babe. I'll see you at home." Kris tried not to sound upset as she pulled into their driveway.

Chad

As he pulled in the driveway, he felt his palms starting to sweat already. This morning everything was somewhat back to normal between he and his wife. Now, it was likely that things were going to go south. Nancy quitting this morning was like a huge relief, but the afternoon was a punch in the face when she appeared as Amanda, Stanley Ahearn's daughter. She'd threatened him. He knew that it only be a matter of time before she'd be using their affair in a way to screw him and his life as he knew it now.

Krista was in front of the TV watching a rerun of The Voice, and drinking a glass of red wine when he walked in. "Hey, there, how was your day?" He asked, trying to sound as upbeat as possible.

She got up from the couch and gave him a hug. "It was interesting, that's for sure." On closer inspection, Chad noticed her eyes were puffy and red, her face blotchy, which always happened when she'd been crying.

"Kris, what's wrong?" Chad gave her a kiss on the cheek. Krista was silent for a moment.

"How can you tell something's wrong? I'm fine." She sniffed, trying to hold back the tears that were welling up again.

"Kris, I know you. You've been crying. And you're getting ready to cry again. What's going on?" Chad asked, moving over to the couch and put his arm around her. What if Amanda had already called her and told her about the affair? His heart began to pound as he realized this was more than a possibility. "Is it your dad, or someone at work?" Chad was hoping to get a grasp on what was going on before he actually found out. He wanted to be prepared.

"No nothing like that. Well, part of it is my dad, given the circumstances, I guess." Krista brushed her sleeve across her eyes. She took a deep breath, as if working up to tell him what was going on. "So, I know you think that psychics are a bunch of phonies and make up stuff, but since I've had all these dreams, I decided to go back." Kris started.

"Kris, you didn't. Really?" Chad tried to conceal his annoyance, knowing she was already upset.

"I know. I know what you think. But this girl knows things about me that I've never told her, or even knew myself. So anyway, she told me that I had a sister. A twin sister, named Karen."

"That was that name written on your calendar." Chad remembered.

"Exactly. She said that Karen died when we were very young, around three years old. She says that Karen has been watching over me and that I'm in danger, as well as my mom and dad!"

Chad was still trying to take in that this psychic had suggested she had a twin sister. "In danger from what or who? And what do you mean, your mom? You haven't seen your mom since you were a kid. I thought she took off. You and your father both made it sound like she wasn't alive anymore."

"I didn't think she was. But Nadine insists that she is alive. She kept saying that we were in danger. She told me to pay attention to the dreams. She said Karen is trying to help." Krista said. Tears were streaming down her face now.

"Kris, first of all, how sure are you that she's right? I mean, you said she knows what she's talking about, but there really isn't proof." Chad tried to hide his irritation that Kris would go back to that psychic. He was almost certain that all that Nadine was doing was filling her head full of potential nonsense.

Krista grabbed a Kleenex and wiped her tear-stained face, blew her nose. "I know there isn't concrete proof, but I remember talking to my imaginary sister when I was little. I could actually see her. She looked identical to me. We would have tea parties and she was my friend, when I went through the usual difficult middle school years. She helped me! Then my dad started taking me to counselors because he was worried about me talking to an 'imaginary friend' and then I didn't see her anymore. That is, until I began having these dreams." Krista blew her nose again, as the tears continued. "You know what upsets me most? My dad has lied to me all these years. I bet he even lied about my mom. He never came out and told me that she had died, but he acted like she had. I can't believe he would do this to me." Krista broke down and sobbed in Chad's arms.

Chad wasn't sure what to think about Krista's news. He had no faith in psychics. He thought they were quacks and took innocent people's money. He also knew that Krista's dreams were real, at least to her, and that it was affecting her and their lives together. He held her while trying to come up with a plan to talk to William.

"I don't know how to begin talking to my dad about this. I know my mom is a hard topic to bring up with him. But the fact that he hasn't ever told me that I had a sister, that she was killed; that just makes me feel.......well, like I can't trust him. As if I'm not worthy of the truth, I guess. Does that make sense?" Krista asked.

"I understand, Kris, I do. But I also know your dad. I really think he was just trying to protect you." Chad knew how William doted on Krista. But if the twin sister had in fact existed, he felt like William owed it to Krista to tell her the truth when she was old enough to understand. Yet, he also understood how much William didn't want to upset his daughter.

"I know he cares, but I'm an adult. He should have told me. I'm not even sure how I can face him now, let alone talk to him about this." Krista's tears were rolling again. She wasn't sure how she could have any tears left after this afternoon. "Then, there's my mom. I mean,

Nadine said she was alive, and in danger. He made it seem as though she was gone. He never said it, but I thought she had died."

Chad held her and tried to come up with a solution that Kris would be able to handle at this point. "Let's sleep on it. Tomorrow, we'll come up with a way for you to get the answers from your dad. After all, you do remember, all these new revelations are coming from a psychic? I mean, she could be wrong." Chad didn't want to push that issue, but he wanted her to recognize that all this heartache might be just a ploy for the psychic to get her to return.

"I know. I honestly wish she was wrong, Chad. I do. If I had a choice, I'd like to go back to how amazingly simple our lives seemed to be just a few weeks ago." Krista gave her husband a hug. She suddenly felt closer to Chad than she had in a long time. Chad hugged her back. "I'm here for you, Kris. We'll talk to your dad together. When you're ready, okay?"

"Thanks, babe. I love you." Krista said, feeling emotionally closer to her husband after all these weeks of awkwardness and arguments. "I love you too, Kris. I'm always here for you." Chad gave her a kiss. "Let's just relax tonight and we'll tackle this in the morning."

"At least I won't have to deal with Jane anymore!" Krista joked. She couldn't believe she'd forgotten this morning's drama. She smiled at Chad's surprised face. "Yeah, she quit today. It was kind of weird. She didn't give a notice. "Oh, yeah, she destroyed my office today! I don't have proof, but I know it was her. This is how my day started. I had to file a police report." Krista couldn't believe she'd forgotten to tell her husband about this morning. She told him about her office, the principal's reaction and the police.

"What? Are you kidding me?" Chad sat up. She definitely won the prize for the worst day between the two of them!

"Yeah, that was my morning. My office was destroyed, talking to the principal and making a police report. I don't know what I was thinking about going to the psychic, but I already had an appointment." Krista laughed suddenly.

Chad watched his wife laugh after discussing her morning of a violation of her office and making a police report. "Are you okay, Kris? Seriously?" He was concerned now. Maybe she was having a nervous breakdown?

Krista smiled and gave him a hug. "Honey, don't worry. I'm fine. I'm not going to lose it now. I'm okay. Actually, it's good that she's gone. Less stress for me! I'm pretty sure everyone that works in my office feels the same way. Besides, the police will find out, and if it isn't her, then they'll find out, right? I have more important things going on now."

Chad gave his wife another huge hug. "Honey, I'm so proud of you. You've had the worst day, and you're dealing with it so well." Plus, it meant that he didn't have to share what happened with Nancy-Amanda today. At least not tonight.

William

He was just entering his office the next morning, when Kate, the new receptionist said, "Mr. Carson, you have a call from Stanley Ahearn on line one. Should I take a message?"

"No. Please give me a minute. I'll take the call. Thank you, Kate." William gave her a smile as he unlocked his office. He didn't usually lock it, but since Nancy turned out to be sketchy, he wasn't taking any chances. He took a deep breath as he saw the red light blinking on hold and picked it up.

"Hello, Stanley. Thank you for returning my call." William wasn't sure what would come of this call, but pretty sure it was going to be interesting.

"What's going on Bill? You're the one that called me." Stanley said in an irritated tone.

"I guess I'm curious to know if you had a hand in your daughter working for me and scheming under another name. Really, Stanley? After all this time, do we have to still play games like this?" William didn't mince words. If there was any moment in time that he wished he'd never met Stanley Ahearn, it was now.

"What do you mean? I guess I don't get what you're saying, Bill. My daughters are adults. They have their own lives. I don't monitor them or what they do!" Stanley's surprise was apparent at Williams' accusation.

"I mean, your daughter, Amanda, came to my company and worked for almost a year under an alias, quit with no notice, then showed up at your Block Island property when one of my colleagues was preparing for a sale. Are you kidding me, you really didn't know about this?" William wasn't buying it.

"Bill, I honestly didn't know. Amanda has told me that she's been in Boston for the past year, working as an intern at Massachusetts General, going through nursing school. I haven't seen much of her in the past year, come to think of it." Stanley sounded confused.

"Well, I think it's beyond what we had agreed on. I've done what you've asked. I've had to keep the truth from people I care the most about. The least you could do is keep your family members from meddling with my business and my employees. I was also under the impression that you were in agreement to sell your property." William was straight to the point.

"I am in agreement, Bill. I believe I told you that the last time we spoke." Stanley raised his voice. He didn't like being challenged by anyone.

"According to one of my sales associates, your daughter did everything in her power to interfere with the sale, including trying to intimidate him with threats." William wasn't backing down either. He drew the line at Krista being threatened.

"Bill, I swear I didn't know any of this. I will find out and put a stop to it. The property is for sale, regardless of what my daughter's wishes are. I know she is fond of the place. But I own it, and I will talk with her. Trust me, she won't be a problem going forward." Stanley said.

"I hope not. After all, your wife is the one that contacted us, Stanley. If you didn't want to sell, I'm sure you would've told me that the last time we spoke." William was still skeptical about Stanley's intentions.

"I get it, Bill. I will talk with my daughter and set her straight. Okay?" Stanley sounded irritated.

"Thank you, Stanley. I appreciate it." William replied. "The next time I talk to you, I hope it will be to close on the sale of your property." He hung up, and tried to picture Stanley having any kids at all. It still shocked him that he had a daughter. He'd never seemed like a family type. He was always about himself and his work, so it wasn't surprising that he didn't have a clue what his daughter was up to. He just hoped that Stanley could do as promised and keep her out of the sale from now on.

Chad knocked on his door a few minutes later. "Hey, Bill, how's it going? Did you get a chance to talk to Stanley about the nonsense that went on yesterday?" Chad looked anxious as he sat down in one of the chairs in front of William's desk.

"As a matter of fact, I just got off the phone with Mr. Ahearn. I'm not sure, but he sounded as surprised as you and I were about his daughter being employed here and then showing up at the house. Either he's taking acting lessons from his Hollywood stars, or he's really in the dark about his family. I'm thinking he probably doesn't know his kid very well. He says he thought she was in a nursing program at Mass General, which is far from what she was doing here."

"I would have to agree with you, Bill." Chad said. All the while he was waiting for the other shoe to drop about their affair, but William said nothing. 'Maybe she kept her mouth shut for once.' Chad thought.

"Well, I contacted a former colleague that will be in town tomorrow. He's an IT guy that will check out the computer systems for breach of security. I don't trust Stanley's daughter anymore than I trust him. It'll cost me but I'm not taking any chances." William assured Chad.

"Good thinking. She sure didn't give much of a notice, and she was acting pretty sketchy before she quit. She seemed to be on the phone with personal calls and running an hour late coming back from lunch." It was halfway true anyway. He was still worried that she would make a call or show up to talk about their affair.

William patted him on the shoulder. "I'm sure she didn't make too much of a mess of things that my IT guy can't fix." Chad nodded in agreement. It would be less stressful for them to know that there weren't any viruses in their software, but he honestly didn't think that Nancy had been that smart to implement any kind of computer malfunctions. She wasn't dumb, but she wasn't all that smart either. She had missed the train when it came to her father's brilliance at directing movies for sure.

Krista

The new receptionist, Sara, who was transferred from another department, was a godsend. She was young, probably in her mid-twenties, good-natured and eager to please. Krista was relieved that work did not involve Jane any longer, but she felt a different black cloud over her head now. She knew she needed to confront her father about Karen's existence.

After hearing from Nadine, she was ready to head over to her father's house and have it out with him. Now that she'd had some time to think it over, she kept hearing Chad's voice of reason. That maybe Nadine was wrong, that she never existed after all. It was a hard sell after thinking about it over and over again. She knew she needed to talk to her dad, but she also needed to approach it when she wasn't so emotional. Yesterday would've been a nightmare if she'd called him. Now, she was hesitant. She was fearful about bringing it up, but she knew she needed to. The dreams were enough to question the past and she needed to know.

She spent the rest of the day seeing students here and there. Jane's sudden departure made her day considerably easier though. Despite her internal conflicts, she was able to manage now. Although she still was having some dreams that woke her up, she wasn't sleepwalking. She also realized there hadn't been any strange items or references that couldn't be explained. It was another reason why she was hesitant to talk to her father about Nadine's insistence about Karen. What if he thought she was crazy? What if Chad thought she was crazy? 'I need to stop worrying about this,' Krista told herself. Her phone rang just then.

"This is Krista," she answered. All she could hear on the other end was a static noise, almost like the wind. "Hello? This is Krista?" She could faintly hear a small child's voice in the background. "HELP!" The wind noise grew louder. "Hello, this is Krista, can I help you?" She became more concerned. What if it was one of her students?

"HELP ME!" The shrillness of the voice scared her. Krista shook her head, trying to figure out what to do next. Her office door was slightly open and she looked around, hoping to catch someone's eye about this strange phone call. The voice sounded like a young child, so there was no way it was one of her students. Sara saw her waving and came into her office. "Mrs. Burton, is everything okay?"

"Hello, hello, is anyone there?" Krista asked. The phone went dead. She hung up and looked at Sara, trying to compose herself. "Yes, Sara. It's fine. They hung up. It was probably a wrong number." Krista tried to play it down, and rummaged around in her desk drawer to distract from the fact that she was trying not to panic. That voice! She'd heard it before.

"Are you okay, Mrs. Burton? You look pale." Sara observed. Krista collected herself and took a deep breath. "I'm fine, really, Sara. It was just a strange call that's all. I'm fine" she repeated, hoping she'd feel as fine as she was assuring Sara she was. But the child's voice was disturbing. Just when she thought she'd escaped the strange happenings around her. Sara watched her for a moment, and left after Krista insisted.

Krista tried to get herself back together. Just when she thought everything was back to normal. She kept hearing the child's voice in her head. She tried to shake it off and dialed Chad's number to get back to someone familiar. Even just to hear his voice would help her move out of the place that she was in now.

"Hey, Kris, you okay?" Chad answered on the third ring. He was surprised that his wife seemed fairly stable over the past few days given the news about her sister and her mistrust with her dad.

"No. I'm not. The day went fine, until just now. Someone called me. It was a child's voice. It sounded like Karen." Krista was panicked, trying not to cry.

"Honey, I'm sure it was someone that got the wrong number. Are you sure it was a child?" Chad was just leaving the office, and decided to head toward the school. He could tell Krista was on the brink of losing it.

"It was a child's voice. I've heard it before. It's the voice I hear in my dreams, when I've been sleepwalking. It's the same." Krista insisted. She refused to believe that it was a 'wrong number' or her 'imagination.'

"Okay, Kris. I'm headed to the school now. It's almost 4:00, so why don't I just drive you home and we'll pick up your car later?" Chad suggested.

Krista almost agreed, but suddenly remembered something that Nadine had told her. Karen could appear in dreams, give her signs, but she couldn't present herself in a physical way. If what Nadine said was true, there was no way that call could have come from anyone except from someone that was alive.

"No, I'm okay. I need to deal with this. I really need to find out what's going on. I'm going to find out where that call came from." Krista wiped her tears and focused on how to resolve her suspicions. Someone was obviously out to get her for what reason, she had no idea. And that someone wasn't her sister's spirit.

"Are you sure, honey? I'm only 5 minutes away." Chad asked.

"I'm sure. I'll call you back in a few minutes okay? Really, I'm okay. I was upset, but I'm okay. But thank you. Love you." Krista said.

"If you're sure, Kris, okay. I'll see you at home. Love you too." Chad was concerned, but he could tell that she was being reasonable and more logical than she had been in the past month.

"I'm sure. Talk to you soon." Krista said and hung up. She opened her office door and asked Sara if she knew who the landline carrier was for the school. "Verizon, I believe," Sara answered. "Did any calls go through you in the past 15 minutes, Sara?" Krista wanted to know.

"No, Mrs. Burton. I didn't receive any calls asking to be directed to you." Sara said. "Is everything okay?"

"I'm fine, Sara. Can you do me a favor? If a call comes in for me through reception, find out who they are, and why they're calling? Thanks!" Krista didn't wait for an answer and went back to her office. She dialed Verizon and asked for customer service. "Yes, I need to know who called 401-583-2938 in the past 15 minutes." Krista insisted after waiting on hold for what seemed like hours.

"Is this a business line, ma'am." A southern belle with a drawl named Daisy on the other end inquired. "Yes, it is. It's actually a high school landline. I have an extension to the main number, but this specific number is direct to my office phone." Krista crossed her fingers.

"Thank you. Do you mind holding a few more minutes? I'm sorry for the delay." Daisy asked. 'Such nice people down south, I should move there!' Krista thought randomly. "No, that's fine." She answered. She hoped that she would have an answer in the next few minutes. It would be a start. She waited anxiously on hold for what seemed like hours and finally Daisy came back on the line. "Ma'am? I'm so sorry for keeping you on hold for so long. It seems that someone dialed your number, during the time you requested, from a residence in Block Island, Rhode Island."

"What's the name of that residence? Can you tell me that?" Krista held her breath.

"Yes, the residence landline subscriber is Caroline Ahearn, ma'am."
Daisy said. Krista took a deep breath. "Thank you, Daisy, you've been
more than helpful. "She hung up even though Daisy was launching
into her 'anything else I can do for you' monologue. Her mind was
racing. Caroline Ahearn? It took a moment for that to sink in. Why
did that name seem so familiar? She knew she'd heard it before. Wait!
It was that woman who was selling that house that Chad was listing!
The woman on Block Island whose husband was some important
movie person! What the hell! Her mind was racing and she wasn't sure
what to think or do now. Verizon didn't make this up. They gave her
the number and it was Caroline Ahearn's landline. She couldn't dial
Chad's cell fast enough.

"What's up, Kris? You okay? I just got home." Chad picked up on
the first ring.

"What do you know about this Caroline Ahearn, Chad?" Krista
asked, sounding frantic.

"What do you mean? She's a client of ours. We're listing her estate
with us. I've told you that. Why?" Chad sounded confused.

"Because I checked with Verizon and that phone call came from
her landline! What's going on,Chad? Why would she do that?" Krista
asked.

"Hold on, Kris. There's got to be a mistake! I mean, I've met this
lady. There's no way she made that call!" Chad was insistent.

"Well, if she didn't, someone at that house did! Verizon confirmed it! Please don't tell me that you don't believe what they said!" Krista was frustrated. "You know what? I'm leaving now. I'll be home in 15 minutes!" Without waiting for his response, she hung up, grabbed her purse and coat and headed out the door. "Sara, I'm leaving a little early today. Please send any calls to my voicemail. I'll get back to them first thing in the morning." Krista instructed her.

"No problem, Mrs. Burton." Sara answered. "Is everything okay?" She asked, concerned since Krista had seemed frantic just a few moments ago.

"Yes, it's fine. I just realized I'm late for an appointment." Krista told her, as she headed out the main guidance door.

It seemed that it took forever to get home. Traffic was horrible this time of day, and Krista wasn't in the mood for waiting around. Finally, she arrived at home and ran up to the front door, almost tripping over a package that was there. "What the hell?" Krista said out loud. She picked it up. It was a small oblong package addressed to her. She wondered why Chad hadn't picked it up when he came home.

"Chad?" Krista opened the door. No answer. "Chad? I'm home!" Krista called out. No answer again.

"I assume you're looking for your husband." A female voice came from the corner of the dining room. "I think we need to have a conversation first." Krista stopped, horrified and dropped the package she was holding. It was that bitch of a secretary, Jane! She looked completely different; she wore a tight fitting pair of jeans with tight red cold shoulder-sleeved top and red stacked heels. Krista noted that she had makeup on, which she'd never worn at her job. She looked less mousy, but still not a beauty by any stretch. But the look of triumph on her face told Krista she certainly thought she was somebody and she wasn't taking no for an answer.

"What the fuck are you doing in my house? How did you get in here? Where's my husband?" Krista was furious, finally finding her voice.

"I'm the one who will do the talking here, Krista. You forgot to lock that sliding glass door, silly girl. As for your husband, I'm sure he's out running around, trying to come up for an explanation for why he isn't here." She laughed. Krista looked around her for a potential weapon. This woman wasn't right in the head. "Chad?" She called out hoping that he would answer. He didn't. "What did you do with him?" Krista faced the woman she'd hated from day one. She had never wanted to physically harm anyone in her life, but she felt the urge to throttle this woman!

Jane laughed again. "Please, Krista! Give me a little credit! He left before I let myself in. He doesn't know I'm here." She smirked as if she'd just tied someone to the railroad tracks.

Krista took a step back and felt around her purse for her mace that she carried with her. Jane was watching her.

"No need to spray me with your mace that I assume you're looking for. I'm just here to make sure you got the package and a message. Tell Chad that he can't sell that property on Block Island. That's it. That's all you have to do. Then everything will go back to your life. Although it seems a little boring if you ask me."

"Why would you want me to do that?" Krista was still trying to wrap her head around this woman being in her house, but knew she needed to keep her talking. She'd watched enough ID channel series to know that she might be packing a gun.

"You don't need to know that. All you need to know is that you need to convince your husband to not list the Block Island property." Jane insisted. She turned to the package that Krista had dropped. "Why don't you open your package, Krista? Right now." Jane's evil smile returned.

Krista was still trying to assess whether Jane had a weapon or not, and decided that it was better to comply at this point. Just when she thought the day couldn't get worse! She picked it up and opened the brown wrapper. She slowly opened the box up and almost dropped it again. Inside was a photo of Chad having sex with another woman, whom she didn't recognize at first, but at closer glance, she saw her profile and remembered her from Chad's work party. It was Nancy! Not that it mattered who she was. The pictures showed enough of Chad's face to know that it wasn't someone that just looked like him. Jane smiled like someone who'd just won the lottery when she saw Krista's expression. "That's right, Krista. That's your husband. He's having sex with another woman. He's not quite your knight in shining armor is he?" She laughed again. "Enjoy, there's more photos. And don't try to convince yourself those are photo-shopped. You're a smart girl, I'm sure you can tell the difference. You have 24 hours to get your husband and your father to stop going forward with the sale of that Block Island property."

"What if I don't?" Krista asked, still reeling from this crazy woman breaking into her home and the pictures. Her hands were shaking and the pictures dropped to the ground.

"Do you want to find out? I don't think you do. My father is a powerful man. He can make things happen." Jane said. She acted as though her father was a boss in the Mob.

"Who's your father?" Krista wanted to know. After all, Jane seemed to think she was so important.

"Stanley Ahearn. I'm sure you've heard of him. Everyone has."

"Nope, doesn't ring a bell." Krista feigned any knowledge of Stanley. After all, she really didn't know who he was until Chad had made a big deal about him.

"He's only the biggest director in Hollywood, he's connected. He's worth millions. He's willing to spend millions to get what he wants. Is that enough for you?" Jane smirked, enjoying this. Krista didn't give a shit, but she knew that people with money would pay what it took to hurt other people and she just wanted this to be over.

"Okay. I'll see what I can do." At this point she'd be willing to say anything to get her out of her house. Where the hell was Chad?

"See that you do. You have 24 hours. I'd better not hear anything else about that property having an open house or being listed." Jane warned, and walked out the door. "Oh, and if you're thinking about calling the police, think again! The minute you get police involved will make me have to bring in the bigger guns that will take out your husband, your father, and then you! You're being watched, so I will know. You seem to love your family, so I'd be careful and follow the rules if I were you!" Jane warned, laughing sadistically, as she walked out the door, leaving Krista in disbelief.

Krista wasn't sure if she wanted to scream or throw something so she did both. She picked up a huge vase on the end table and hurled it across the room, smashing it into pieces. "Why?!" Krista screamed. She was furious, and heartbroken. She slowly sank to the floor with the pictures of Chad and another woman scattered all over the floor and held her head in her hands.

William

Still feeling unsettled after his conversation with Stanley and Chad about Stanley's daughter's sneaking around in his business, he wanted to check in with Krista. He hadn't heard from her in a day or so, which was strange, as they usually talked every day. He dialed her cell, hoping she'd pick up. It was after 6, she should be home by now.

"Dad?" Krista's voice was barely audible. She sounded upset. "Let me put you on speaker phone. Dad, are you there?" Her voice sounded as if she'd been crying and she was blowing her nose.

"Kris? Are you okay? What's going on? You sound upset, honey!" William was worried. What the hell had happened now? It seemed like life had been nothing but chaos over the past few weeks. The only other time he remembered everything so screwed up was the accident and when Maria left. He had a gut feeling that things were about to be haywire again just by the sound of her voice.

"Dad! I can't even begin to tell you! This woman, Jane! She broke into my house! She was here when I came home! I can't even believe it. I can't…." Krista's voice faded off and William could hear her crying in the background. "Kris? I'm coming over right now, okay? Hang in there! I'll be there in 10 minutes, honey! Stay on the phone with me!"

William headed for his Lexus SUV and was on the road in seconds, hoping that she was okay. "Kris? Should I call the police?"

"I'm here, dad. No, don't bother calling police. She's not here anymore, but...." Her voice broke as the tears began again.

"But what? Is there someone else there, someone that came with her?" William was frantic.

"I'm okay, dad. I'll talk to you when you get here okay?" Krista hung up. She was tired of trying to talk on speaker and also aware that Chad would probably walk in the door at any given moment. In fact, she was still wondering why he wasn't here when she'd arrived. He said he was at home.

William was knocking at the door 5 minutes later. Krista came to the door, tear-stained face and gave him a hug as soon as he walked in the door. "Dad! I don't even know what to do! That woman, these pictures, Chad, I just can't believe it, but there they are!" Krista said between sobs.

"What woman? What pictures?" William asked, but then he noticed pictures scattered over the floor. Pictures of Chad and his former secretary, Nancy and they were explicit. He couldn't see Chad's face in all of them, but the ones that showed his face, it was clear that these weren't photo-shopped! His trusted son-in-law had just crossed the line and he was furious. "Where the hell is Chad?" He asked Krista through clenched teeth, who was sitting on the couch with a Kleenex clutched to her face.

"I have no idea, dad. He was here when I called and said I was on my way home. He must have gone out. At least I hope. Who knows, maybe that crazy woman Jane kidnapped him!" She almost asked her father to call the police, but then she remembered Jane's warning. Maybe she was bluffing, but Krista knew she couldn't take that chance.

"Kris, calm down. Who was here? Do you know who it was?" William's first instinct was to call the police, but he needed more information.

"It was Jane, that secretary from the school that was so horrible to me all the time! Crazy Jane is what I called her. I didn't know her last name until today. She's Jane Ahearn, dad! She's Stanley Ahearn's daughter! She made sure to tell me that, and said that if the Block Island property is listed, she's going to make me sorry. What is going on here, dad?" Krista looked up at him, as if he could solve everything, give her an answer and that it would be okay.

William took a deep breath. Just when he thought he was done with Stanley and his surprises; they just kept coming! Stanley had another daughter? How many kids did this guy have? Clearly, they didn't have his legal means of making an income. They'd rather extort people for their own means and live off daddy's money. He tried to remain calm, but inside he was exploding with anger toward Stanley, his two money-grubbing daughters and now Chad had deceived his daughter. He wasn't sure where to start. But right now he was furious with Chad and wanted to punch him in the face. He knew it wouldn't solve anything, but he was so furious with him, it was the first thing that came to mind.

Chad came walking in the door with a dozen roses and a brown sack with wine a few seconds later. "What the hell?" He saw the pictures all over the floor, his father in law looking as though he wanted to kill him and his wife crying with mascara running down her face. "Did I miss something here? What's going on?"

"I really wish I could get away with punching you in the face, Chad! I can't believe I trusted you! I helped you out when you needed a job and this is how you repay me? By cheating on my daughter?" William was livid and his face was beet red. He stepped closer to Chad, but Krista stepped in front of him, afraid of what her father might do. She'd never seen him so angry.

"Bill, let me explain!" Chad hadn't messed around with Nancy in weeks! Not that it made a difference, but where the hell did these pictures come from? They'd been in the office, alone. Who the hell took these pictures?

"Explain what? There's nothing to explain here! You did this! This is your office, with your secretary!" Williams' voice rose even louder.

"Dad, please! I need to talk to Chad now. Can you please just take a minute, go outside, take a walk, drive, whatever? This isn't helping." Krista regained her composure over the initial shock and knew that nothing good was going to happen if her father stayed here right now. She didn't need the police showing up to the house for a domestic situation between her father and Chad. Somehow, she felt vindicated about her suspicions, as she considered the strange confidential phone calls that Chad had tried to smooth over in the past several weeks.

"Are you okay, Kris? I'm not leaving unless I know you're okay being here alone with him." He said pointedly toward Chad.

"I'm okay, dad. Thank you for coming by, but I need to do this on my own." Krista assured her father. William nodded and gave Krista a hug, then glared at Chad before walking out the door.

"I'd consider polishing up your resume, Chad. Your time at my agency may have just ended!" William slammed the door behind him and the sound of his tires squealing out of the driveway could be heard around the block.

As he drove away, he tried to not think about how much he'd trusted Chad, and he'd ultimately betrayed Krista and himself. He headed toward his house, when he had an idea. He dialed Stanley's personal cell number. He was sick of his kids and their stupid infiltration into his life. If he'd known that Stanley had kids, he'd have never made the agreement that seemed like a good idea for them at the time. Surprisingly, Stanley picked up on the second ring. "Ahearn here." He said in his standard curt manner.

"What the hell, Ahearn? We had an agreement! I never reported anything to anyone. You were supposed to disappear from our lives." William was so angry that he wished he had Stanley in front of him right now.

"What's the problem now, Bill? Seriously, these conversations are getting to be way too often and dramatic." Stanley was angry.

"For starters, you didn't tell me that you had yet another daughter trying to mess up my life! I know you are out to win, but this is beyond necessary!" William was seeing red.

"What do you mean? I don't believe our agreement included disclosing the number of children that I have!" Stanley said. "Really, Bill, I'm starting to think that you're in need of psychiatric treatment, along with your daughter!"

William tried to ignore the reference to Krista and moved onto the problem at hand. "What the problem has become is that one of your daughters that worked for my agency decided to seduce my son in law and take pictures. Your other daughter broke into my daughter's home and threatened her this afternoon! Seriously, Stanley, I would hope your kids growing up with everything would have better manners." William decided to be as obnoxious and up front as Stanley.

"If your son-in-law is too weak-minded to deny my daughter, that isn't my problem Bill!" Stanley retorted.

"I don't dismiss his behavior, but I also know that if she wasn't bent on destroying my daughter's life, maybe this wouldn't have been a problem! That also doesn't explain why Jane worked for the same school where my daughter works. Is that a coincidence? I don't think so. Let's not forget she broke into my daughter's home. I believe that's called 'breaking and entering', Stanley. Seems like some of your offspring are ticked off about our agreement and don't like that you're selling the Block Island property. That seems to be the theme here."

"Theme? What theme?" Stanley asked. Bill could see him rolling his eyes.

"Jane told Krista that she needed to convince my agency to not list your property for sale within 24 hours or else. Not sure what the "or else" would be, but given the damage they've done already, I'm not going to subject my daughter to anymore of your offspring's bullshit! Remember our agreement, Stanley?" William felt the need to go where he hadn't gone before with Stanley. He knew it was risky, but he also knew they needed this sale, and there was a reason that these daughters came out of the woodwork now. Stanley always had a reason for what he did, every move and if he was willing to sell this property despite his daughters conflicts about it, there must be a reason.

After a few moments of silence, Stanley finally spoke up. "Okay, Bill, I get it. My daughters are clearly overstepping their bounds! They want me to keep this place. My wife wants to sell, and I agree with her. It's too seasonal, it's expensive and we aren't there very often. I will talk with them, and make sure they leave your daughter and son-in-law alone. I find it hard to believe that Jane broke into your daughter's home, but then again, anything's possible with her. Did your daughter call the police?" Stanley sounded surprisingly concerned, which shocked William.

"No, she did not, despite my insistence that she should. My daughter is a good person, and doesn't want to make other's lives miserable." William said pointedly.

"Well, that's good. I'm glad that someone has their wits about them. I will take care of this, William. I certainly don't need anything negative, truth or not, to get into mainstream." Stanley agreed.

"Then we understand each other, Stanley. Because if there's another incident, I won't be calling you, I'll be calling ET, CBS, NBC, and any network that will listen! I'll be letting them know just who was responsible for that accident that killed my daughter, as well as these recent shenanigans that your children have created! I'm sure you don't need any drama considering you have a new movie coming out next week." William smiled, knowing that he had just won this battle.

"Just one more thing, Stanley. I'm assuming you're still on board with selling; that you're not backing out." William wanted to make sure that there were no more 'misunderstandings.'

"My plan is still to sell. That's what my wife and I still want! My daughters aren't in charge of what I do!" Stanley sounded angry now, affirming as only he could, that he was in charge. Stanley hated not having control. William was convinced that Stanley had an idea of what his children were up to, and he also knew that Stanley would not let anyone stand in his way, including his conniving daughters.

"Very well, Stanley. We'll be in touch with your wife to finalize details of the property sale." William smiled as he hung up.

Krista

As she stood in the living room with her husband who'd obviously cheated on her with an evil and less than attractive woman, she was overwhelmed with emotions. She wasn't even sure what to say so she moved to the kitchen in an effort to keep busy. Chad followed her. "Kris? We need to talk about this, you know that. Please. I want to make things right again. I love you!" He pleaded with her, wanting to somehow explain his actions, despite knowing there wasn't a good explanation.

Krista was looking through the fridge for anything to distract her from this conversation, and she honestly couldn't look at him right now. She pulled out some chicken tenderloins and vegetables to make a salad. "How about chicken salad tonight?" she asked trying to keep her emotions in check. She wasn't sure what to say or do anymore, and she was still in shock at the photos.

"Krista! We need to talk! I don't want to discuss the dinner menu! I did something wrong and I want to explain to you what happened, why it happened!" Chad was desperate to explain. He felt like the elephant in the room would never be addressed. Chad almost wished she'd screamed, called him names and insisted that he leave the house.

She paused for a moment, trying to gather her thoughts. She wasn't sure how to react anymore. The last few days; no, the last few weeks had been nothing short of awful and this was just something that needed to sink in. She knew that something was going on with Chad in the past month, but to have it thrown in her face; and the way it happened, was almost too much. Then she remembered the situation at the bar last week. That had to have been Nancy, trying to make her look crazy and make Chad leave her. She took a deep breath before she spoke, trying to remain calm.

"Honestly, Chad. I don't know what to think or feel or what to do anymore! The pictures speak for themselves. Clearly, Nancy was the person using your phone that night and probably planted that article in my car. She's a crazy lunatic, I get it! The problem is that you decided to follow what your dick wanted at the time, rather than thinking of me! So yeah, we have a lot to talk about and I'm willing to do that. But not now! I want to eat something. Oh, and by the way, you're sleeping on the couch tonight." Krista busied herself with making dinner. She was physically and mentally exhausted. She just wanted to get something to eat and relax; try to remove herself from the non-stop drama.

Chad backed off, knowing that he was lucky that Krista hadn't thrown his ass out of the house. Not yet, anyway. He retreated to the couch and watched the news channel while she was in the kitchen. "Are you making enough for me?" He asked half-heartedly, knowing he was risking getting hit in the face with something from the kitchen.

"You can have anything that's left over, if there is any." Krista replied curtly. She didn't care at this point. She was going to take care of herself and he could too. She was still too stunned to take it all in.

"I'll take that as a 'no.' Chad replied quietly. He picked up his phone and ordered a pizza.

"That would be a good idea," Krista said. 'Yeah, have fun with that. You get pizza, I get to make dinner. That figures!" Her anger just refueled and she threw together the chicken and salad and retreated to their bedroom to watch "Friends" reruns. She wasn't ready to talk to Chad about this affair, and wasn't sure what to do. A part of her wanted to kick him out and leave him forever, but at the same time, she also knew that they were dealing with a potential sociopath, and Krista was scared. If Jane was breaking into their house in daylight, there was no question that she would follow through with her threats. She was afraid for herself and Chad. This wasn't the time to force him to leave when their lives might be in danger.

"No problem. I'll be on the couch. Let me know if you need anything." Chad said, as his pizza arrived.

As she was falling asleep, Krista heard a noise at her window. She sat straight up in bed and opened the window. She didn't see anyone. She could hear the wind and an occasional bird. She thought about asking Chad to come upstairs, but she knew that he would take that as she'd forgiven him. She hadn't, and she wasn't sure if she could. She also knew that the Ahearn sisters were crazy and trying to break them apart. It made her want to fight all that much more for this relationship. She wasn't about to let two vindictive bitches ruin her marriage. She fell asleep almost immediately out of sheer exhaustion from the day.

She was suddenly on a cliff, hearing footsteps behind her. As she looked down, there was nothing but broken rocks and water at least 500 feet down. The only way out was to jump, because she could hear the rustle of the leaves, footsteps coming behind her, looking for her. She looked to her right and Karen was standing there, completely identical to her, down to the blue yoga pants and pink tank top. "Karen? Is that you?" Krista asked, just to be sure. Just knowing that she had existed had somehow erased the terror that Krista felt when she'd first seen her.

"You're in danger. You need to finish this." Karen replied. "I'll be there when you need me, but you need to do this yourself. You can do this, Krista." She walked away and seemed to disappear in a sudden fog cloud.

"What do you mean? Why am I still in danger? Karen, are you there?" Krista began running after her, but her legs were heavy, and as she looked down, she realized she was trying to run through deep mud. "Karen!" she called out. "Karen, please come back! Please help me!" Her legs were so heavy with the mud and she could hear footsteps behind her. She looked behind her, and saw a tall dark silhouette following her. She ran through the bushes, trying to follow Karen, but it seemed that every step she took, she wasn't making any ground and suddenly the figure was within feet of her. She screamed as she struggled to free her legs from the mud. The edge of the cliff seemed to move closer and closer. Just as the figure reached out to grab her, she was jerked awake and was back in her own bedroom. It was quiet, except for the sounds of the birds in the window. She instinctively reached out for Chad, but there was an empty space there. Then she remembered. He'd cheated on her. He was on the couch. But she missed him, and she was so afraid. She crept downstairs to see if he was awake.

"Chad?" Krista whispered, loudly enough that if he was awake, he'd here her. No answer. She crept closer to his sleeping form on the couch. "Chad?" She whispered in his ear.

"Huh, what, Kris what's the matter? You okay?" Chad sat up, disoriented, but clearly concerned.

"I'm sorry to wake you. I just had another nightmare. Karen was there again. But this time, she left me on the cliff and said 'you need to finish it'. I'm just really scared." Krista realized she was shaking uncontrollably.

Chad gave her A hug. "Honey, these dreams, I know that they mean something to you. But they are just dreams." He held her close to him, glad that she felt able to come to him even though he'd screwed up in a very bad way. He knew that he had a lot to make up for, and he planned to do just that. Krista resisted the urge to pull away. She was still shocked about the affair with Nancy, but this dream was

217

especially frightening. Karen had left her alone on that cliff with the dark figure. She didn't try to help her, and now she was really afraid. What was it that she needed to finish?

Chad

When the alarm went off at 6:00, Chad got into a wrestling match to turn it off. He sat up, disoriented for a moment. He found himself on the couch with Krista lying next to him. He gave her a hug, remembering how she came to him in the night with her dreams and tried to get up without waking her. It didn't work.

"Chad? What time is it?" Krista yawned and stretched her legs out that had been shoved under his legs on the couch.

"It's 6:00, sweetheart. Go back to sleep. Maybe you should stay home today." Chad encouraged her. He would do anything to rectify the affair with Nancy that turned out to be a set up.

"No, I need to keep busy. Staying home will just make me think too much. Besides, I left early yesterday after that phone call. I can't keep leaving like that. I can't afford to lose this job." Krista was insistent on going to work today. She got up and went to the kitchen to make coffee. Chad admired her work ethic and also the outline of her body in her tight leggings and t-shirt that she'd slept in. He realized for the millionth time in the past 24 hours what a fool he'd been, even thinking about cheating on her! What an idiot he'd been! What the hell had he been thinking? He got up and followed her to the kitchen.

"Let me get the coffee. I know how you like it. Relax and go take your shower if you're going to work. Do you want something to eat? I can make something."

Krista turned around and smiled. "You know what? I would love that. How about some French Toast and bacon?" She almost laughed out loud, knowing that they had none of the ingredients to make that, but would enjoy watching him scramble around to try and find them. He wasn't getting away with this without some payback.

" Um, okay," Chad had no idea how to make French Toast. Bacon was easy, but when he looked in the fridge, he didn't find any. He tried the freezer, hoping for a miracle. Nope. "Kris? There's no bacon." Chad called out to her, but she was already upstairs and the shower was running. He was tempted to run upstairs and ask about the French toast, but then decided he'd better not bother her. He'd figure it out. He googled a recipe for French toast and managed to mix up some egg mixture and added what he thought was cinnamon to it. After a closer look at the spice container, he realized it was cayenne pepper. 'Shit! This isn't going so well!' He thought. But he'd already made a few pieces of it on the pan. 'Maybe it'll be okay.' A few minutes later, he looked at the messy piece of bread that was burnt beyond belief and decided it was better to take Kris out for breakfast.

"Kris, get ready. We're going out for breakfast!" He called out, as Krista stepped down the stairs, looking like a model straight out of Vogue. Wearing a blue pencil skirt and a coral colored blouse that hugged her curves, and a pair of black heels, he was struck by how beautiful his wife looked. He whistled, "Wow! You look amazing!"

"Thank you." Krista said, with a little more warmth in her voice. Maybe this affair had brought them closer together? Chad could only hope. He sure as hell didn't want to lose her. Burnt cayenne pepper French Toast wasn't going to do him any favors. "Where would you like to go?"

"Let's go to our old hangout, The Lighthouse. We haven't been there since we started dating!" Krista suggested. The Lighthouse was a small diner in Johnston that they had found early in their relationship, and used to have a ritual to go every Sunday morning. That is, until life got in the way; marriage, busy careers and no time to even think about the small things.

"Perfect, I love it!" Chad smiled and was glad that his wife was on the same page with him. He was thinking just the same thing. Nothing like bringing back the good memories of the past to try and move forward. He knew that she was scared and likely the reason she wasn't throwing him out of the house. He knew he deserved it.

As they headed out for breakfast, Chad couldn't help being so thankful that his wife was so classy about this whole nightmare. He looked over at her and squeezed her hand. "I love you, Kris. I hope you know that I'll do anything to fix this."

She gave him a quick smile. "I know, Chad. It'll take awhile, but I think we can get through this. Just know it's going to take some time to trust you again." She squeezed his hand back as they drove in the Lighthouse parking lot which was already packed. It was popular place and they'd probably have to wait for a table. "Looks pretty busy! Do you have the time to wait, Kris?"

"After what Jane has done, they can wait. I don't have anything scheduled until 10. It's only 8:45 now." She smiled at him. It was nice to see her smile again, not being so stressed out by that horrible bitch.

As they sat down, Chad got a text from William. 'Where are you? Caroline Ahearn is calling, wants to talk to you ASAP!' "Oh, shit! Now what?" Chad said out loud after he read it.

"What's the matter?" Kris asked, although she already knew it was work, as usual. She was still surprised that her father would be trying to contact him after last night. It must be really important.

"It's your dad. Ahearn's wife is calling, wanting to speak to me. I'll have to call in. Sorry, babe, it'll be just a minute. We ARE going to finish our meal, by the way!" He winked at her as he walked outside to call William.

"Bill, what's going on? I'm taking Kris out for breakfast before work." He hoped that whatever conversation they had would help with his relationship with his father-in-law, especially since he was ready to fire and disown him only last night.

"Caroline Ahearn is calling. She wants to speak to you right away. She wouldn't tell me what it was about, but she wants you to call her back. Immediately!" William was all business. He spoke in a clipped tone and was clearly still upset with him, but he knew that if Ahearns' wife wanted to talk to Chad, he had no choice.

Chad wished his father in law had never found out about that horrible affair, but there was no going back. "I'm on it, Bill. I'll call her back right away."

"See that you do. Get back to me immediately after and let me know what's going on. You're not in the clear with me, by the way. Maybe Kris is making her peace with you, but I sure haven't." William's tone towards him was cold.

"Will do, Bill." Chad hung up and immediately dialed Caroline Ahearn's home phone. He peered into the window to see Krista sitting and looking around. Why did today have to be the day Caroline decided to move on this deal? He went back in quickly. "Kris, I'm so sorry. I have to call Ahearn's wife back right now. It's bad timing, I know. Order me some French toast and bacon, okay?" She looked more than a little irritated, but nodded her head. That was all he could hope for. "I'm sorry, honey. The fact that your dad called me tells me it's that important. You know he plans to fire me right?" Chad reminded her.

Krista's face softened. Her father was pissed and it would probably take more than Chad's lifetime for her dad to get over this, but he needed to try. "I understand. I'm sorry if I sounded bitchy. Go make your call. I hope it goes well." She nodded.

Chad felt relief wash over him. At least Kris was on board for trying and understood. She knew her father better than anyone. "Okay, thanks, sweetheart." He gave a quick kiss on her cheek and returned outside. As he dialed Caroline's number, he found himself shaking with anxiety. His situation with Bill at this point was uncertain; just last night, Bill told him to 'polish his resume' and Bill was many things, but one thing was certain. He was steadfast when it came to Krista, and anyone that crossed her had to answer to him.

"Hello?" Caroline's voice answered on the second ring.

"Hello, Mrs. Ahearn, uh, Caroline, it's Chad Burton from Carson Realty. Mr. Carson advised me that you wanted me to call you." Chad tried to sound calm, although he felt anything but.

"Thank you for calling me back so quickly, Chad. I wanted to speak with you about several things. First of all, I sincerely apologize again for my stepdaughter interrupting your last visit to my property. Her arrival was so unexpected and I had no idea that she was opposed to the selling of the property. I apologize for her inappropriate behavior as well. Apparently, despite the good schools that she's attended, she still has an edge to her when it comes to her temper." Caroline's voice came across as crass, almost indifferent. Chad found it strange, but chalked it up to her being embarrassed at their last meeting.

"Not a problem, Caroline. That didn't impact my evaluation of the property at all. It's a wonderful home that should sell quickly." Chad said, wanting to avoid the conversation about her stepdaughter.

"Thank you, Chad. I know that she was more than annoying, but you're a trooper." Caroline kidded. "I also want to apologize for my other stepdaughter who apparently came to your home and scared your wife last evening."

Chad was silent for a moment. How did she know that happened? Should he say something about it? He decided to be honest. "I have to say, Caroline, it was pretty upsetting to my wife. Her visit caused quite a problem to say the least. But I'm still willing to work hard to sell your property if you want me to continue as your realtor." He was trying to stay positive. He wasn't even sure that Bill would let him continue on, but he'd wanted him to speak with her directly, so that must mean something.

"Of course I do, Mr. Burton. I think you're the best person for the job. I just wanted to be sure that you still wanted to be part of this considering… the unexpected." Caroline finished her thought after a moment. Chad was certain that she must know about the threats that were made as well.

"I'll do my best to get the best offer. It is a beautiful property. My plan was to get it listed today, and I expect you'll have prospective buyers within a few days." Chad crossed his fingers that he'd still have a job, but clearly Caroline Ahearn wanted him for the job. It would mean the difference between Bill firing him because he was pissed about the affair, or giving up a high dollar commission on a Block Island mansion. He hoped Bill wouldn't be that petty to let the deal go.

"Thank you so much, Chad. I feel like I can trust you. I will do my best to see that my stepdaughters don't interfere again in the process, so that we can move ahead with the sale." Caroline sounded confident, and Chad suspected that several people that tried to interfere may have gotten the wrath of their father. And maybe a promise to cut off their allowances!

"No problem. I'll call you later this afternoon after I've posted the listing and we can go from there." Chad assured her, although it would ultimately be up to Bill.

"I'll be in touch then. Thanks for calling me back." Caroline said and hung up. Chad felt relief wash over him. The last thing he needed was Caroline backing out, especially with William on the fence about keeping him employed because of the affair. He dialed William immediately. He picked up on the first ring.

"Hi, Bill, uh, William, I just spoke with Mrs. Ahearn. She wanted to apologize for the other day with Amanda at the house. She also apologized for the incident with Jane breaking into the house. How the hell did she know about that? We didn't call the police." Chad asked.

"She probably found out because I had a conversation with Stanley. Stanley wasn't too happy about the incident and I'm sure told her to go ahead with the sale. I do know how to deal with clients, Chad. You should know that by now." William was being sarcastic and still very distant.

Chad knew that if he and Krista's marriage was going to survive his infidelity; he and William needed to call a truce. Otherwise, it would end up a disaster. Krista was too close to her father for him to continue this vendetta against him. "William, I'd really like a chance to talk with you about, well, you know. I promised Kris that this will never happen again. I know that I really screwed up and I'm willing to do anything to earn back your trust, as well as Kris'." Chad said earnestly, crossing his fingers that his father in law would eventually agree to give him another chance.

There was a long silence which seemed like a lifetime to Chad. "I need some time, Chad. I need you to finish this deal with the Ahearn property. We'll talk after that. I'm going to keep you on staff for that reason only and I expect you to be on your game. You're going to have to earn back my respect." William said. "In other news, I'm happy to say that Ray, my IT tech, checked out any potential hacking with our servers and everything appears to be secure."

"That's great news about the security!" Chad was relieved. "I'll work day and night to finish this closing, but Kris is also a big priority for me now." Chad said. "I'm truly sorry about what happened."

"Krista should always be that priority to you, Chad. Please don't ever forget that again. She's all I have and I'll protect her even if you can't because you're too busy with other 'activities." William wasn't budging. "Call me later with any details when you get them about the Ahearn property." He hung up.

Chad leaned against the building, feeling exhausted. He had a lot of work to do, literally with the Ahearn property, and with rebuilding his relationships with his wife and father in law. 'I need to get this right, make this right,' he thought to himself, as he walked back inside to have breakfast with his wife.

Krista

After the surprisingly pleasant breakfast with Chad, Krista was in a better mood headed to work. Very late, but she'd let Sara, the receptionist know that she would be in later and she had no scheduled appointments. Still, the fact that her father hadn't told her about her sister was something she was still upset about and knew she needed to talk to him as soon as possible. She dialed her father's office number on her blue tooth and waited for him to pick up. "Kris? What's going on? Are you okay?" Her father's voice sounded concerned.

"I'm fine dad. I assume you're worried about me and Chad. I'm still confused and angry, but let me deal with it, okay?" Krista decided to be straight-forward with him. She loved her dad, but he needed to let her deal with her own relationship problems.

"Okay, I know. You're an adult, but I'm still your dad." Bill was still upset about the affair, but he knew better than to press Krista for details.

"Dad, I really need to talk to you about something important. Can I come by later today?" Krista suddenly felt the urge to bring up the fact that she had a sister over the phone but stopped herself in time.

"Sure, honey. When do you want to come by?"

"Actually, could I come by your house when you get home?

It's not something I want to talk about at your office." Krista knew that it was going to be a difficult conversation.

"Sure. I'll be home around 6:00. Is that okay? Are you okay, sweetheart? Is this about Chad?" Bill couldn't help but ask.

"No, dad. It's not about Chad. I just need to talk to you, okay?" Krista knew that if she mentioned anything about the past, she'd end up on the phone for two hours and she needed to get to work.

"Okay. 6:00 it is. I'll see you then. I'll pick up your favorite pizza from Luigi's too, okay?" Bill sounded more upbeat, glad to have some alone time with Krista. "Is Chad coming as well?"

"No, he's not. I'm not going to talk about that. Okay? Please don't bring it up when I come over either." Krista insisted. She wasn't going to get into the details of her marriage with her dad. There was so much he needed to explain to her. She needed answers. She called Chad to let him know she was having dinner with her father. Chad's reaction to the mention of her spending time with her father was similar to Bill's, only more obvious.

"Kris, I hope we can work this out between us. I mean, I know your dad is furious with me now, but please, can't we work this out alone?"

"Chad, this has nothing to do with us, trust me. It's about Karen and everything that's been going on, okay?" Krista tried to keep the annoyance out of her voice.

There was a pause. "Of course, Kris, I hope it goes well. Call me when you're on your way home. Love you." He made sure he said those words, even if she didn't believe them right now.

"I will. Talk to you soon." Krista hung up without saying the words back. Too much had happened in such a short time, and quite frankly, she wasn't sure how she felt at this point.

The day went by with regularly scheduled students coming in, some needing help, and some that didn't need help, but trying to get out of class. Krista knew them all too well. At the end of the day, she was shutting down her computer when the phone rang. She was tempted to ignore it, but knew she would wonder about the call for the rest of the night. "Krista speaking, can I help you?"

There was silence on the other end. "Hello? This is Krista, can I help you?"

She repeated. It sounded like poor cell reception in the background, fading in and out. "Kris......" She could hear her name, but the rest was faded out.

"Hello? Are you there?" Krista was almost shouting into the phone.

"You need to watch out. They are after you. You need to be careful." It was a young girl's voice that came through clear this time.

Krista didn't recognize the voice at all, but knowing the antics that the Ahearn sisters had displayed, she was certain one of them was behind it.

"Okay, Jane, or Nancy or whatever the hell your real name is, you've got a lot of nerve calling. I've already talked to the police. Don't think you're going to get away with harassing me!" Krista yelled into the phone. No response.

"Hello? Are you there?" Krista was certain they hadn't hung up yet.

"You need to watch out, Krista. Be careful." The girl's voice said and then she heard a click. She'd hung up. What the hell? Krista suddenly felt paranoid, looking around her office and checking in the closet. No one was there. The receptionist had gone home already, so this person, whoever they were had her direct line. 'Jane! This must have been Jane doing this again!' Krista thought. It was almost 6:00 and she was supposed to be at her father's house. She looked around the office again and then left, looking behind her all the way to her car. She breathed a sigh of relief once inside and dialed her father.

"What's going on sweetheart? I'm here, are you running late?" William sounded concerned.

"I'm on my way, dad. Yes, I'm fine." She tried to sound as normal as possible. She just needed to get to him, needed to find out what was going on. "I'll be there soon, just running late, okay?"

"Okay, see you soon." William sounded relieved.

Krista and William

As soon as she hung up with her father, she dialed Verizon. She needed to find out where that call came from. But after multiple transfers to different departments, the answer was the same. "We don't have a number. There's nothing recorded." As she sat in her dad's driveway, she felt defeated. There was nothing else to do, except to go confront her father with the information about her sister, and suddenly she felt so unprepared. "I can do this!" Krista said out loud. She shut off the engine and forced herself to get out and go inside. He'd come out soon since she knew he'd seen her pull into the driveway. Sure enough, as she got of the car, he had the front door open and waved to her. "Hey, Kris! Come on in, sweetheart."

Krista pulled herself together and gave him a hug. This wasn't going to be easy, but she needed to talk to him. "Hi, dad, I really need to talk to you."

"I need to talk to you, too. Do you realize that if I get this property sold, I'll be able to spend less time at the business?" Bill seemed happy about the prospect and it made her heart sink. But she needed to do this.

"Want a drink? Maybe a glass of wine?" Bill offered. A glass of wine, or maybe an entire bottle was her thought. "Wine would be great, dad.

Thanks." Krista said. She was trying to put the call in the back of her head. She needed to be able to focus now. Her hands were shaking as she sat down on the couch. The Red Sox game on TV in the background. It was somehow comforting, reminding her of the afternoons watching games with him.

"Here you go, Kris." He handed her a glass of white wine. "I didn't forget your favorite Margarita pizza from Luigi's!" Bill reminded her as he retrieved some plates and the pizza. He settled down in his recliner with his glass of beer. "What's going on, Kris?"

"Thanks, dad." Krista nodded to the dinner and wine. She knew she was stalling.

"C'mon, Kris. Something's on your mind. Talk to me."

Krista took a deep breath and blurted out, "Why didn't you tell me I had a sister?"

Bill looked shocked for a moment and sat straight up in his chair. "Who told you that, Krista?" His voice changed from jovial to ice-cold in a second. He took a long swig of his beer as he waited for her to answer.

"Well, you know I've had these crazy dreams, and strange things happening at work, so I, well, I decided to see a psychic." She braced herself for a tirade, but instead, her father was sitting quietly in his chair.

"Okay, I'm listening." She could tell he was refraining from saying more.

"This psychic, she insisted that I had a sister. I didn't believe her the first time I talked to her a week ago. Yes, I talked to her twice." Krista added before he could say anything. "The second time, she told me that she was my twin sister; that she died when we were very young. Is this true, dad?" Krista suddenly felt tears forming in her eyes. It was enough to hear it from a stranger, but to talk to her father was so much more difficult. It was becoming real. He could speak to what was the truth with no second guesses.

Her father sat up in his chair and walked to the kitchen. 'Dad? Are you okay?" Krista got up and followed him. He had his head in his hands on the counter. "Dad, please. Answer me. I need to know." Krista put her arm around him. His shoulders were shaking, and the sobbing came out of nowhere.

"Dad!" Krista put her arms around him and he embraced her, still crying. "I'm so sorry, Krista. I tried to do the best I could. I'm so sorry," he repeated. Krista held him for a few minutes. She was beginning to regret this discussion after all, but it was out now. Maybe it was time to confront the past, however painful.

He finally sat back down in his recliner after claiming another beer out of the fridge. He looked suddenly pale and tired, and almost, well, old at that moment. Krista was beginning to regret bringing this up, but she also knew it was time to know the truth.

Finally, her father spoke. "Krista, it's a long story. A long and sad story, I'm afraid. One that I had hoped I'd never have to tell you. I wanted to protect you."

"I know, dad, but I really need to know. It's impacting my life now." Krista insisted.

"Where do I begin?' William sighed. He leaned back on the couch as he continued. "Your mother and I were very happy together. When she became pregnant with you, we weren't expecting it, but we were happy. We were so in love." His eyes became teary as he spoke about her mother. "When she was in labor, we had our beautiful daughter. That was you. The doctors were attending to you when your mother began having more pains. It turns out, she was having another baby. Back then, technology wasn't as it is today, so no one knew that your mother was actually having twins. She came out a few minutes later, just as beautiful as you." Bill's eyes were filled with tears with the memory, and Krista felt as though her heart was pounding out of her chest.

Bill continued as if it was actually happening now, "We were just so happy. We didn't expect to have twins, but we felt like the luckiest parents ever. The two of you were just so perfect in every way and when we took you home, we had to dress you in different colors so we could tell you apart! As you got a little older, it became easier to tell the difference between you with your personalities. You were so sweet, and just wanted people to hold you and spend time with you. Karen was different. She only wanted your mother. She would cry and was inconsolable if anyone else held her."

It was the first time Krista had heard her father actually speak Karen's name and she felt as if suddenly her sister was actually real. "Karen. Yes. That was her name. That was what the psychic said, that her name was Karen."

"Are you okay, Kris? Do you really want to know about this?" Bill was still shaken by his daughter's discovery and now going back for him was much more difficult than he'd ever expected.

Krista brushed off the tears. "I need to know dad. This is my life. I need to know who used to be part of it." She honestly was shocked despite the ongoing predictions that she had a sister, and now it was real. Her father had just confirmed that it was.

Bill continued on after taking another long swig of his second beer. "Anyway, you girls were so close from the beginning. It was almost as if you knew what the other one was thinking, even though you were just babies. When you started to walk and talk, you seemed to rely on each other. You were true identical twins. But when it came to your personalities, it was easy to tell you apart. You were more sociable, eager for attention and Karen held back. She was shy. We could tell in the way that she would let you go first at everything. She would follow, but if you were doing something that might be dangerous, she always held back, always made sure that you were okay. She acted almost as if she were your older sister, always keeping an eye out for you." Krista nodded. She could sense that about her. Especially after what Nadine had explained about Karen's wish to help her.

"It happened late one night after we were driving back from a housewarming party. You two girls were in the backseat. It was a raining so hard, so I was going slower than usual. We were coming around a turn and there was a car coming directly toward us. It was so hard to see with the rain and I tried to swerve out of the way. But it was too late. The car hit us head on, and all I remember is getting out of the car. It was on fire, and your mother and you were on the side of the road screaming. Your sister was still in the car, and I tried, Kris, I tried so hard to get her out." Bill was crying as he choked out the words. "But…..the car… it exploded before I could get her out." He put his head in his hands. "I'm so sorry. I wish I could've gotten her out!"

Krista was speechless for a few minutes, just trying to process what she'd just heard. For a split second, she had a flashback of a fire, her parents crying, and then being picked up by a stranger that had put her in an ambulance. She didn't remember what had happened or why everyone was so sad. She could still see Karen in the ambulance, sitting next to her mother, holding her hand. Karen had been around during the hospital stay and went home with her. How could she have been there?

"Dad, I'm not upset with you. It was a long time ago. You did what you could. But I need to know everything", Krista wasn't sure she was going to like what she heard, but she needed to know. She held her father's hand and squeezed it. "I need to know."

Bill took a deep breath. "Are you sure?" She nodded.

He took a deep breath and reached for a tissue before he began. "After your sister died, your mother became a different person. She didn't talk to anyone. She barely ate or slept, and spent the days sleeping or staring out the window. She stopped taking care of anything, including you, so I hired babysitters during the week, until I got home from work. The only time she spoke to me was to blame me for Karen's death. Your mother sat in your room, next to Karen's bed and cried for hours. I remember I came home from work one day and she was suddenly busy filling a gold-colored box, but she wouldn't show me what was in it. She just smiled and said that 'Karen told me to make this.' I was worried and tried to get her to see a therapist, but she refused. She kept insisting that she could see Karen and that Karen was telling her things."

"Did she say what she was telling her?" Krista whispered, almost as if to speak louder would break the spell of what her father was saying.

"She said that Karen was talking to her. That Karen was telling her she needed her to come back to her." William's voice shook. "I'd planned to take her to a doctor to get some help right away. I'd had it planned for the next day, but when I got home, she was gone."

"What do you mean, she was gone? Where did she go?" Krista asked softly.

"I came home from work and found you with the babysitter who said, 'Mrs. Carson hasn't returned yet.' I was frantic and called the police, but they didn't begin looking for her until two days later. They tried all her friends, and relatives but it was as if she just vanished. I never heard from your mother again since that day, Kris. I still miss her. I still hope that she's still out there." Bill held his head in hands. He was exhausted. So much of the past had been dredged up, but he knew that Krista needed to know. How could he have thought it was the right thing to do to keep such a secret from someone he loved most in the world?

"There was one detective, Mr. Sumner. He worked hard on the case for several years. I actually tried to contact him a few weeks ago, after you started to have these dreams and strange things happening and hoping he could help me out. I recently found out he died suddenly. Some kind of accident, I guess." He shook his head.

Krista sat in silence, tears running down her face. "Dad, if she was just missing, why did you let me believe that she was dead?"

William took a swig of his beer and then took a deep breath. "Honestly, Kris, it was such a loss after your sister died. You were having a tough time. You kept talking to Karen, as if she were still there. It was as if she had never left. I remember one day you were in your room, having a tea party with your dolls. I watched as you talked to your dolls, but then you kept talking to someone in an empty chair, as if they were actually there. It scared me and I was worried that you were having psychological problems. I brought you to several therapists. Do you remember?"

Krista nodded. "I do. I remember they kept insisting that she was my 'imaginary friend' that was helping me because I was sad."

William nodded. "That's what they told me too. They said you were working through it in your own way. I guess they were right. After you started first grade, I didn't hear you talking to her or telling me that she was trying to get you in trouble. It was as if she had just disappeared and you seemed fine. You made friends, seemed to enjoy school, and never talked about her again."

Krista suddenly remembered that day. She was getting ready to start school and Karen had said that she needed to leave. "I remember, dad. She said she needed to leave for awhile, but she would come back someday. I was sad and I would try to find her, like she was hiding in the closet. But I couldn't see her anymore. I always missed mom, but then I missed her more because Karen wasn't there either."

William reached over to Krista and enveloped her in a huge hug. "I'm so sorry that I didn't tell you about her, but you were doing so well. By the time I considered bringing it up again, you were sixteen years old and enjoying your life. I didn't want to risk your stability at that age. When you asked about your mother, I tried to be vague, because I didn't want you to know that she had just left. I hope you can forgive me, Kris."

Krista returned her father's embrace. Although she wished she'd known, she could understand why her father had kept it from her. "I understand, dad, I really do. I just wish that I knew what happened to mom. I think she's still out there, and I want to find her." She looked up at her father's face.

"So do I, Kris. So do I. I've never really believed that she's dead. I still look for her on every street corner. There's one other piece to this that no one knows about with the exception of your mother. But I'm going to tell you, because you deserve to know everything. The driver of the car that caused the accident was drunk. It was Stanley Ahearn." William seemed relieved as he said the words, as if he'd been waiting a lifetime.

"What? The same Stanley Ahearn that wants you to sell his house? Why? Why didn't you tell police back then if you knew? I don't understand, dad!" Krista wasn't prepared for this.

"To make a long story short, he had money, a lot of money. And I didn't at the time. He was becoming a well-known director on the Hollywood scene. He didn't want anything to hurt his reputation with regard to the accident. At the scene of the accident, he immediately approached me with an offer at the time that would help us financially. When the police arrived, I gave a statement that made it appear as though it was just an accident, not mentioning that Stanley had been drinking."

"So he should have been charged with a DUI, resulting in death." Krista said bluntly. She couldn't believe what she was hearing. She was shocked that her father would even think about letting Stanley get away with killing her sister in exchange for money? That didn't seem like something he would do.

William nodded. "By the time police questioned him, Stanley had sobered up and police didn't question him further. He gave me enough money to start this real estate business and buy our home, with my promise that I wouldn't go to the police with what really happened." He fell silent, waiting for Krista to scream at him for what he'd done. He felt it was deserved and if he could turn back the clock, he never would've agreed. At the time, he and Maria had been struggling financially. Maria didn't agree with it despite their financial troubles, and he knew that was a huge part of why she left. "Your mother was so upset. Between that and losing Karen, she left one day and didn't come back." William was silent for a moment.

"Kris, I can't take back my past decisions, but I hope you can understand them. I did what I thought would help at the time. But after your mother left, I knew that I should've just been up front with the police."

"Dad, I'm not sure what to say. It's a lot to take in. I can understand the financial aspect of it, but I think he's a coward for offering in the first place just to save himself." Krista shook her head. "Especially under the circumstances; your child died, you were in shock." Her counseling mindset seemed to take over just then. She wasn't happy that her father had made that choice, but he was still a good person. "We're okay, dad. I think you've made decisions you regret, but you're still my dad. I haven't wanted for anything, except that I wish mom was still here. But that's not your fault. She made the choice to leave." Krista wiped her tears and reached for her father's hand.

William gripped Krista's hand and gave her another hug. "Thank you, sweetheart. It's been a weight on my shoulders for so long."

William's cell phone broke through the silence with a loud piercing old -school ring tone. William groaned and looked at his watch. "I wish I could let that go, but given that it's after 9:00, I think it might be important. Do you mind if I get this?"

Krista nodded. "Of course. I hope it's good news." She was sure it wasn't, but was trying to be positive.

William answered and was suddenly on edge. "Chad, what? What happened? Where is she?" His face was suddenly pale. Krista moved closer to try to hear Chad on the other end. "Dad, what's going on?"

William shook his head at her and mouthed, 'just a minute,' as he was listening. "Okay, okay. Well, I'll plan on going there myself as well. I'm as concerned as you are." He cut off the call and turned to Krista. "That was Chad. He just got word that Mrs. Ahearn was brought by airlift to South County Hospital."

"What happened and why did Chad know about it?" Krista was confused and suspicious at the same time. After all, she was just his real estate client, and a new client at that. Then she realized what he had said about Amanda Ahearn and her threats.

"The police said that she wanted him to be called. I'm not sure why, but maybe she was in shock. He just saw her today and I know that Stanley is out of town right now. I need to go and see what's going on." William concluded.

"Of course, dad. You should go. Is Chad there right now?" Krista had been so focused on her conversation with her dad that she'd forgotten about her husband and their current circumstances.

"He's on his way. You should go home, though. It's getting late. I'll give you a call later, okay?" William gave her another hug as he grabbed his keys and headed for the door.

"Okay. Have Chad call me and keep me in the loop. Let me know what's going on. I love you, dad." Krista kissed him on the cheek.

"I love you too, sweetheart. No more secrets, I promise."

Chad

The phone rang just after Chad had settled down with his second beer and leftovers for dinner. Feeling irritated, he looked at the number and groaned. It was a local area code, so he picked up as it might be a client. He couldn't risk William getting more upset with him right now. "Chad Burton," he answered crisply.

"Mr. Burton? This is Officer Daniels with South Kingstown police. We were asked to contact you by one of your clients, Mrs. Caroline Ahearn."

Chad's slight beer buzz evaporated. "Yes, officer. How can I help you?" He was confused but concerned as well. He hadn't forgotten about Caroline's creepy step-daughter.

"We were given your name and number by Mrs. Ahearn. There was an accident and she had to be airlifted to the nearest hospital. She insisted that I inform you."

Chad was shocked. Why would they call *him*? "I'm so sorry to hear that. Is she going to be okay?" Did they think he did something?

"She slipped and fell down the stairs a few hours ago. She's at South County Hospital now. We don't know her condition right now, but we're suspicious that the fall wasn't an accident."

Chad tried to maintain his composure and keep his voice from shaking. "Mrs. Ahearn is a new client of ours. I'm not sure how I can help you, Officer."

"As I said initially, she asked that I contact you to let you know. Of course, we would want to speak with you as well, but just a formality because she had asked for you." Officer Daniels' said. Chad could tell he wouldn't get any details from him. He decided to let William know of the circumstances. "I understand. I'll contact my supervisor and will be in touch." The officer gave his number and hung up.

Chad's mind was all over the place. He hated to bother William when he knew he was with Krista, but he felt he had no choice. William sounded very irritated initially, but after the explanation, calmed down and agreed to meet him at the hospital. He sighed as he looked at his now- cold leftover chicken parmesan on the coffee table. 'Screw it, I'm going to finish eating.' Chad said to himself. He hadn't eaten much all day and knowing how hospitals worked, he was sure this was going to be a long night.

Fifteen minutes later, he got into his car, and called his wife. She picked up immediately. "Chad? Are you okay? I was with my dad when you called." She sounded concerned, not irritated with him as he had thought.

"I'm fine, Kris. I'm sure your dad filled you in. I'm not sure why she gave my name to police, but we should both go and find out what's

247

going on. I'm especially suspicious with her crazy step daughter's threats to us." He pulled out onto the highway.

"How was your talk with your dad tonight?" He wanted to focus on something else.

"It was intense. So much that I didn't know until I started getting answers. I feel overwhelmed but like a weight's been lifted at the same time." Krista admitted. "I'm okay. Just let me know what's going on. Do you want me to meet you there?" It was an afterthought, but suddenly, she felt like she should be around for support.

"No, Kris. It's fine. Let me and your dad deal with this. It shouldn't take long and I'll be home. Just relax and take some time for yourself tonight. It sounds like you had a lot to take in tonight." Chad didn't like the situation and he was still skeptical about Ahearn's daughters that had already wrecked havoc in their lives. He was sure they had something to do with this.

"Are you sure?" Krista asked. She was worried.

"Absolutely. Get yourself in a hot bubble bath with a glass of wine and I'll see you in a few hours. Just relax, ok?" Chad insisted.

"Alright, I will if you insist. Call me and let me know what's going on, ok?" Krista was worried about her husband and her father. Why did the police want them to come there?

"I will. Call you soon. Love you, sweetheart."

"Love you too." Krista said, hoping that he would be coming home sooner than later.

Chad hung up, relieved that his wife wasn't headed into what was sure to be a drama filled evening. Twenty minutes later, he pulled into the South County Hospital parking lot and took a deep breath. As he was walking toward the entrance, he could see William outside, pacing nervously.

"Bill, what's going on?" Chad asked, foregoing the formal greeting with his father –in- law, given the circumstances. "Did you find out what happened? Why did the police want us here?" Chad fired his questions rapidly. William was clearly nervous, which wasn't a good sign. On closer inspection, he noticed his father- in- law was pale and shaking slightly. "Bill, are you okay?"

William looked grateful to see him. "Chad, thank god you're here." He embraced him, which shocked Chad. Yesterday, he'd been the enemy. He held onto the hug for a moment. "Bill, you're shaking. Is everything okay?" Chad repeated.

William held him at an arm's length. "I wish it were." He shook his head. "The ER staff said she's headed for emergency surgery. She apparently fell down those stairs in the front hallway and has some internal injuries, and likely several broken bones, along with a concussion.

"Did they let you see her?" Chad asked. William nodded.

"They said no, but I did manage to peek in on her when they were taking her into surgery." William looked away, and brushed his hand across his face. He coughed and brushed his eyes again and faced Chad. His eyes were blood shot, as though he'd been crying, which struck Chad as strange. He'd never met Caroline. Why was he so upset?

Chad put an arm on his shoulder. "Bill, what's going on here? I mean, I know its upsetting that this happened. She's a nice person and a new client, but you seem really upset." He decided to get straight to the point.

William walked away a few steps and sat down on a nearby bench, and put his head in his hands. "I wish that were true. That she was just a nice person and new client, I mean. But it's more than that. I'm not sure why I suspected, but I didn't actually think......" His voice drifted off.

Chad shivered as he sat down next to him. Kris was better at dealing with this kind of thing. Maybe he should call her. "Suspected what, Bill? What's going on?"

William lifted his head up, "I know Kris has told you that her mother left when she was young and that we thought she had passed away. But I always felt like she was still out there, and I was always looking for her." He looked at Chad for confirmation.

Chad nodded. "I know Kris struggles with not knowing what happened to her. Kris always told me that she thought she had died and that's why she never came back." William lowered his head again, his shoulders heaving as he began sobbing uncontrollably. Chad put his arm around him. "Bill, what's going on? Do you know Caroline?"

William looked up at Chad, "Yes, I do. I've known her for so long. But she isn't Caroline. She's Maria. She's my wife. She's Krista's mother." His words hit hard and Chad had to sit back instead of falling off the bench in shock. "She's what? She's your missing wife, Kris' mother? Bill, are you sure?" Chad was beginning to think he needed to take his father–in–law in for a psychiatric evaluation.

William stood up suddenly. "I know it's Maria! I've loved that woman over half my life and I'd never forget her, no matter how much time has gone by!" His voice lowered to a whisper. "I know it's her. Why did she leave and marry that asshole and then contact you? Why? And now, she's……she …she might not…" He couldn't finish and broke down again. Chad's mind was racing. 'What should I do? Call Kris? No, that wouldn't help, how would I even explain that to her? Who else would I call?' His thoughts were interrupted by two police officers who were suddenly standing over them.

"Are either of you Chad Burton?" the short officer asked in a loud voice. His taller partner stood next to him, as if he were his watchdog. Chad stood up. "I'm Chad Burton. How can I help you?" He tried to keep the nervous quiver out of his voice.

"Mr. Burton, I'm Officer Daniels. This is Officer Allen. I spoke to you earlier this evening about Mrs. Ahearn."

"Yes, I remember. This is William Carson, my father-in-law and the owner of Carson Realty." Chad felt the need to include William in the discussion, especially after his last statement about Caroline actually being his estranged wife.

"Mr. Carson," Officer Daniels offered his hand out to him and William shook it. "Officer, do you know anything about what happened? I don't think this was an accident." William said with conviction.

"Mr. Carson, just what is your relationship to Mrs. Ahearn? I understand she is a new client of your realty business, but you seem to be presumptuous about what happened to her." Officer Daniels looked at him with more than a little suspicion. William looked at Chad for a moment. "Before I get into it, has her husband been contacted?" He needed some time to process Maria's reappearance, and he was hoping that Stanley would be around soon to give him some answers.

Officer Daniels gave him a strange look. "Yes, we have. He's on his way back from California and should be in tomorrow. Do you know Mr. Ahearn?"

William nodded, "Yes, I've known Stanley for years. I spoke to him recently with regard to selling his home on Block Island."

"How long have you known him?" Officer Allen had been quiet up until now, seemed suddenly interested in how much William knew about Stanley.

"I'm not sure, maybe twenty years total. We aren't close or anything." William was being vague and the officer could tell.

"How did you meet Mr. Ahearn?" Officer Allen pressured. He was at least 6 foot 3 and was very intimidating.

"We were in some classes together at the University of Rhode Island." William said quietly, wishing they would both get off his back. He didn't want to get caught up in the investigation with Stanley. He didn't want to reveal what he had done years ago. "I do know that he has two daughters. One of them visits his Block Island home quite often. Her name is Amanda Ahearn. She took a job as a secretary at my business under a different identity." He told him about Amanda's threats towards his daughter if the Block Island property was listed. "Is there a way you can prove those accusations, Mr. Carson?" The officer wanted to know.

"I have her application and W2s that she signed upon employment with my company. Of course, she gave a false name, but I can get them for you," William offered.

"There's another daughter, officer." Chad spoke up. "Her name is Jane Ahearn. She worked with my wife as a receptionist for Johnston High School, and then quit around the same time that Amanda quit William's agency. Jane broke into our home and made threats towards my wife."

"Were police reports filed on either of these incidents?" Officer Allen was definitely interested in this information.

"Someone broke into my wife's office at the school a few days ago. It was the same day that Jane Ahearn quit her job there. A police report was made, although there was never anyone arrested. Unfortunately, a report wasn't made on the break -in at my home." Chad answered quietly, suddenly realizing how strange that must seem to the police.

"I remember the report your wife made at the school, but why didn't you report the home break in? This woman broke into your home, threatened your wife." Officer Daniels wasn't letting go of it.

"My wife, has been dealing with a lot lately. She wasn't harmed and I just didn't want to involve police at that time." Chad knew his excuse sounded lame, and also realized that it was a big mistake on his part, in retrospect. Why hadn't he called police? Then he remembered. William had insisted that they didn't call police. Maybe he was part of this. Suddenly he didn't trust anyone. William glared at him, as if telling him to let it go.

"Well, a police report should have been made in regard to the home break in," Officer Daniel chastised. "If either of you have further contact with Amanda or Jane Ahearn, you need to let us know immediately!" Both William and Chad nodded in unison. "Here's my card. Please call me if you hear or see anything. We will be in touch." He shook William's hand and Officer Allen nodded as they walked back into the hospital.

They both took a deep breath and sat in uncomfortable silence for a few minutes.

"Whoa, that was intense." Chad broke the silence.

"You're telling me? I was starting to think I was being interrogated for what happened to her." William sat back, suddenly exhausted. Chad nodded, "I got the same feeling. I hope Mr. Ahearn gets here soon, so he can take the hot seat!" He tried to joke, but he felt as though he had just hit a brick wall. "What do we do now?" Chad asked.

"I'm not sure. I wish I could know how she's doing, but they aren't going to tell either of us anything right now. We should probably head home. I'll try Stanley in the morning."

"Do you think her crazy stepdaughters have anything to do with Caroline's 'accident'?" Chad was suspicious.

"I definitely think that at least one of them did. Amanda was dead-set against that property being sold. It hasn't been long enough for us to even put up the listing, but maybe she's sending a message. There's got to be more to this though. I can't believe anyone would try to kill someone over a house. I mean, Stanley's a billionaire. He could buy them a house anywhere they wanted." William was thinking out loud and suddenly he stopped talking. Stanley was a billionaire, and if he was married to Maria, it was likely that all his money, and assets would go to her if something happened to Stanley. He knew that wouldn't go over well with Stanley's daughters. They definitely knew about Krista and knew that she was Maria's daughter. He picked up his phone and dialed his daughter's home number. "Please pick up, Kris, please pick up," he whispered as the phone continued to ring and then went to voicemail.

"Chad, call Kris and see if she'll answer. I just tried her and it went straight to voicemail." William insisted, as he paced back and forth. He didn't think she was angry with him, but considered that Krista might be taking some time to digest the information given to her, and just not picking up his calls.

"What's going on? She's fine. When I left, she was taking a bath and headed to bed. She actually wanted to come with me, but I wanted to keep her out of this." Chad said. Still, he tried to call Kris. It went straight to voicemail. "Same here. Voicemail." Chad shook his head and hung up.

"Let's get to your house! I'm worried! Listen to me!" William gave him his thoughts about the Ahearn sisters and their possible involvement with Maria's accident. "The only other person standing in their way from an inheritance is Krista. That's why they've been threatening her. Maria wouldn't leave her out of her will. They know that. Krista's not safe, Chad."

Chad went into protective mode. "Let's go!" His heart was pounding as they got in Chad's car and took off for the 40- minute drive to their home. The entire drive he continued to call his wife with each call going straight to voicemail. He left several messages for Krista to call him immediately, but she hadn't called back. He only hoped it was because her phone was on silent, and Kris didn't hear it because she was relaxing.

Krista

Krista filled the bathtub with some hot water and added her favorite bath scents. It was so much to take in. She left her phone in the bedroom, tired of reading about everyone else's life on social media. She thought about her sister, her mother and all these years that she'd never known anything about them until today. After the tub was filled with scented bubbles, Krista lowered herself into the tub and sipped her glass of chardonnay. Her mind was whirring with the recent confirmation that her mother might still be alive and Karen. She was upset that her father hadn't told her the truth until now, but she put herself in his place, and realized that he'd only tried to protect her. She laid her head back on the tub and tried to relax into the fragrant lavender- scented water.

Just as Krista was settled, and feeling calm, the sound of breaking glass jolted her out of her relaxed state. Her senses were on high alert, and she sat still, hoping that it was just the neighbors outside. Her heart was pounding and she tried to breathe slowly, telling herself she was being ridiculous. Yet, she could hear a muffled voice, and it was definitely coming from inside her house. She stepped out of the tub, quickly dried off, and grabbed her robe on the back of the bathroom door. She opened the door slowly and looked out.

"Chad,?" She called out, hoping her husband was home and didn't want to wake her. No answer. She crept to her bedroom and quickly pulled on some old yoga pants and a sweatshirt, along with some sneakers. 'I must be hearing things.' She thought to herself. 'I'm just going to go downstairs and get in the car. It's fine,' but she was shaking as she walked into the hallway. She felt as though she were in one of her nightmares, as she tip-toed to the stairs and turned on the hall lights. She didn't see anyone and crept slowly down the staircase. As she came down the last stair, she noticed a figure moving slowly toward her.

"Hey! Who are you? What are you doing here?" Her heart was pounding, and instinct commanded her to run back up the stairs. The intruder followed her, taking two steps at a time. Krista tried to make it to the upstairs bathroom, but tripped on the hallway rug and sprawled on the floor face down. As she struggled to pull herself up, she was suddenly tackled by the intruder from behind and screamed as her face hit the floor. "Stop! What do you want from me? What are you doing?" Krista was screaming, feeling blood in her mouth. She wrestled as they sat down on her legs to pin her down.

"It'll be okay. You're just going for a little ride. I hope you don't get seasick." The woman's voice laughed, taunting her. "Don't worry. You won't remember a thing."

Krista twisted around and tried to get a look at her assailant. She was wearing a cheap plastic princess mask that was from the 1980s, and

259

dressed entirely in black. 'Jane', Krista thought to herself. "Jane, I know it's you!" She reached up and tried to rip the mask off her head, but another person with a Scream mask emerged and grabbed her arm.

"Oh, no, you can't do that, Krista! That would ruin everything! You see, you should have just let things go, but no, you can't do that!" The voice was muffled but clearly another woman. She held her hands tight. "Give me the rope, please. I thought this was going to be easy!" She said to the woman on top of her. "Hold her still so I can give her this injection. It'll knock her out, at least for now." Her captor nodded. 'Go ahead, I've got her."

Krista knew that if she was drugged, she might not wake up and continued to fight by kicking and trying to free her arms from the woman's grip to get free. "No! Why are you doing this? I didn't do anything!" She screamed as she fought. The masked woman managed to get one of Krista's hands free and grabbed at the gold half-heart necklace that was hanging from Krista's neck and pulled. Krista watched in horror as it fell to the floor and tried to grab it, only to be wrenched upwards in a choke hold. "Stop! I didn't do anything!" Krista knew that they weren't going to let her off easy, but that didn't mean she wasn't going to stop trying. The necklace meant everything to her. She'd had it since she was a little girl.

"No, of course you didn't! You're such a good girl, you're so perfect! You get whatever you want!" The woman in the princess mask sounded sadistic. "You get what you want, but I get nothing! It doesn't have to be that way, though!" She laughed, as she and the other woman held her hands tight behind her back and tied a rope around them to the point Krista thought she was going to lose circulation. "Okay, give it to her," the woman said to her accomplice, who was ready with a syringe filled, poised to inject Krista's left arm. "No! No!" Krista continued to scream, as she felt the needle puncture her vein and cool liquid was injected. "Dad, Chad, Karen! Help me!" Krista continued to fight, but whatever drug they'd injected her with began to kick in. She tried to fight the drowsiness and haze that had taken over.

Chad and William

Chad had driven the 40 -minute drive in less than 30 minutes when he pulled into the driveway. The house was dark, except for a few lights on upstairs, and Krista's car was still there. He grabbed the flashlight and a tire iron out of the trunk and headed up the front stairs. As he approached the front door, he could see broken glass close to the doorknob. "Oh, my god! Call the police, now!" Chad shouted to William as he came up behind him. William nodded as he dialed 911." There's been a break in at 511 Hartford Lane! Please hurry, I think my daughter is in trouble!" He went on to explain some of what had been going on. "Please let Officer Daniels know. He's been involved with this case already." He turned to Chad. "I wish we'd insisted that Kris come with us." Chad nodded in agreement. "I know, but we couldn't know this was going to happen at the time." He pulled the door open slowly. "Be careful. They could still be here." He whispered to William.

They carefully walked into the dark house. Chad suddenly wished he'd been one of the guys that liked to shoot guns at the range and had one in the house. "Kris? Kris, are you okay?" Chad called out. He noticed that the long hallway rug was rumpled and a lamp had been knocked over. Chad ran up the stairs yelling "Kris, Kris!" He walked into the bathroom, and spied a gold object on the floor. "It's a

262

necklace." He recognized it as a necklace that Kris had worn since she'd met him. In fact, it was something she'd told him at the beginning. "It's something I've never taken off."

"Bill! Come up here! Someone's taken her!" Chad yelled down to his father-in-law who came running up the stairs.

Bill recognized the small gold half-heart charm hanging on the chain. It was the charm he'd given Kris when she was young. The other half belonged to Karen, but it disappeared along with Maria. Kris never took that necklace off, except to change out the chain that it hung on throughout the years. "She didn't leave on her own. She'd never take that off!" William was beside himself. First finding out about Maria, now his daughter was missing.

"I'll bet the Ahearn bitches are involved! I know it!" Chad said as he and William sat on the front step of the house to wait for the police. "I wish I'd never met Caroline. Maybe then, we wouldn't be here." He'd never felt as helpless in his life. William was as fearful as Chad, but knew one of them needed to keep it together. William patted his shoulder as he sat next to him. "Chad, we will find her! Trust me. There's no way I'm going to let anything happen to her." His voice shook, but he had an idea of where they would find her.

Five minutes later, two police cars were racing into the driveway with their lights on. Both Chad and William ran up to the first car as Officer Daniels stepped out of the car. "One at a time, guys, please," Daniels tried to keep them calm while they both told him about Krista.

"Do either one of you know who would do this?" William nodded. "I think the Ahearn sisters were involved. I'd be willing to bet that they took her to Block Island."

"I appreciate you telling me about your theory about the Ahearn sisters, but why would they take her there?" Officer Daniels wanted to know.

"It only makes sense. Their father owns property there. It's remote and very little police presence." William replied, hoping that Daniels would see the common sense behind it.

Officer Daniels nodded and gave his order to the officers. "Put out an all points bulletin on Krista Burton, white female, blonde hair, blue eyes, 5 foot 4, 28 years old. Possible suspects are Amanda and Jane Ahearn, potentially at or en route to Block Island." The other three officers nodded and passed along the message over the radio. Sirens began flashing as one of the cars headed out. Officer Daniels turned to Chad and William. "I hope you're right about this. If you're not, and we're going all the way out there, we'll be way behind." He warned.

"I think it's the only place she could be. She's my daughter. I wouldn't tell you to look, if I wasn't sure." William assured him. Daniels nodded, "Okay, then. I'll be in touch. In the mean time, sit tight. I don't need you two disappearing." He added, hinting that he wasn't ruling either of them out as potential suspects. "Now, wait a minute, what do you mean?" Chad picked up on his suspicion. William grabbed his arm, "Just let it go. That's what they do." He whispered to him. "Don't give them a reason to interrogate you." Chad nodded. He was right. "Will do, officer," he said obediently, biting his tongue.

As the police cars left, Chad and William were left sitting on the front step quietly. Chad was stewing. "I can't sit here and wait! We have to do something!"

William nodded his head in agreement. "I know. I wish there was a way to get to the island now. The ferries aren't running now and even if they were, we'd probably cross paths with the police."

Chad suddenly started searching though his phone. "It's a long shot, but my friend Paul had a boat at one time. It's not a yacht or anything, but it's docked at Point Judith and could get us there." William nodded, as Chad dialed. Voicemail picked up immediately and he left a message to call him back as soon as possible.

William was quiet for a few minutes then dialed his phone. "Who are you calling?" Chad was curious.

"Stanley Ahearn. I'm done with his bullshit for good now. He owes me a favor or two." William said. He seemed eerily calm for the situation. He held up a hand to cut off Chad as Stanley had surprisingly answered his call.

"Bill. What do I owe you to talk at this time of night?" Stanley said. William was shocked that Stanley knew who was calling. "Yes, I do have your number in my phone. I'm not that old and out of touch with technology, Bill." Stanley said, as if he were reading his mind.

William was lost for words for a moment and suddenly, anger replaced the shock about 'Caroline.' He couldn't believe his wife had left him and married this pretentious asshole. "As you probably know already, your WIFE, who used to be MY WIFE is in the hospital and my daughter is missing and I let police know that I think YOUR daughters are involved! By the way, how is it that you ended up marrying my wife, Ahearn? How is that even possible? As far as I'm concerned, our little agreement is off the table! If I'd known that Maria was your wife now, I'd have given you up a long time ago!" William was shouting into the phone now. Chad had never witnessed him being this upset before, even when those pictures of him and Ahearn's daughter showed up. What was he talking about, 'given him up a long time ago?'

"Hold on a minute, Bill! I'm on my way to T.F. Green airport now. I should be landing soon. Meet me there in an hour and we can talk on the way out to the hospital." Stanley was suddenly agreeable, and his voice lost its usual condescending tone. "There's a lot that I need to explain to you. I didn't go against our agreement. There's a lot that happened after the fact that you need to know. Please, Bill. Let me explain before you start saying things you may regret later." Stanley sounded surprisingly sincere; pleading with him.

William was cautious; worried that Stanley was being sneaky. His curiosity and knowledge that he was probably the only person that had any answers at this point won out. "Okay, Stanley. I'll meet you at the airport. I'll listen to what you have to say. In return, I need your help. My daughter was taken tonight. I believe she was taken by one or both of your daughters, or someone that was hired to take her by them. I sent the police out there, but I need a boat chartered in order for her husband and myself to get out there. I can't just sit here!" Williams' throat was burning and tears fell as the gravity of the situation finally hit him. Finding Maria after all these years only to find out she was married to an arrogant ass like Stanley, and Krista missing was like a nightmare. It was almost too much to comprehend.

"You've got it. I'll call one of my regular contracted staff to be on standby and get you out there tonight." Stanley didn't hesitate to agree.

"Please do it as soon as we hang up. I'll send her husband out now to catch the boat, so that he can be on his way." William said. He was still angry, but glad that Stanley was acting almost human for a change.

"I'll do it as soon as we hang up. Husband's name is Chad Burton, right?" Stanley didn't waste any time.

"Yes." William breathed a sigh of relief.

"Tell Chad to get down to Point Judith right away. The crew of the Sunset Queen will be waiting for him at the dock." Stanley said. "I'll see you in an hour."

"Thanks." William said but Stanley had already hung up. He shook his head and turned to his son- in- law. "Chad, head down to Point

Judith right now. A boat will be waiting for you. The boat is called the Sunset Queen."

"Really? How did you manage that?" Chad was surprised.

"Chad, stop asking questions and just go! I'll meet you there later. I'm meeting with Stanley tonight. Go right now!" William raised his voice. This was no time to waste.

Chad nodded and ran to his car. "Keep me posted!" He said before he sped off for Point Judith. William nodded, then turned to get in his own car and headed for the airport to meet Stanley. He couldn't even begin to wonder what Stanley could possibly say that would make any sense of this unbelievable reality that was unfolding.

Krista

As Krista managed to get her eyes open, she could make out shadows of a rope swinging overhead, and feel a rocking motion that was making her more nauseous by the second. 'Am I dreaming?' Krista wondered. She was flat on her back on a small mattress with her wrists painfully tied behind her confirming she was not dreaming 'I'm on a boat. This is real.' Looking around, there were two portholes on either side, with water lapping over them. There were a few wooden polished stairs that led up to the deck. She was still groggy from whatever they'd given her, but knew that she'd better find a way to get out of here. She thought about crying out for help, but suddenly realized it was better to keep quiet. Let them think she was still unconscious. As far as she knew, there wasn't anyone on this boat that was going to help her.

Krista could hear voices faintly from up above that were somewhat recognizable. She knew without a doubt it was the Ahearn sisters and better figure out how to get away. She wrestled her hands to see if she could loosen the ropes with no luck. They were far too tight, and hoped that she could loosen them enough to get circulation back into her tingling hands.

The voices became louder and she could see someone headed down the stairs to what had become her prison. She immediately shut her eyes and pretended to be unconcious. The footsteps came closer. "Hey, Jane, our little mermaid is still down for the count. When are we supposed to be there?" Krista recognized that voice. It must be that bitch, Amanda, that had lured Chad. She fought to keep quiet, tamping down the urge to stand up, scream and strangle her.

"Oh, Amanda, she'll be out for at least another hour or two. That was strong shit that we gave her. Besides, we're almost there. Kyle said another 15 minutes." Jane sounded like a giddy teenager.

Krista forced herself to stay calm and breathe slowly as Amanda came closer to her. She tried not to make a face as she smelled the stench of whiskey while Amanda hovered above her face. She seemed to hesitate for a moment and suddenly pinched one of her toes. Krista did her best not to move or make a sound.

"Yeah, you're right, she's still out. Let's get this done already." Amanda was slurring her words now, and worked her way back up the stairs.

" I'm just here to get you all where you need to go. I'm not going to hurt anyone!" A male voice objected.

"You'll do what we paid you to do, or you get nothing! That's the deal you made, Kyle." Jane reminded him. Krista couldn't hear anything from Kyle, so she assumed he would be no help to her. He was still obviously on board with drugging and kidnapping.

Krista breathed a sigh of relief that they didn't catch on that she was awake, but knew she didn't have much time. "Karen, where are you? Can you hear me?" Krista whispered, and knowing her chance of communicating was slim to none. She waited and continued to work on loosening the ropes on her hands. After a few minutes, she was exhausted and sleepy from the drugs still in her system. "Karen…really need you ….right now…." Krista managed to whisper, before succumbing to the drowsiness.

"Krista, Krista…I'm here. I'm going to try and loosen your ropes. I'm here. Help is on the way I promise." Karen's now familiar voice was in her dream. "You have to run! Get away from them!" Krista suddenly woke up. She moved her arms and noticed the ropes that bound her hands were slightly loosened, enough for her to work her way out with some effort. She wrung her hands to get circulation again. She could still hear voices on the deck, and tried to plan her next move. Her sister's appearance in her dream was ironically comforting to her now. "Thanks for looking out for me, Karen." Krista whispered.

'I need to stay focused; act as though the rope was still keeping me here, then make a run for it.' She could hear the engines of the boat slow and knew they were close. She quickly wrapped her hands loosely in the ropes so that it appeared she was still unable to move.

She could hear the footsteps again, as the boat came into dock and came to a stop. "Okay, now, let's get this bitch out of here, and get rid of her. No one will find her." Jane's caustic voice was loud as she came

271

close. Krista focused on staying still, eyes shut, and oblivious to what was happening. The strong smell of alcohol was on their breath as all three of them picked her up and carried her up the stairs, not caring that her forehead smacked against the stairwell or that they plopped her down on the dock like a piece of furniture. It took all of Krista's resolve to avoid crying out after being smacked in the face on the stairs and being dropped. She remained still, waiting for her time to make a break for it. She was just glad that no one noticed that the ropes were loosened.

"I think we should drop her into the water here." She could hear Jane's voice. "She's tied up, can't swim, drowns, and maybe they'll find her in a few weeks."

Amanda laughed at her sister, "Are you kidding me? They find her with ropes still tied, and they think it's not a homicide? Seriously, Jane? It's only a matter of time before cops come sneaking around here. No. We need to do it the way I said. It needs to look like a suicide."

Krista opened her eyes halfway to figure out where she could go. Clearly, they had no intention of letting her live. If she made a run for it and they caught her, she'd never have a chance. She could tell she was on a small boat dock and could see the house in the background. Suddenly, she saw Kyle looking her way and immediately closed her eyes. Krista kept her eyes closed and her breathing slow, but now the guy that brought her there might know she was coherent. She waited for him to tell Jane and Amanda and braced herself.

"I think Mandy's right. We can't just dump her off here. That would be obvious," Kyle said quietly, as though he was waiting for Jane to criticize him. Krista thanked him silently. Maybe he hadn't seen her eyes open after all. Or maybe he was starting to have a conscience and help her out? She'd have to gamble on that later.

"You're right. We'll have to drag her up to the house and go from there." Jane finally agreed. "Well, lets go, we don't have a lot of time. I'm sure that husband of hers is going to be coming for her. Although, Amanda, he was into you for some time." Krista wished they had given her earplugs for this conversation.

"Yeah, but he was kind of a dud. He wasn't very kinky. In fact, he was kind of boring; not my type." Amanda joked. Krista wanted to get up and punch her in the face at that moment. She was still upset with Chad, but this woman was clearly a manipulative piece of shit. Despite her anger about Chad's infidelity, she still loved him, and would give anything to see him considering her circumstances.

"I'm glad I didn't have to deal with him. It was enough having to deal with this crazy girl!" Jane replied. Krista swore to herself that if she got out of this, she would make sure that Jane and her bitch sister would get what they deserved!

All three approached her then. "Let's get this done!" Jane insisted. Kyle hesitated and then picked her up, flinging her over his shoulder. Krista did her best not to make any movement, despite the pain in her wrists and the headache developing from her head banging against the wall and the drugs. "Where are we taking her?" Kyle asked.

"You don't need to know that. Just follow instructions. You'll get your money, as long as you cooperate, Kyle." Amanda shut him down for the moment. "You just need to do what we say and then we're done. Understand?" Her tone of voice made it clear that she wasn't playing around. Krista's idea that Kyle might stand up to them dissolved immediately. She had to save herself. She remembered Karen's voice telling her to run once they hit the dock. Clearly, that plan was out, but when she *had* the chance, she'd run! There wasn't any other choice.

Chad

As he headed to Point Judith, Chad continued to try Krista's cell, even though he knew it was probably pointless by now. It went straight to voicemail each time, and each time he called, it made him worry that much more. "I'm coming, Kris! I won't let anything happen to you. I love you." He left a message for her even though she wouldn't get it, at least for now. 'But she will later. She'll get it after we find her and get back her phone.' He forced himself to be positive in order to stay focused.

After what seemed to Chad like an eternity, he pulled into the Point Judith marina and went to the dock that Stanley said would have a crew waiting. Sure enough, the Sunset Queen was right in front of him. It was huge and hard to miss with the lights on and a crew standing on board. He locked up his car and ran down the dock.

"Mr. Burton?" A tall dark haired man asked him as he neared the boat. "Yes, I'm Chad Burton." He managed, out of breath from running. "Make yourself at home. Mr. Ahearn said to take you straight over to the Bluffs." Chad thanked him as he walked on- board. As he looked around, he thought 'boat' was not accurate for the Sunset Queen. More like a mega-yacht that he'd seen sitting in the harbor in Newport that were owned by millionaires, celebrities. He was welcomed immediately by a shorter blond young man in a white uniform.

"Welcome, Mr. Burton, please follow me. I'm Quentin, lead stew on board. Can I get you a drink?" His British accent made him feel like he was on vacation in Europe. Chad's first instinct was to decline, but what the hell. Bourbon on the rocks would settle the nerves. He ordered one from Quentin and was ushered up to the upper deck where he sat in a cushioned deck chair. Within 3 minutes, Quentin returned with his bourbon and he was able to sit back and breathe for a moment. 'If this is the life of a director, I sure could get used to it.' Chad thought to himself.

His phone rang and he picked up immediately. "William! What's going on? I made it onto the boat, although, I would say yacht would be a better description!" Chad began. "Good! There's no time to lose! I just pulled into the airport and to meet Stanley. Let me know when you dock." William sounded frantic.

"Bill, I'm not going to let anything happen to Kris. She means the world to me! I'll call you as soon as we dock." Chad assured him. He hung up and sipped slowly on the bourbon that helped warm him. It was chilly, especially on the yacht, and the wind was blowing. He could see storm clouds ahead and started to worry if it would cause problems getting to the island. His thoughts turned to his wife and praying she was there, safe and sound. He couldn't allow himself to consider the worst.

William

William sat in the arrivals area of TF Green Airport, waiting for Stanley. He was told his plane just landed so it was a matter of minutes before he would come face to face with the man that had destroyed and changed his life in a matter of seconds. He hadn't seen him since that morning after the accident, and was grateful for that. It would've been a constant reminder of what could have been. It had been difficult just dealing with him on the phone over the past twenty-three years.

As passengers started to emerge on the escalators from the arrivals, William sat up in his seat near the escalators nervously. He spotted Stanley in a blue suit, his graying hair perfectly in place. Next to him was a stunning woman who obviously had traveled with him, considering he was flying in his private jet. She was tall and gorgeous, with long blonde hair cascading down her back. She was clearly no older than 25, and wearing a designer light blue suit and skirt with ivory heels. He spoke to her as the escalator moved toward him, and she laughed as if they were sharing a private joke. It was only after he noticed William waiting for him that he stopped talking and appeared reserved again. He smiled and waved, as if they were good friends, getting together after over two decades. William felt his stomach churn with anxiety and building anger, as he went to meet with his 'ally'.

Stanley apparently had no fears about meeting up with him. "Bill! We finally meet again after all these years!" He said, as if they were meeting up for a bachelor party. The leggy blonde hung back, while Stanley moved forward to hug William. William was shocked, and his arms felt like stone as he managed a slight hug back. The strong smell of whiskey was on Stanley's breath, and it didn't take a genius to know he was more than a few drinks in. The blonde woman moved in closer. "Oh, Bill, I want to introduce you to Aubrey. She's my new assistant and public relations person." Bill grasped her hand lightly and let it go, hoping to move on from these ridiculous niceties. "Bill's been a good friend for many years. I can always count on him." Stanley continued on. William winced at the words 'good friend.'

"It's great to meet you, Bill. I'm sorry that we all had to meet under these circumstances." Aubrey seemed to understand the situation and hung back after the introductions.

"Thank you, Aubrey, I appreciate that." He said honestly. He turned to Stanley. "I believe you needed to talk to me, which is why I'm here instead of looking for my daughter." He was losing his patience by the minute. Stanley nodded, "Of course. There should be a limo waiting. Let's talk in there." William was ready to explode with rage. Stanley's wife was in Intensive Care and his own daughter was missing and now likely at the mercy of his psycho daughters on Block Island. "NO! We are going to talk now!" William said loudly, as the few passersby looked at him.

"I'll be in the limo while you two talk, "Aubrey said politely. "Nice to meet you, Bill," she acknowledged, and walked away. Clearly, she was much more perceptive than Stanley about discreet conversations.

William didn't waste another second. "What's the deal, Stan? Please explain to me how you are married to my wife now? I've kept my end up for the past twenty-three years, even though you destroyed my family. Now, I find out that your wife, "Caroline", is actually Maria. How is it that you're married to her now? Is that shit even legal? I doubt it!" Something in William snapped, and he couldn't stop. "If that wasn't enough, your crazy kids have been playing games with my daughters' head and now she's missing. Is that a coincidence? I don't think so!" Stanley was quiet for once. He sighed. "It's a really complicated situation, Bill. I promise, I can explain, but you have to calm down." William knew he had to get himself composed and nodded. "Okay, you're right. I'm listening. I deserve an explanation that makes sense. That is, if there is one." He couldn't help with the added dig.

"Should I be worried about being arrested now? I just want to know," Stanley asked. He seemed almost paranoid, looking around for any sign of law enforcement as he spoke. William laughed, "Of course not, Stan! They're all out looking for my daughter and figuring out if your wife's accident was a murder attempt! But if I were you, I wouldn't be parading around that woman you brought along as your "assistant." This isn't Hollywood, Stan! Bottom line is your negligence cost me a daughter and my wife! Now Krista is missing after being stalked by those crazy women that happen to be your daughters. I know that we made a deal after the accident. I've kept my end of the bargain, and I've never said a word. But this needs to stop! I'll remind you of the details. We were driving along and you hit us head on, killing one of my daughters. You got out of the car and offered me the deal of a lifetime; set me up in my own business and financed anything I needed going forward, if I would cover for you. Well, I've done that! I went through hell and back. I took your deal, and made the business successful. But, then Maria left, and both Krista and I suffered terribly." William tried to keep the tears from forming, but not before one escaped and ran down his cheek. "And now she's your wife! She's hurt and she's in the hospital in ICU. So please try to explain this to me, Stanley. I'm dying to know." William held his head in hands, trying to hold back the emotions.

Stanley sat silent for what seemed an eternity. His eyes became misted with tears as he finally spoke. "Meeting Maria was an accident. I did not seek her out, William. I had never met her except for the accident. After that, I did as I had promised. I set you up with the financing for your business. I never went after your wife. I swear to you." Stanley seemed sincere, and William found himself believing him. "I had just bought the house on Block Island and took the girls there on their summer vacation. It was one morning that I woke up early and went down to the cliffs and saw a woman standing on the ledge near the property. She was clearly upset and crying. I walked toward her and saw that she was preparing to jump from the cliff and then ran toward her, but I was too late to catch her; she jumped before

I could reach her. I had my cell with me, so I called 911 and then ran to the area where she had been. She had jumped, and fallen about 20 feet down. She had a severe concussion, broken ribs, and a broken arm, but she healed. All except that she still couldn't remember anything prior to the accident and it was determined that she had amnesia and didn't even remember who she was, or give names of family numbers to contact. I didn't' realize who she was at first. She seemed familiar, but I couldn't pinpoint why until I saw the news about Maria missing."

William was trying to wrap his head around what Stanley was saying. "So you're saying Maria showed up near your house to jump off the cliff and you found her, knew who she was and didn't bother telling the police or anyone else." His tone was acidic. Stanley was more of an arrogant ass than he thought possible.

"She didn't know anything. She didn't even know her name, so I gave her the name 'Caroline.' She was suicidal and a complete invalid for quite some time, Bill. You have to understand. I gave her around the clock care until she was well, and then she didn't want to leave. She didn't recover her memory and she wanted to stay. She was so beautiful, vulnerable, and she seemed to need me. I knew that I loved her and I didn't want her to go. After a few months, I did bring her to several different doctors in an effort to restore her memory. But after several months, she still didn't remember her real name and seemed to have no recollection of you, Krista or the accident that killed your other daughter."

"Karen." William said between gritted teeth. "What?" Stanley was confused.

"Her name was Karen. She was Maria's and my daughter, Krista's twin. She was a little girl who died unnecessarily. I would think that you would at least have the decency to remember her name. After all, if it hadn't been for you driving while you were drunk as shit, that accident would've never happened. Or have you forgotten that too?" William spat at him. "Did YOU ever talk to Maria about any of us, or did you just let her believe that she was a suicidal woman, wandering around the cliffs and clueless about who she was or any family?" Stanley seemed to be listening. Finally.

"She had a picture with her when I found her, still clutched in her hand. It was a picture of her and the twins. She still has it framed in the bedroom and she still looks at it, as if she's trying to remember. She claims that she sees a young girl wandering around the cliff area at the house at Mohegan Bluffs and it frightens her. It's the main reason why she wants to sell the place. But she's never told me that she remembers anything about any of you. Yet, she still wants that picture. Yes, I did try to ask, but all of the professionals insisted that I shouldn't interfere. William, I did try, and by the time I realized who she was, it was too late to go back. I didn't want her to unravel and risk losing her." Stanley brushed his hand across his eyes, trying to mask the tears forming there.

William was floored by this information and Stanley's reaction. Stanley didn't strike him as an emotional person, but then again, he only knew that 'Hollywood' Stanley. "What about Aubrey? If you're so in 'love' with Maria, what are you doing with that bimbo?"

"Hold on Bill! I don't appreciate what you're insinuating here! If you're referring to Aubrey, she is my assistant, and a damn good one! Just because she's a good looking woman, doesn't mean that I'm having an affair. Far from it! She's married, and has a child back in California. She came here with me to help with any publicity that needs to be handled while I'm here. I've never cheated on Caroline!" Stanley's face turned beet-red with the accusation, and his fists were clenched. "Speaking of Caroline, I really should get going. I came here to see my wife who's injured and that's what I intend to do!" Stanley grabbed his bag and headed toward the limo, leaving William behind.

"Stanley, wait!" William called out. He wasn't sure what he wanted to say, but he knew that leaving things as they were with Stanley would only hurt the situation. Stanley took a few more steps toward the limo and stopped. "What?" He asked without turning around.

"Look, Stan, It's been a long night and I'm stressed out of my mind. I was wrong to bring up accusations about you and Aubrey. I really need to know that I can count on you to help with......with this situation." He didn't want to state the obvious, that his daughters were involved, as Stanley held the cards to help Krista. Stanley turned around.

"Bill, I may be a lot of things, but I'm not one to tolerate illegal or violent behaviors from anyone, including my own daughters, despite what you might think. I'm going to the hospital now to check on Caroline. I've told the staff at the house on Block Island to keep an eye out and report anything to me and the police since I heard about what happened, but I can't control what my grown daughters do. I can tell you that I'll help you out with whatever you need in the meantime. I'm not here to argue about the past."

It was as close as an apology he would ever get from Stanley. He was right. There was no time to throw accusations or try to make sense of what was now past. William knew that he needed to work with Stanley, despite the fact that Maria belonged to him now and how much he hated that.

"Okay, Stanley. I'm going to trust you. I hope that Mar-, I mean Caroline is doing better." Bill stumbled and wanted to tell him he was thinking of her, but suddenly knowing he couldn't.

Stanley nodded, "Okay. I plan to go out to the house later on, maybe in a few hours, depending on how she's doing. I'll call you and we can meet up at the dock and head out. Are you up for that?" William agreed without hesitation. "I am. Just call me and I'll meet you there." He only hoped they wouldn't be too late.

Krista

As Kyle carried her off the boat like a sack of potatoes, Krista did her best to remain motionless as if she were still unconscious. It was tough, considering that they'd drugged her up and then wacked her head against the side of the boat several times. She knew it was her only chance. She opened one eye occasionally to see how far they were from the water to get an idea of what her escape plan might be. She could see the steps to the house closer, worrying about her fate once they got there. "What's your plan, Amanda? How are we gonna make this look legit?" She could hear Jane's shrill voice, like nails on a chalkboard.

"I'm thinking we should bring her inside. Maybe give her some more prescription cocktails, enough to take care of her for good." Amanda replied, slurring her words.

"That's the worst idea I've heard in a long time. I believe you're drunk, little sister. I've got a better plan." Jane sounded confident, and scarily lucid. She was the monster that Krista had always thought she was when she worked at the school. She was a textbook sociopath. "She's out of it. I think she might have an "accident" and fall off the cliffs in the backyard area. After all, there isn't a fence. She might have just been walking along, and you know…fell suddenly, or jumped is more like it." Jane laughed maliciously. "She was always on the edge anyway. It wouldn't be a surprise. Especially since her mother is the same way. Like mother, like daughter, isn't that what everyone says?"

Krista was caught off guard with mention of mother and moved her head slightly without realizing it until it was too late. "Like her mother is?" What did that mean? Jane spoke of her mother as if she knew her, as if she were still alive. Her mind raced and she struggled to maintain her composure as a comatose victim, when she really wanted to bash their heads in. Her head movement did not go unnoticed by Jane. "Is she awake? She just moved her head. Anyone else see that? Maybe our little princess is waking up and the fun has just begun." She could feel Jane's breath within inches of her ear.

"Hi, Krista! Welcome to our home away from home! I hope you enjoy what time you have left here!" She laughed sadistically. They continued through the front door, through the foyer, long hallway and down some steep stairs to the basement. Although it was a huge space, it was dimly lit by a single overhead bulb and clearly a storage area. There were stacks of boxes, along with old toys and furnishings that had been abandoned and forgotten. They continued down a long hallway and through a door to a small, prison-like room with a small window that allowed enough daylight to peek through. Jane shut the door behind them and Kyle dumped Krista onto an old folding chair as she continued to feign drowsiness from the drugs.

Krista didn't move or try to speak. She wasn't sure what they had planned, but was sure that talking to these bitches wasn't going to help. Surely her father and Chad had figured out by now that she was gone and hopefully were looking for her. In the mean time, she wasn't going to make this easy for them to get rid of her. "Oh, the princess is pretending to still be sleeping?" Jane's voice rasped with venom. She stomped on her left foot which caused Krista to cry out despite her resolve to remain quiet. "Yeah, that's what I thought. When I talk to you, you'd better answer! Got it?" She slapped her in the face. Krista's eyes flew open, glaring with anger. "Well?" Jane asked again.

"Yeah, I got it." Krista managed between gritted teeth and it was all she could do not to add 'you bitch' to her response.

"Good. I'm glad you understand that you're not in charge here. You may have been a thorn in our side for a VERY long time, but not anymore. You see, you're standing in the way of a lot of money that we deserve, and I'm afraid that we can't let that happen." Jane snarled at her as if Krista was the cause of all her problems in the world. Krista was stunned. So this was about money? She and Chad didn't have enough money to warrant this kind of behavior.

"What? What money are you talking about? I don't have a lot of money and neither does my husband." Krista couldn't help but respond. They were trying to kill her and she wanted to know why.

Jane laughed. "Oh, poor deluded Krista. You really don't know do you?"

"Know what?" Krista's voice rose, almost as demanding as Jane's.

"Since you've been left in the dark by your devoted father, I'll fill you in. Your mother is married to my father, Stanley Ahearn. I'm sure you've heard of him? The movie director?" Krista shook her head. "No, my mother disappeared! That's impossible! My mother died! You have the wrong person!" She screamed at Jane.

"Oh no, dear Krista. Your mother is very much alive, unfortunately for us. She has been for many years. My father married her years ago when we were still little girls, isn't that right, Amanda?" Amanda nodded. "She wasn't really ever in her right mind, but my dad was blind, he didn't care!" Her eyes were blazing as she said the words. "He didn't care about us anymore! All he cared about was his precious Caroline!"

"Caroline?! That's not my mother's name! You're a lying bitch!" Krista spat at her, despite her compromised situation. What the hell was she talking about? Jane was definitely delusional! Her wrists still had the loosened ropes, but she remembered not to show them she could move. It was three against one right now, and it wasn't likely she could make it out of the room with those odds.

"Maybe not her given name, but since she didn't remember it, that's her name now. And she's a big problem, which also makes you a big problem. You see, your mother will inherit most of my father's money and assets when he dies." Krista shook her head. "Oh, yes, it's true. Your mother is our stepmother, and she's been interfering for far too long. Then, there's you. My father had a clause put in his will in regards to her child. You, well….. you WERE supposed to get a huge

288

amount of his money." Jane laughed. "But then again, if you aren't alive, I guess that you wouldn't have a need for any of that, would you?"

"I don't want your father's money! Just let me go and I'll make sure I'm taken out of his will. You're lying about my mother! She would never be married to someone like your father and put up with bitches like you!" Krista yelled at her now. Knowing that her mother might be alive was almost more than she could bear. She couldn't believe anything that Jane said. She had to admit, she wished she was right that her mother was alive. All the more reason to get away from these people before they went through on their crazy plan to kill her! She clenched her fists behind her back, still with the loosely tied ropes, preparing for attack if needed. She wasn't going down without a fight.

Jane brought her face to Krista's, her face beet-red with anger. "If I were you, I'd shut my trap! It's only because of my sister and Kyle, that you aren't floating with the fish right now! As for your mother, it's true! She's been around for years, more than I care to count. She can be such a drag; encouraging my dad to send us to college, or Europe or somewhere out of the way. She seems to think that would make us 'more respectful and get a good education.' She really does mean well, but in the end, we just disappoint her anyway. Honestly, I don't give a shit! She isn't my mother! But, I guarantee this, Krista, she IS your mother. It's just too bad that you won't be reacquainted with her."

Krista gritted her teeth and fought back tears, but she refused to let them see any sign of weakness. "I'm sure she wanted you far away, considering she knew what useless shitty people you turned out to be!" She couldn't help throwing that in Jane and Amanda's faces.

Jane lunged at her "You fucking bitch! How dare you!" She grabbed Krista by the neck from behind and began to strangle her. Amanda and Kyle rushed forward to stop her. "Jane! Stop! You can't do this," Kyle yelled at her. "Janie, stop it!" Amanda was behind him. "If you do this, it'll never look like an accident!" Her words seemed to reach Jane in her moment of insanity. She let go of Krista.

Krista was struggling for air and lying on her back. She knew that the next chance she had, she'd make a run for it. There was no other way. She could only hope that Chad and her father had figured out she was kidnapped; that they called the police. Even if police were notified, she needed to figure this out. There wasn't much time left.

Chad

Chad was sitting on the top deck of Stanley's yacht, looking into the distance and hoping that he could get to his wife in time. The storm clouds were closer, and the wind had picked up in the past few minutes, making him that much more uneasy. Quentin appeared out of nowhere. "Another drink, sir?" he asked.

"No, thanks. Are we almost there?" The bourbon hadn't done a thing for his anxiety. "We're almost there, Mr. Burton. However, we have to dock a few miles from the Bluffs. There aren't big enough dock slots for the yacht at the Bluffs. There will be a car waiting for you when you get there." Quentin advised him. Chad was frustrated, but knew there wasn't anything to do but wait. "Quentin, are there any weapons on board?" Chad asked.

"Weapons? You mean guns, knives? No, I don't think so. Mr. Ahearn usually takes this vessel to the vacation areas of the world. No, he doesn't carry those on board, Mr. Burton," Quentin answered, sounding surprised that Chad had asked.

"Of course." Chad said, deciding not to explain himself, and suddenly saw a Coast Guard vessel 20 yards from them with their lights flashing and headed toward the Bluffs that he could now see straight ahead. The impending storm was creating huge white caps and he noticed that the smaller Guard vessel was getting caught up in the huge waves crashing in on the Bluffs. "They must be headed to the house! Thank god!" Chad said, breathing a sigh of relief.

"Like I said, we'll get you over there as soon as we've docked, Mr. Burton. No worries there." Quentin assured him. Chad thought for a moment and then got up and headed downstairs to the galley. "Thanks, Quentin!" He said as he made his way down.

"Mr. Burton, you can't.......You're not supposed to go down there......." Quentin's words were lost to Chad as he headed downstairs to find something, anything to use against these people who took his wife. The galley was small, dark, and empty and it was hard to find his way around. He looked around for a knife block and spied one off to the side. He grabbed a large butcher knife, hiding beneath his coat as he made his way back to the upper deck.

"Mr. Burton, I'm glad you're back! Guests aren't allowed down in the galley area." Quentin chastised him as he came back and sat down.

"Sorry, I was just....just looking for a bathroom." Chad improvised as best he could. Quentin didn't look convinced, but didn't argue with him. "We'll be docking in 5 minutes, Mr. Burton. If you like, you can make your way toward the stern. Chad nodded. "Thank you, Quentin." He pulled out a fifty -dollar bill to tip him, but Quentin shook his head. "Oh no, sir. I can't take that. Mr. Ahearn has taken care of it already. Be careful, the wind is picking up, I think we're in for a storm."

"Thank you." Chad said and headed toward the stern for docking. He knew he still was at least 15 minutes from the bluffs, and the wind was blowing in gusts now as the black storm clouds loomed up ahead. He looked at his phone and then tried Krista's number again, knowing it was useless. After two rings, he was ready to hang up when suddenly, it was answered. "Hello? Kris? Is that you?" Chad asked frantically. He could hear noise from whoever had picked up the phone. "Kris! Answer me!" He was almost yelling now, desperate just to hear her voice.

"Do you really think I'd let your wife have access to her phone?" A woman's voice finally answered. Chad was stunned for a moment, but he was sure he knew who was answering. "Amanda, I know it's you. Give it up! There's no way you're getting away with this. If you let her go, I promise I won't press charges, and all this can go away." The words slipped out of his mouth without hesitation. All he could think about was Krista's safety.

There was a woman's laughter intermixed with wind gusts on the phone. He knew she was close. "Chad, you really think it's that easy? After all, we had a pretty good time together, and she wasn't paying much attention to you when you needed it. Am I right?"

Chad was furious. "No! It was a mistake on my part, it wasn't her fault! Listen, I won't list the house! I'll step away and you won't have to worry about Carson Realty ever again, if you'll just let her go!" He tried to keep the fury out of his voice, which was nearly impossible. He had never felt so scared, angry and helpless all at the same time.

"First of all, I'm not Amanda. But she did share all the naughty details. Second of all, your time was up 8 hours ago. I will give you a hint of where she is though. Those cliffs do seem pretty steep. Especially when someone isn't paying attention." There was sadistic laughter again before the phone went dead and Chad was left gaping at the phone, knowing that he didn't have any time left. "Shit! I need to get there now!" He shouted through the wind out to the deck staff preparing to throw out lines to dock. "Just one minute, sir and you can leave. "One of the deck staff assured him. He just hoped that the police or Coast Guard was almost there, ready to help.

Just as he was about to step off the boat, he could see a car waiting for him. "Thank god!" Chad shouted as he ran off the yacht, toward the black Lexus with the lights illuminated. The driver rolled down the window. "Chad Burton?"

" Yes!" Chad jumped into the back seat. "Please get me to the Ahearn house as fast as possible!"

The person driving the car had a black ball cap on and as he looked closer, he noticed that he or she had blonde hair sticking out from beneath. Chad wasn't sure why, but he felt uncomfortable. "Looks like a storm is headed here!" He attempted to make small talk. The driver didn't answer right away.

"It does, sir, but we've had storms before." The driver was clearly a woman and she sounded strangely familiar, but he couldn't place it. He was sure that he'd heard that voice before. Then suddenly he knew where he'd heard it. She sounded exactly like Caroline Ahearn. But how? His heart was beating out of his chest, as he tried to remain calm. "How long have you worked for Mr. Ahearn?" Chad asked as he looked around. The car windows were tinted like a limo. No one would see him in here.

"I just started here." Again that voice. He could swear it was Caroline. Yet, that was impossible! Caroline was in the hospital. The car was swerving around the bend up toward the Bluffs as the rain started and came down in sheets.

"What's your name? I didn't get your name." Chad was increasingly nervous, grabbing the armrest as the car sped up. He had a gut feeling that this person wasn't here to help him.

"You don't need to know my name, Mr. Burton. I have to say, I enjoyed showing you around the mansion the last time. It was almost as if I actually was the lady of the house."

"Caroline? Is that you?" Chad asked. The driver laughed. "I wish I was! They live the good life! No worries about money, or where you're going to live. They don't know the meaning of being homeless." Her voice became shaky, tearful.

Chad was silent, remembering the second meeting had been different. Her whole persona was different; the way she greeted him, allowing Amanda to follow along. Even her mannerisms were different. The first meeting, Caroline always made eye contact and smiled. The second time around, he remembered, she avoided his eyes whenever possible. Then there was the opportunity to take pictures of her on the property. Her response was as though she were being asked to pose for Playboy.

The car pulled off to the side of the road, and she turned around to face him. "Look, Mr. Burton! Just let me get you to the house! Stop asking me so many questions!" She turned back around and continued to drive. "Should've never taken this job. Knew it was a risk....don't want to be involved." She muttered to herself loud enough for Chad to overhear her.

He suddenly remembered her refusal for him to take her picture and now it made sense, as did the strange apology for "my step-daughters behavior" that she'd brought up when she'd called to schedule the last visit to the house. The soft-hearted person that he'd met was gone. He was facing a monster now. Her eyes glittered with hate, and it shook him to the core. He pulled on the door handle, which refused to budge, since she had locked them from the driver's side. "I'm afraid I can't let you go. You know too much."

"I don't know anything, except that I met with you to sell your house! Since you're not Caroline, who are you?" Chad demanded to know.

Her face softened for a moment. "My name is Estelle. I'm an actress. I've lived outside of Hollywood for almost five years now, trying to get a break. I was working as an assistant for Jana Evans who was acting in one of Mr. Ahearn's movies. When she told me that one of Mr. Ahearn's daughters wanted to hire me for an acting job. I couldn't say no." Estelle seemed somewhat regretful and teary. "They gave me videos of Caroline and told me to study her. That this was my 'audition', agreed to pay me well, and promised that I would get a role in one of their fathers' next movies." It was all starting to make sense to Chad now. "So who is the person in the hospital, Estelle? We're all under the impression that it is Caroline."

Estelle nodded. "It is Mrs. Ahearn. She had an accident." She sounded sincerely upset. "Did you see it?" Chad asked, hoping she'd give away a clue about what happened.

"No. Not really." Estelle replied vaguely as she wiped her eyes. The phone sitting next to her rang and she pulled off to the side. "Yes?" She answered. Chad couldn't hear the voice on the other end, but knew that it was likely one of the Ahearn sisters. "Yes, he's here. I'm on my way." She hung up and kept her eyes forward. "Estelle! Listen to me! You don't have to listen to them! They want to kill my wife! They want to kill me! Do you want to be an accessory to that!?" Chad was almost shouting as he realized what a hold they had on this person. Estelle ignored him and continued driving. "I'm sorry, Mr. Burton, but if I back out now, I won't get the rest of my paycheck."

"You're not going to have anything, if you're sitting in a jail cell next to those two girls! You think about that! You're only helping them with a life sentence!" Chad yelled at her in desperation. He dialed

William's phone. 'Pick up, please pick up, Bill!' Chad prayed silently. When he heard his voice, Chad sighed with relief. "Bill? I need help here. I'm in a black Lexus. The driver who picked me up on Block Island is in on the kidnapping. It's someone hired by Stanley's daughters! I'm not sure he even knows! Tell the police. I….". Suddenly he realized he was talking to silence and wasn't sure how much Bill heard. He only hoped that he'd gotten enough to know that he needed help to save Krista.

William

William was on his way to the dock to meet Stan to head over to the island when Chad called and he picked up immediately. "What's going on?"

Chad's voice was faint and he sounded stressed out. He could barely make out what he was saying. "Need help.....black Lexus ...driver picked me up...in on the kidnapping... hired by someone...... Stanley's daughters. .not sure if he knows.....tell the police." The call was dropped. William pulled over and dialed him back, desperately hoping that Chad would pick up, but it went straight to voicemail. "Damn!" William tried again, but it was no use. He dialed Stanley's number as he headed back to the Point Judith marina. After three rings, Stanley picked up. William breathed a sigh of relief. "Stan, I just got a call from Chad. He got to the island. It was poor service, but I got that the driver who picked him up was someone that was 'hired' and in on the kidnapping. What the hell is going on?"

"What are you talking about, Bill? I didn't hire anyone. I've had the same driver for years!" Stan insisted, but William wasn't going to let this go. "Stan, think about it! Your daughters don't want the house to be sold. What if they did hire another driver, someone who would help them to get their way?"

Stan was silent for a moment. "Stan? You still there?" William was frantic. "Yes, I'm still here. It still doesn't make sense why my daughter's would hire a driver, when we have one.....wait a minute. I remember one of the actresses this week talking up her assistant. Something about recommending her for a role. It was strange. She went on and on about her." Stanley was thinking out loud.

"What are you getting at?" William asked.

Silence on Stanley's end. "Stan? Are you still there?"

"Yes, I'm here. I'm still not sure about what's going on, but I'm 5 minutes away from the dock. Where are you?" His voice sounded strange, as though he was finally getting how serious the situation was becoming.

"I'm almost there. I'll meet you soon!" William hung up and sped toward the dock, anxious to get to his daughter and son-in-law. He arrived at the unlit dock with a few overheads lighting the way. He got out of his car, just as the rain started pouring down and the wind picked up. As he looked up at the sky, he knew they were in for a treacherous ride to Block Island. That is, *if* Stanley's crew were even willing to take them there in this weather. Stanley's limo pulled up just then and he jumped out.

"Bill! This isn't weather that we should be sailing in!" He was yelling over the wind that was taking on a life of its' own.

"I don't care! I'll swim there if I need to! Krista's being held hostage there, and now Chad's been taken too! I don't know! I can't reach either of them! I need to get over there! Please, Stan!" William hated to barter with anyone, but in this situation, he was desperate. Stanley stood for a moment, then nodded. "I'll get you there." He seemed almost human now, as if the great Stanley Ahearn had finally been brought down to earth again. He spoke to the deck hands and captain of the small boat named the "Caroline" and then nodded to William. "Let's go. We need to go." William nodded and immediately got on board, despite his fear of the impending storm. Stanley followed behind him.

When they were on board, the small yacht surged forward and they were immediately faced with waves that threatened to smash over the bow of the yacht. The deck crew said something to Stanley. William couldn't hear them due to the sound of the waves, and then Stanley was rushing toward the captain's deck to speak with him. He could see him talking with the captain, and his heart sank as he saw him throw up his hands and walked back to William. "The captain says we can't go out there in this weather." Stanley said. He looked genuinely upset. "I know how important it is for us to be there, Bill, but he isn't willing to risk it. Unless you want to sail yourself out there, I'm afraid we're not going to get there until this storm lets up. I'm really sorry, Bill." Stanley turned away just then. "I'll contact the police and the Coast Guard. They must be there by now and have some answers."

William bowed his head. "Thanks, Stan. I appreciate everything you've done. It can't be helped." Stan stood silent for a moment, looking unusually sympathetic, then spoke, "By the way, Caroline is stabilized. The doctors say she should be okay. Just needs a few days in the hospital, but she'll recover. I thought you'd want to know." William didn't reply and walked away. He didn't want to hear about his wife. Not when she was now known as "Caroline." She was once 'Maria', but there was no chance for him. She would remain in his past. It still hurt but at least she was stabilized. They both walked off the boat in silence.

As they reached the parking lot, Stanley turned to William. "I'm calling the police again now. Do you want to wait with me in the limo while I try to get hold of them?" The wind was gusting to 60 mph now and blowing the rain in sheets. William knew he couldn't go home and just sit, so he nodded. "Thanks, Stan. I think I'll take you up on that!" He tried to make light as the wind blew a branch his way and he was forced to duck to avoid being hit.

"Get in!" Stan yelled through the wind at William who gladly jumped into the limo as fast as he could and Stanley followed. The limo was nothing short of spectacular, and William found it hard to not stare at the luxurious interior. The limo was big enough for at least 12 people with a full bar, a 50 -inch TV and blue lighting to set the mood. For once he was glad that he knew someone with the kind of money that warranted this extravagance, and importance. He only wished that he could've been headed out to the island. He wouldn't be able to relax until he knew Krista and Chad were safe.

Stanley was on the phone with the police and he could overhear his end of the conversation. "Yes. I'm glad you're on the island. Be aware that there's a black Lexus headed towards my estate on the bluffs." Stan shook his head at Bill, as he continued on the phone. "The person driving is not my employee. I'm concerned that this person is connected with the kidnapping." William tried to tune out the rest of Stanley's phone call. "Yes, yes, I understand. Please call me as soon as you have any information." Stanley finally hung up.

"Well? What's going on?" William was hungry for details. "They're on the island now and headed toward the house. They'll let me know anything that's going on when they get there. I guess the storm is worse there." Stanley said. They could both hear the wind howling and slightly shaking the limo as they were talking and William was silent. "Bill, I'm sorry we couldn't get there." Stan sounded sincere.

"I know. I just wish I knew what was happening. It's almost like reliving that night...all over again." William said as he looked out the window.

Stanley was quiet and at a loss for words for once. He knew William was referring to the night of the accident. He remembered it all too well and hoped he'd never have another like it. "I know, Bill. I'll do what I can to help. I should've known that something was going on. I know Caroline wanted to sell the property, and she did talk to me about it. When you called me to confirm about selling the property, I knew Caroline was at the house when your son-in-law visited. But the second time Chad was out there, well, something didn't add up."

"What do you mean "didn't add up?" William asked.

"I mean that when you told me Chad came out for the second time and you told me about my daughter being there....it didn't occur to me until later." Stanley was stalling. "What? What, Stan?" William asked, his entire body was tightened up.

"I remember that Caroline was visiting friends on Martha's Vineyard that day. She wasn't home. I know she wasn't. She was aboard one of my yachts headed to the Vineyard that morning shortly after I left the house."

William shook his head. "You just remembered that? So it's more than likely that this stranger, whoever she is, *was* pretending to be Caroline!" He was dumbfounded. Stanley shook his head. "Honestly, Bill. I have to admit, I'm a little scatterbrained when it comes to details about my family's whereabouts. I was headed to LA that morning, so it didn't click until just now. I'm sorry about everything; the accident, your daughter, your wife. If I could go back and change it, I wouldn't hesitate to do it." Stanley seemed sincere. William noticed a few tears roll down his face before he quickly brushed them away with his shirt sleeve.

"I appreciate that, Stan, but you can't go back in time. You can't take back the accident, or Karen's life. You can't take back that you married my wife that I thought was dead. It's done. Just help me bring my daughter and son–in-law back and I'll go back to my same life. I won't bother you or Maria again." William assured him, tears threatening to break free. All he cared about now was Krista and Chad. They deserved a chance. Stanley nodded and held his hand out to William. "I'll do whatever I can. Can you forgive me? I really didn't know about any of this. Apparently, I need to be in touch with what's really important." William shook his hand. "I believe you, Stan. Now let's finish this!"

Krista

After almost being strangled, Krista was still trying to get her bearings. Jane had stopped right before she'd passed out, but only because the others had insisted. She knew she needed to get out no matter what. She hoped that by now, Chad and her father knew she was missing, but she couldn't count on them or the police to save her at this point. She looked to her right and saw a door. The only question was whether it was locked or not. She said a silent prayer to Karen in her head and began unraveling the ropes that had been loosened around her wrists while keeping an eye on her captors the whole time. Amanda was still wrestling with Jane to calm her down and Kyle looked like a deer in headlights, unsure of what to do next.

Krista remained quiet, pretending to struggle for breath and knew it was time to make a run for it. She noticed a small plastic bucket near her foot and decided she needed a distraction and kicked it as hard as she could. It had the intended effect. They looked around to find the source of the noise, as she pulled herself away and ran toward the door that she prayed wasn't locked. As she turned the knob and she was able to get through she said "Thank you, Karen."

She had no idea if her sister had anything to do with it, but she was grateful for an opportunity to be free, as she slammed the door hard behind her. Their voices were loud and she could hear footsteps running. Krista started down the dark hallway, seeing some light up ahead. She continued to follow it, running as fast as she could, her heart beating out of her chest. 'I've gotta get out of here! They'll kill me if they catch me!' She ran up the steep stairs to find herself on the first floor of the mansion. The front door was in sight, but she heard footsteps and voices getting close. She knew there wasn't time to head for the door, which might be locked. Krista chose to hide in a niche underneath the staircase instead. Panic set in, but Krista focused on keeping her breathing slow just as she'd taught so many students to overcome anxiety over the years.

"I know she came this way." She could hear Jane's voice above the mumbling, her shrill annoying voice that could peel paint off the walls. She heard another woman's voice that wasn't familiar to her.

"He's here. I've got him with me, Ms. Amanda." Who the hell was that? Who was "he?" She could hear a man's voice muffled in the background. "Krisssss, Krisssss!" He was trying to call out. She recognized the voice immediately; it was Chad! Her relief lasted only a second, as she realized that he was being held captive by these psychotic people that had taken her.

She resisted the urge to call out to him, let him know she was okay, but knew she couldn't take on three people by herself. She needed to do something, and searched for a weapon, anything, but there was nothing along the staircase that would help. She poked her head around the corner to see Chad with a piece of duct tape over his mouth and his hands tied behind his back coming through the main foyer. Amanda and Kyle were forcing him forward, despite his resistance. Jane and a woman with blonde hair were following behind. She immediately pulled back, 'Oh my god! What am I going to do?' Where was Karen when she needed her? It was almost as if Karen had led her to this place to now be stuck. Did she want her to die and be with her? It crossed her mind now.

'Karen, if you're here to help me, I could use some help right now.' She thought, hoping that her sister would hear her. As she looked around, she noticed a huge brass candlestick holder across from her on a small table. She gasped out loud, then clapped her hand over her mouth as they walked past her, forcing her husband. She was trying her best to not panic. 'Karen, I'm scared. But I can do this. I know you're with me.' Krista thought. Somehow, the knowledge that Karen had existed made her feel confident that she could make it through this. 'We're getting out of here!' Krista decided. She was done being afraid!

She waited until they passed into the living room. 'I've got to go for it,' she thought and quickly crept over to the candlestick, grabbed it, and hurried back to her hiding spot. 'What do I do now?' Krista was frantic.

She could feel her heart pounding as she could hear them close by. She crept around the corner near the kitchen and saw a faint light from the stairs that she'd come up to escape. She could hear voices down the stairs and held the heavy candlestick tightly as she was descending back down into the dungeon-like basement that she'd just escaped from. On the third step, the old wood made a creaking noise, and Krista stopped, praying that they hadn't heard it. The voices continued on, and she carefully continued her way down.

As she got to the last stair, she quickly hid behind a stack of boxes. She could hear talking, the sound growing louder as they came closer. "You'd better tell that wife of yours to show herself, or you're going to be fish food! Do you understand me?" She recognized Jane's voice. She gripped the candlestick so tight her knuckles were turning white. That bitch! She crept closer around the corner and could see Chad lying on a wooden table, wrists still duct taped, along with his mouth. He was struggling and shaking his head. "No! Neverrrr!" His voice was muffled by the tape, but she could make out the words. She could hear Amanda laughing.

"I'm afraid it doesn't work that way, baby. You see, if she isn't here in about 5 minutes, you'll be getting a lethal cocktail injected into your arm. Then you won't be much help to anyone, including your crazy-ass wife! I suggest that you call her out here, because we know she's in this house. The doors are locked, she didn't leave. I also suspect that she knows that you're here and despite your 'indiscretions' she somehow still cares, although I'm not sure why. You weren't worth it in the first place." She giggled as she tore the duct tape off his mouth. "Go ahead, Chad. Let her know you're here. I want to hear you beg her to save you." She sounded like a sadistic witch and Krista racked her brain, trying to figure out her next move. She knew that if she went after them and didn't succeed in getting her husband free, they'd both be dead. Chad shook his head and remained silent.

"That's not the begging I was looking for, Chad. Let's try again. I'll give you to the count of five. One….Two…"

She knew she needed help and pleaded, "Karen, if you're here, I need your help. I need your help to save Chad. Can you help me?" Krista whispered desperately. "Three…Four….." The countdown continued.

For what seemed like eternity, nothing happened, but then she heard the words although she wasn't sure if they were her own or Karen, 'Run! Run, the door is unlocked. Just run!' 'But I can't leave him here!' Krista thought. She needed to do something, and whether it was Karen giving her direction or herself, she needed to do whatever she could to save him. She took a deep breath and gripped the candlestick, gave it a practice swing. It was heavy enough to cause some serious damage. Krista took a deep breath and ran out, taking them all off guard, and headed straight for Amanda's head swinging as hard as she could. She made contact with her head and Amanda went down to the floor. The syringe she was holding went flying, along with the candlestick. She could hear Chad's voice, telling her to run. Jane and Kyle dropped to the floor to check on Amanda.

Krista hesitated long enough to glance behind her. She could see a pool of blood spilling from Amanda's head. 'Oh, my god. She's dead.' Krista thought, suddenly horrified that she was responsible.

Jane looked up at her with venom. "You've killed my sister! You fucking bitch!! Now I'm going to kill you!" She got up and ran to a nearby cabinet, pulling out a shotgun.

Krista knew the only way out to save herself and Chad was to run as her sister had told her. She ran up the stairs and down the hallway to the front door which was thankfully not locked. Once outside, she was immediately pelted with a downpour of rain blown sideways by the wind. Her eyes tried to adjust to the darkness from the storm. Taking a moment to get her bearings, Krista raced past the pool toward a wooded area hoping to hide in the trees. Suddenly, she slipped in the wet grass and found herself flat on her back. Huge raindrops clouded her vision for a moment, then she managed to flip over and low-crawl to a nearby bush. She could hear Jane's footsteps stop suddenly. She held her breath, hoping that Jane hadn't seen her. Luckily, she didn't.

"Get up! The police are on their way." She could hear Karen's voice clear, as if she was there. She got to her feet and continued through the trees only to stop at a cliff with nothing but huge rocks surrounded by churning waves below. "What do I do?" Krista screamed into the wind. There was nothing, but the sound of the waves that were churning below, and as she turned, she was faced with Jane, with a shotgun in her hand only yards away.

Just when Krista didn't think Jane couldn't be uglier, she managed it. Her dark brown eyes were narrow with anger, like a venomous snake. Her long hair was wet and matted to her head, and an evil smile was frozen on her face. She brought the gun to her shoulder. Krista knew that she was in trouble. She couldn't go any further and it was unlikely that even if Jane wasn't a sharpshooter, she wouldn't miss from 5 feet away. If she moved another foot, she was falling into the ocean. Krista had a sudden flashback of her nightmares with the same scenario. 'Karen was warning me.' Nadine had been right.

Krista envisioned Chad and her father now. How she wished she could have said goodbye. She thought about her mother and the chance to see her again. 'I'm not giving up! This isn't a dream! I will find a way out!' Her resolve to survive strengthened. She steadied herself as Jane grew closer. "I see you've run out of room, Krista. I think it's time to say goodbye. I have to say that your husband was most helpful while Amanda worked at his office." Jane laughed as if this was the most enjoyable moment of her life. Krista could see Jane raising the shotgun to her shoulder.

"Let him go! He didn't do anything wrong!" Krista shouted. Instinctively, she tried to move away from the gun that was pointed at her head, but the rocks underneath her feet were giving way and she grabbed at a tree branch to steady herself. Next to the tree branch was a glimpse of gold. She tried to dig around it, but it was almost impossible with one hand and Jane was closing in quickly. She was only 10 feet away. Krista wasn't sure what Jane's skills were as a sharp shooter, but no one needed to be from that range.

"He's already involved! He knows! No reason to keep him around. He's served his purpose!" Jane laughed again. "Actually, so have you. I think your time has run out, Princess."

Krista looked around for an escape, but there wasn't any with the exception of jumping off the cliff into the angry waves threatening below. Maybe if she jumped far out enough, she'd hit the water, instead of the rocks below, but it left her little chance of surviving.

Just then, she noticed a tree trunk, on the cliff a few feet down. If only she could distract Jane for a minute, it could buy her a few seconds to crawl to it. She saw Jane moving closer, the gun pointed at her head, as she cocked back the bullet. Krista cringed, knowing she was out of time, and prepared to jump off the cliff. Suddenly she heard a male voice, "Put it down now!" Jane seemed frozen with surprise, her finger on the trigger.

Suddenly, she heard Karen's voice in her ear, "Crawl down to that tree trunk! Right now!" She moved back cautiously to the cliff's edge and crept down, trying not to look down at the waves and jagged rocks which seemed miles below her. "Keep going, you'll be okay. Just listen to me." Karen's voice was clear and Krista trusted her. She grabbed onto grass clumps until she reached the trunk. She grasped onto the tree trunk with her arms while her feet swung free with nothing beneath them except the rocks and waves below. "Stop! Put the gun down! Don't move!" A male voice called out. Suddenly, a loud gunshot rang out. Krista closed her eyes, waiting for the bullet.

A hand reached out to her. "It's safe to come up now. You're safe." It was the same soft, consoling voice that she recognized from her dreams. For the first time while she was awake, she could see her sister. She looked exactly like Krista, down to the clothes she was wearing. Krista could still hear Karen's voice, her sister's hand reaching out to hers. "I miss you. I wish you could always be with me." Krista said as she grabbed the hand. "I'm always with you. I'm always here." Karen's voice was very clear. "Karen! I can see you! Please stay!" Krista pleaded.

As she was pulled to safety, Krista was shocked to realize that the hand helping her off the cliff belonged to a police officer. The young officer looked confused as she got her feet back on firm ground. "Mrs. Burton, are you hurt?" She stared at him for a moment, confused. Where was Karen? "Where is she?" Krista asked, suddenly looking behind him to discover Jane Ahearn lying motionless in a pool of blood. She began to shake uncontrollably from the cold and shock of what had just happened. "Where is *who*?" The officer asked her quizzically. "Are you hurt, Mrs. Burton?" He repeated.

"I..I don't think so…she saved me I.. mean… you saved me. Thank you." She fumbled over her words as she realized that Karen wasn't there. The young officer looked confused, as the EMS team headed over. "Where's my husband? Where's Chad?" Krista was frantic as the medic team assisted her onto a stretcher, asking her if she had any injuries. "I'm okay, where's my husband?" Krista couldn't relax until she knew he was safe.

Chad

As Chad watched Krista run from the house with Jane following her with the gun, he had never felt so helpless. His hands still tied behind his back and he wrestled around, desperate to free himself. He managed to roll himself off the table and moved towards Kyle and Estelle, who were hovered above Amanda, both of them muttering amongst themselves. He wasn't sure if Amanda was alive, but he was looking for a chance to catch them by surprise. He clung to the hope that the police were able to get to the scene in time, but he also knew that with the weather, it might be a long shot. His wife had potentially killed her sister, and Jane was already unstable. As Chad was trying to loosen the tape around his hands, he could hear footsteps coming down the stairs and suddenly three officers in SWAT attire had guns drawn on himself, Estelle and Kyle

"Get up and get your hands in the air! Now!" One of the officers commanded. Estelle's jaw dropped and she moved away from Amanda with her hands in the air. "Officer, I can explain. I was just hired by this woman! I didn't do anything!" Chad watched as she continued her monologue with the officers as they ignored her insistence that she 'wasn't involved.' Kyle ran like a scared rabbit, only to be captured by the other officer a few seconds later. "Please, I didn't hurt anyone!" Kyle's dramatics fell on deaf ears as they cuffed him and led him up the stairs. Estelle was hand-cuffed, despite her insistence that she wasn't 'really involved' and continued to sob her innocence during the trip to the police cruiser.

A medical crew followed, and immediately went to work to assess Amanda's condition. "She's still got a pulse! We need to get her out of here STAT!" The medical team worked on getting Amanda onto a stretcher and up the stairs. Chad was shocked to hear that Amanda was clinging to life, but then again, it was just like her. She wasn't going to let anything go. Ever.

"I'm Chad Burton! Please help me! I need to find my wife!" He lifted bound fists behind his back.

"Mr. Burton! Are you alright?" The remaining officer helped him remove his bindings. "I'm fine. But my wife is still out there and Jane Ahearn followed her with a gun!" Chad advised. "Please just go! They're headed out toward the cliffs. Please hurry!"

"An officer is outside right now." He spoke into his radio, "Is the suspect down?" He waited a few seconds. Seconds that felt like hours, when Chad finally heard the news. "Suspect is down. Mrs. Burton is safe. We're on our way back to the house."

"Your wife is fine and headed back to the house, Mr. Burton." The officer repeated to Chad. Chad bowed his head and covered his face with his hands with relief. "Thank you! Thank you!" He was openly crying, for once not giving a shit about how he appeared. He just wanted to see his wife again.

She finally came through the door a few minutes later, completely drenched and covered in mud with a few scratches, but unharmed. Chad couldn't get to her fast enough.

"Kris! Oh my god! I thought you wouldn't get away! I thought I'd lost you!" Chad hugged her, refusing to let go, even after Krista told him he was holding her too tight.

Krista's eyes were glazed over and she seemed disoriented, but she returned his hug. "It was Karen. She helped me. Is she still here?" She looked around. Chad held her as her body seemed to sink toward the ground. "I think we need a vacation!" She giggled incoherently. Chad kept her upright. "Yes, we do and we will, sweetheart!" Krista closed her eyes and clung to him, as the officer motionedhim toward the EMT rescue that had arrived. They were both led to be evaluated in the ambulances. Krista continued to ask where Karen was and Chad gave the EMT staff a short version of what had been happening over the several weeks. Krista seemed to be lucid after receiving some fluids for dehydration and began asking about her father. "We're on our way to the mainland, and he'll meet us there. He knows what's happened." The medical team reassured her.

William

"Bill, wake up!" Stanley shook him, as William sat up disoriented for a moment. His neck felt cramped from lying on what seemed to be a comfortable seat in the limo. "What? What's going on?" He scrubbed his eyes with his hands. It was still dark, but the downpour of rain had lessened to a drizzle.

"They found Krista and Chad!" They're on their way back!" Stanley told him, sounding relieved, almost happy; for Stanley anyway. William sat up. "They are? When will they be here?" He grabbed his jacket and yanked the limo door open to look outside. The drizzle lightened and he could see some light from the moon appear from behind the clouds as they parted. The waves were still high from the storm, but he could see a Coast Guard vessel with red lights flashing coming towards them in the distance.

"Yes!" William shouted, tears coming to his eyes. "They're both all right? They aren't hurt?" Stan nodded. "According to the police, they're just pretty shaken up." Stanley said looking away, his shoulders shaking.

"Thank you, Stan. I appreciate your help. I'm not sure this would have turned out well without it." Stanley didn't turn around. "Stan? Are you okay?" William could tell he was struggling.

"Amanda is being taken to the hospital with some serious injuries. I wish this could've ended differently. Jane...she didn't make it." Stanley shook his head, in shock from the news.

"I'm sorry, Stan." William's sentiment was sincere. He knew first-hand what it was like to lose a child.

"My girls have behaved in a way that put them where we are today. I don't condone what they did. In fact, I'm horrified that they came up with a scheme to kill people for money. But they're still my daughters." Stan's voice trailed off as he wiped his face and turned to face Bill. William was shocked. Although they'd been directly involved with his daughter's kidnapping, he was empathetic to Stanley's situation. Stanley sat down on the hood of the limo and put his head in his hands and began to sob. William instinctively went to Stanley and put an arm around him. "I wish this would have been a good ending for you."

"So do I, Bill. So do I." Stanley said quietly. "There's a lot I wish I could've done differently. But I'm glad that your family is safe. There's something to be said for being a family man." Stanley returned William's hug. The Coast Guard vessel was headed into dock and both men got up to meet them.

"Stan, has there been any word about Maria...I mean Caroline?" William had to know. He knew that Maria was never going to be in his life again, but he still hoped for her well-being.

"I just got word from the hospital that she's been stabilized. She still not out of the woods, but she's a fighter. I'm hopeful that she'll pull through. Amanda's being transported there right now. I could give you a lift." Stanley offered.

"Are you sure, Stan? I mean, I appreciate it, but….it might be a little strange." William was hesitant. "I won't go in and see her. I'd rather leave things as they are now."

Stanley nodded his head. "Krista and Chad will be taken there to be checked out. It's up to you if you want to check in with my wife. But I know that someone else might want to see her after all these years."

"Krista. Are you saying that you'd let Kris see her?" William wasn't sure what to say, but knew that it was better to not ask too many questions. Stanley nodded. "Caroline is her mother. She's been frustrated over the years because she has never forgotten that she was a mother to her and Karen. My girls were not hers, and they gave her a hard time over the years. I believe it would help her to see Krista. I think it would help both of them to reconnect and have some closure." Stanley said.

"I think you're right, Stan." William agreed. He'd included Karen, because he knew that if his former wife missed one twin, she'd missed them both. Stanley looked confused for a moment, then nodded. "Yes, it would be good for all of them."

Krista

Krista never imagined she'd ever meet her mother again, but yet here she was; ready to walk into her hospital room. Her palms were sweating with anxiety, as she gripped Chad's hand. "What if she doesn't recognize me? What if she doesn't want me here?" She rattled on nervously. William was standing behind her. "Kris, she wants to see you. Stanley already talked to her about you. Go ahead." Krista nodded, took a deep breath and opened the door.

Caroline looked pale, and her blond hair was muddled amongst electrodes attached to her temples, but her cerulean blue eyes that were so like her own, lit up as soon as Krista walked into the room. "Krista! My god! You're so beautiful!" Tears were in her eyes. Krista suddenly ran to her as if the years had never gone by. She hugged her gently, careful not to move the intravenous line in her arm. Despite the circumstances, it was a moment she'd always longed for. Krista's tears mixed with her mother's as they embraced after almost 25 years of being apart.

"Mom….I mean, Caroline…." Krista began, but Caroline cut her off. "Krista, I'm your mother. I know I haven't been around for the past 25 years, but you can call me 'mom'. In fact, I'd love it if you're okay with that!" Krista nodded, brushing tears away. Chad backed out of the room, knowing they needed time to themselves.

"I believe I have some explaining to do about why I left and been gone for so long." Caroline began. Krista nodded, glad that her father had told her about the accident and Karen ahead of time.

"After that accident, I couldn't seem to shake the depression that set in after losing your sister. I really tried. I tried to take care of you, be there for you and your father. I saw a psychiatrist who gave me medication, but I still couldn't pull out of it. I'd had enough. My intentions were to go somewhere quiet where I could be alone. We used to take you and Karen to Block Island in the summer so that was where I wanted to go. I sat on the bluffs, drinking the wine that your father and I used to drink. Then, I made that fateful decision to jump off the cliff. Maybe it was because I drank too much, combined with my lack of desire to struggle with depression any longer. When I woke up in the hospital a month later, I didn't know who I was or where I belonged. That's when I discovered that Stanley had found me and saved my life. He had been at my hospital bed every day since the incident. Our relationship grew from there." Caroline stopped for a moment and motioned to the glass of water. Krista handed it to her. "Mom, if you don't want to finish, we can talk another time," Krista could tell she was feeling tired.

"No, I need to finish. I owe you that much, my sweet daughter." Caroline smiled and reached for her hand. Krista squeezed her hand and nodded.

"Stanley and I eventually married and my new life was going well, until I began having memories about my life prior to the fall. The doctors told me I might begin to remember. I began remembering you girls first, almost like a trailer of a movie. That brought on remembering my life with your father. Eventually, I was able to recollect the accident that killed your sister, and who I really was. Unfortunately, that took years, 15 years to be exact. I'd thought about contacting your father, but I didn't want to disrupt his life or yours. Too much time had gone by. I can't imagine what it was like for you or your father." Tears were streaming down her face as she talked.

"What helped me was the picture that was in my jacket pocket when I jumped. It was a picture of the three of us; me, you, and Karen. We'd just finished a great day at the beach and your father had taken it. I brought it with me because I wanted you both to be with me always. It's framed on my nightstand in my bedroom now."

"That was the picture I found stuffed in my desk a few weeks ago!" Krista was stunned.

"You saw this picture?" Caroline asked, but didn't seem surprised. "Unfortunately, Stanley's daughters were not well-behaved, or happy that he'd remarried. They've been a thorn in my side for all these years. They found out about the accident that killed your sister, and that you were still alive. Those girls knew that you were in the will, because as I began to regain my memories, I insisted that Stanley change his will to include you. They likely made a copy of the picture, and planted it there. Maybe they hoped they'd make you think you were insane? Who knows with those two?" Caroline shrugged. Krista realized that she might not know about the Ahearn girls.

"Mom. I don't know if they told you, but Jane died and Amanda is here in this hospital." William and Chad kept her updated on Amanda's condition. Doctors were saying she'd pull through, but would have a long recovery of rehabilitation to relearn motor skills and memory. Krista said it quietly, not sure how she would react.

But Caroline was already nodding. "Yes, I know. Stanley told me. It is sad, especially for him. I can't say that I'm surprised though. Considering their plan, it was a risk. I have to be honest; I'd choose your life over theirs any day." She said with certainty. "Over the years, especially at the Block Island house, I would hear a young girl laughing. Once in a while, I'd catch a glimpse of a small blonde girl that looked just like Karen, walking over to the cliff. I'd run down to the cliff, but I couldn't find her. It was part of the reason that I reached out to your husband. I began keeping up with your life through the internet and knew that you were married to Chad. I wanted to hire him to help sell that house. I had some hope of somehow getting to know you, but I never meant to put you in danger. I guess I underestimated them. I hope that you can forgive me." Caroline's voice was growing quiet.

Krista gripped her hand. "Mom, I'm just glad that I finally got to see you again. I didn't think you were alive, until I began having dreams about Karen. She really helped bring us back together. I've missed you so much!" Krista had never felt as complete as she was at this moment.

"Krista, you said you've seen Karen in your dreams." Caroline began. She brought Krista's hand and held it close to her chest.

"Yes, I do. Do you believe me?" Krista anxiously gripped her hand, as a sudden chill came over her. What if her mother didn't make it? She knew from the doctors that her mother was not out of the woods yet. She had survived the fall down the stairs, but because of another concussion, a collapsed lung and a heart condition that had gone undiagnosed for several years, she was in serious condition.

"Of course I do. Like I said, I've seen and heard her around that Block Island house for years." Caroline's grip on Krista's hand weakened. She suddenly seemed as though she were having trouble breathing, but she continued. "Your father gave you and Karen necklaces when you were almost three years old. You may not remember." Caroline coughed as she tried to catch her breath. Krista helped her sit up further, gave her a sip of water.

"Thank you, sweetheart." Caroline murmured. "Are you okay? Should I let you rest?" Krista asked.

"No. I'm fine. I don't have time to rest. There's still so much to say…." Her mother insisted. "Do you still have the necklace?"

"Yes, I do! I still have it!" Krista said, and put her hand up to her neck. "At least I did. I hope dad found it. I was wearing it during the break-in. It was gold, a half-heart charm."

"I put Karen's in that box and buried it near the cliff. It has the other half of the necklace." Caroline said. "I wanted to have her close to me. I thought it was the end for me. I could've never imagined that we would be here now. But I'm so glad that we are." She reached out to stroke Krista's hair.

"Mom, I saw that box when I was on the cliff! It must be the same one!" Krista said, suddenly remembering. "I know exactly where it is!"

Caroline smiled and weakly gripped her hand. "Go find it and dig it up. You'll find Karen's necklace, and other mementos that I hope will bring back some of the memories we had. I love you, Krista! So very much. I've missed you both so much Please...go ...find it..." Her voice began to fade, and her eyes closed.

Krista nodded squeezing her hand. "I will! I'll do it tomorrow!" She kissed her on the cheek. "I love you, Mom. I'll see you soon. Get some sleep."

Caroline didn't respond and suddenly the monitors in the room went off with a loud shrilling sound. Krista's heart was suddenly in her throat. No! Not now! "Please don't leave me now, mom!'" She ran outside the room. "Help! Something's wrong! Please help!" Within seconds several nurses and doctors rushed in, checking the monitor. "Ma'am, you're going to have to leave." A tall blond nurse advised her and ushered her to the door. "What's happening? She's my mother!" Krista cried out, as she followed her to the door. Chad was on the other side and held Krista as they watched the doctors pull out the defibrillator in preparation. Stanley approached the nurse at the door. "What's going on? What's happening to my wife?" He demanded answers.

"Mr. Ahearn, your wife is in cardiac arrest. We're doing all we can." The flustered nurse tried to assure him.

"I thought you said she was stable!" Stanley wasn't backing down. He continued to stare through the glass paned door as the doctors continued to use the paddles to try and shock his wife's heart back to life.

"Mr. Ahearn, she *was* stable. I'm not sure what's happening. We're doing all we can." The nurse seemed flustered. "Please go to the waiting area. We'll keep you updated." She pointed down the hall.

Chad guided Krista, Stanley and William down to the waiting room, despite their protests. "We need to let them do their job. She's a strong woman. I'm sure she'll be okay." Chad tried his best to comfort his wife. But they were beyond comforting. Krista clung to him as if she'd drown if he let her go. Stanley was pacing the hallway, complaining about the staff in the hospital not allowing him to see Caroline, while William sat motionless, staring into space.

They waited for what seemed like an eternity until one of the doctors came out to talk to them. The grim look on his face said it all. After all her struggles, Caroline had passed away. There was a moment of silence, when Krista heard a voice, "I'm always here with you. I'm with Karen now. Find the box." She thought she was dreaming as she saw a faint image of her mother holding hands with a little blond girl. "I'll take care of her, Krista." The little girl blew her a kiss and then they both disappeared. Krista waved back. "I love you." She said through her tears.

"Who are you waving at, Kris?" Chad asked her softly.

"My mom. My mom and Karen. They're finally at rest now." Krista replied. "Now I need to find the piece to the other half."

"The other half?" Chad asked.

"The other half of the necklace. Karen and I were given a half-necklace when we were young. Dad could never find Karen's half after she died. Mom told me where it's hidden. I just hope I can find my own in the mean time! I think Jane yanked it off my neck when she dragged me out of the house" Krista said bitterly.

"Now that you've reminded me, I have something for you." Chad pulled her necklace with the heart pendant on it that he'd grabbed from the floor. Krista embraced him as the tears flowed. Her mother and Karen were gone, but now she had the missing pieces she'd been looking for her entire life. Chad fastened the chain around her neck and she vowed as she touched the pendant that it would remain there.

Epilogue

Krista stood with her father, Chad, Stanley Ahearn and a handful of acquaintances of her mother's; most of whom she didn't know. It was a small service held on the grounds of the Ahearn mansion near the cliffs. Both Stanley and William were able to come to an agreement that this is what she would have wanted.

Jane's funeral was going to be the following day. Amanda had managed to survive her injuries, but was being charged with 2nd degree manslaughter along with kidnapping and a handful of other charges. Her bail was set at a million dollars, which Stanley paid. She was out of jail for now, but had a long legal road ahead of her. Not to mention the trial, which would likely end in significant jail time, despite the top-notch attorney team Stanley hired. Estelle and Kyle were both still in jail on charges of conspiracy to commit murder, as well as kidnapping charges. Both were talking with the prosecution to make a deal to testify against Amanda in exchange for a lighter sentence.

Stanley was a shell of himself. His usual arrogance was gone, replaced by despair and sadness. William didn't have the heart to leave the planning of Caroline's funeral to Stanley, and had been helping him with the arrangements for their wife; Caroline, also known as Maria. She'd been cremated, as she had instructed in her final wishes. There was a simple marble gravestone that read "Maria Caroline Ahearn Burton. Beloved wife and mother." Stanley had actually suggested adding Maria Burton to the stone. Ironically, it was the woman that they had both loved that brought them closer together.

William found himself spending more time with Stanley and they were becoming friends. Stanley was grateful for William's friendship; he needed the support more than ever.

As the urn was given to Stanley, he turned to Krista and offered it to her. "I really think she would want you to spread her ashes." Krista brushed her tears away and nodded. "Thank you, Mr. Ahearn." She walked to the very edge of the cliff which had almost been her demise less than a week ago. "I love you, Mom. Take good care of her, Karen." She whispered and opened the urn. The ashes flew out, some scattering over the cliff, but some making their way to the ocean.

As the gathering dispersed, Krista began looking for the box her mother insisted that she find. Suddenly she saw a glint of gold near the edge of the cliff. She ran to it and dug with her bare hands. It was small and gold, the size of a child's jewelry box. She picked it up and opened it. Inside were several photos; one of both her and Karen as infants with their mother, another with them with William at around 2 years old in front of their house making a snowman. The third was the same photo that Krista had found in her office that day. It was the one her mother treasured the most, the one that she'd said she kept on her nightstand all these years.

There were locks of hair from Krista and Karen's first haircut, her mother's wedding band, and a piece of yellowed paper wrapped around an object. She pulled out a chain with a tarnished pendant of a half-heart. "This was Karen's!" She whispered

Her hands shook as she smoothed the creases in the paper. In her mother's faded handwriting, there was a poem.

You were both here with me for a brief time
You were my world and my joy all along
Then suddenly one was taken away
Like the tide, suddenly my world went astray
I tried hard to cope but it left a void
Your life so important, I didn't want to destroy
My dear daughters, one here and one waiting for me
I wish I were stronger, but I can barely breathe
My Krista, I love you always, I will always be near
Just as I loved Karen, remembering her brings me to tears
Here's one thing that I can leave you to grasp
This symbol of love from your other half

All my love,
Mom

Tears streamed down her face as Krista read the message that her mother had written so many years ago. "You'll always be here with me, mom. You and Karen will always be here with me." Krista was startled as a flock of seagulls flew overhead. "Oh my god, ..." Her voice trailed off as she noticed two sparrows sitting on a nearby tree branch. They seemed content as they glanced her way. Krista blew them a kiss. The sparrows chirped as if to say goodbye, and then took flight over the ocean.